Amidst the Stones

OF CELTIC IRELAND

Jeanne Crane

GRATITUDE

The Celts found magic in threes. I found magic in three very special people.

Judy Cadle, who offered constructive, insightful and loving feedback from start to finish.

Sylvia Strobel, who first brought Jane and the message to "tell the story" to my attention.

Janice McNamara, who helped me go deeper into my own story and trust my inner wisdom.

Three others were particularly helpful to me in the final stages: Judith Knight, Sally Hamlin and Lynn Ashley. What blessings all.

And, a huge thank you to Suzi van der Sterre of van der Sterre Design for book design, for her cover design and for bringing the book to its published state with ease and grace.

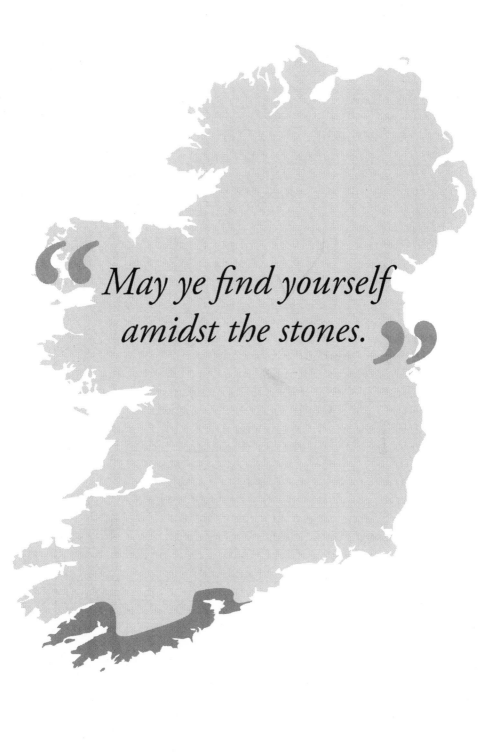

"*May ye find yourself amidst the stones.*"

CHAPTER ONE

You don't look very happy, Abby. Not for a woman who has finally made it to Ireland, who sits over an Irish breakfast with her handsome American chauffeur, in a postcard-perfect town, with four glorious weeks ahead of her." Mark has a teasing tone but a look of concern in his eye as he says all this.

"Listen to you, and you haven't even kissed the Blarney Stone!" I reply with a chuckle. "Actually, I was thinking about the Kenmare Stone Circle we visited yesterday. I have been so looking forward to seeing these stone circles. And, well, yesterday's visit was somehow disappointing."

"Good grief, a third of our trip is planned around these stone circles. Are you saying you aren't into them?" I hear a bit of alarm in his voice as he tries to keep his question light.

"No, I'm still interested, just somehow yesterday wasn't what I expected," I say as my voice trails off into further reflection.

We are sitting in a charming little café in Kenmare, County Kerry on our first day of our first trip together. The relationship is new. We met in October, started dating after Christmas and then started planning this trip around Valentine's Day. Here it is May and we are still feeling out what it is like to be together. I decide to try to reassure him that I am not a moody, difficult to please traveler. So, I add, "I really love it here. Already I can tell I am going to like the people and the pace of things. And even though I was getting too tired to hold my head up after such a long day's travel, I loved the pub last night and the music. And everyone was so welcoming."

"Speaking of welcomes, I took a video of that lovely flight attendant welcoming us to Shannon. Let's see how it came out," Mark suggests as he pulls out his smartphone.

Sure enough, he has captured the redheaded, green-suited Irish "lass" as she makes the announcement: "Prepare for landing. Once more, please be sure your seat belts are fastened, you seat backs straight up, now. We will be landing in Shannon momentarily. You are very welcomed here." And then she repeats it all in Irish, or at least, we assume that's what she says. I myself don't speak or understand a word of it, but it is fun to hear. I think I got the end of it: *céad míle fáilte*, the famous Irish "hundred thousand welcomes".

"I am so glad you recorded that moment, Mark. It was thrilling. I have never been abroad before. And now that everyone keeps welcoming us like that, it has even more meaning. I am so, so glad we are here!"

"Well, that's good to hear. Me too. I couldn't be more content than sitting here with you, an Irish newspaper and a café Americano. What a great start to our first day of vacation."

Mark gets lost in his newspaper as I pull out my journal. Truth be told, if I were on my own I would be anxious to get started. I mean Jeez, we are in Ireland. But life is trade-offs and it is very companionable to sit here with this guy and probably good for me to relax and just take it all in. My phone buzzes before I even begin writing. It's a text from Mike, my younger son:

> *Mom, glad you arrived safely. I have a trip myself to Montana starting tomorrow. Scurrying around to get ready. Have a great time and enjoy those wee leprechauns,* then a series of emoji: heart, Irish flag, leprechaun.

I reply:

> *Love back to you and do be safe.*

I try to be breezy and just a friend, but he will always be my baby boy. And as proud as I am of both boys being on their own and successful, I ache for them to be a bigger part of my life, but they have their own lives to lead. This relationship with Mark has filled some of the void. I still miss them terribly.

"Everything OK?" Mark asks looking up from his newspaper.

"Yes, great in fact. It is a text from Michael. He's off on a business trip to Montana. I can't believe he makes a living taking city folks on whitewater rafting trips, but I am happy for him that he is doing what he loves. I have heard nothing back from Brian. I imagine he is just busy. What about your Cheryl? Did you two connect yet?"

"We did. She sends love to me and greetings to you. I think it's hard for her that I am not here with her mom, but she's happy for me and she's coming around to there being another woman in my life. I told her I would text her a good time for us to FaceTime later in the week. Little Lydia wants to see what Papa looks like in Ireland. Who knows what goes through a four-year old's mind when they see a loved one fly away into the sky. Maybe she's afraid I will turn into a leprechaun or be gone forever like her grammy."

"Might you turn into a leprechaun?" I chuckle but silently admit to myself that I want to redirect the conversation away from his deceased wife. It still makes me uncomfortable when he talks about her.

"Well, I wouldn't mind finding a pot of gold. As for being free and easy, today I am beginning to let go and settle in. I think when I get used to the car, I will relax more. Funny, how I find sitting here drinking strong coffee calming. I guess it is the familiarity of getting into my morning routine."

· · ·

Mark was widowed about a year ago. He had taken an early retirement from church ministry to be with and care for his wife the year before her death. Now he is working through his loss, giving himself some time and space to adjust and taking the risk to begin a new relationship.

As for me, I also recently retired from teaching and am finding my way into this thing called retirement. For so many years, my focus was on raising my two boys and teaching full-time. I never really had the luxury to think about what I wanted for myself or to be reflective about my life. I certainly didn't have time or money to pursue my own travel interests.

A few years ago, Stonehenge was at the top of my fantasy travel list. I always watch those TV documentaries about this ancient site with fascination. I was disappointed when I heard they no longer allow tourists to walk inside the Stonehenge circle itself. I still would like to see it, but these smaller stone circles here in Ireland offer a chance to walk amid the stones and that is really appealing.

I can't really explain why I am so drawn to these places or so intrigued to experience them firsthand, but I am. My curiosity about their purpose and meaning led me to explore Celtic spirituality too. I found a women's group at our local healing center just a few months after school let out last year that proved to be made to order. It consisted of a circle group of eight women of different faiths sharing ritual, poetry, readings and prayers as a path to making meaning in their own lives. I feel I have found a spiritual home I didn't even know I sought.

A few months later, I met Mark in an adult education class at the local community college. Here again, I didn't realize I was looking for a relationship. But as I got to know Mark, I found myself open. Mark and his quiet, low key but attentive way became more and more appealing. The course had nothing to do with

Ireland or the Celtic lands of which Ireland is one, but somehow Ireland came up in the small group work we were doing. We started talking about it. My interest in the ancient rituals, the stone circles and the standing stones kind of overlapped his interest in early Celtic Christianity and its abbeys. We enjoyed talking and learning from each other. Then after Christmas, we finally admitted to wanting more from each other.

One night we were watching the movie *Ondine* and the beautiful scenery of Ireland, the humor of the Irish people and the mysticism of Irish lore really moved us. Come to find out, Mark is fascinated by lighthouses. Right then, we decided to make this trip: lighthouses and stone circles and a chance to get to know each other without the watchful eye of his congregation and our larger community. And now here we are.

"Abby, I think I will run across to the tourist center we noticed last night to get some better local maps before we set out. Want anything in particular?" Mark asks, bringing me out of my reverie.

"No, just whatever you see that you think we will want. While I can read a map, I like those automobile club trip-tik packets my dad used to get. And, to tell the truth, I always delegated the geography projects to my student teachers. So simple tourist maps appeal to me. Do you want me to come along so we can head out from there?" I ask.

"I will just run over. Then, unless you are in a hurry, we can have a final cup of coffee while we mull over the materials I pick up."

I nod in agreement and add at the last minute "Don't forget to look right and then left—I want you in one piece. Remember how we almost got clipped walking out into traffic last night."

Now, he nods and is off. I take the time to begin recalling last night so that I can capture it in my journal. I start by asking myself the question Mark asked me over breakfast: what's wrong? Am I not into these stone circles after all? I begin running through last night in my mind almost as if it is one of Mark's videos.

• • •

"It is still light out. I would like to check out the Kenmare Stone Circle now instead of waiting until morning, if you are OK with that," I add. "I am afraid I won't be able to sleep if I don't."

"How could I say no to that?" Mark answers amiably. "Plus, I think it's exactly the right way to begin. After all, we came for stone circles and lighthouses. Plus, we also get beautiful scenery, good food and music. Let's fill our first day with as much of that mix as we can."

Kenmare Stone Circle is just on the edge of town, within easy walking distance. We both allow as to how good it is to walk and we enjoy being in a residential area for the first time. Of course, forgetting to look right before stepping off the curb breaks the tranquility, when we almost get hit. But we quickly move on, glad to be stretching our legs and seeing things up close and personal.

There is a range of stone circles that dot the countryside in Celtic nations. England's Stonehenge, of course, is the most famous. Built before the pyramids of Egypt on the plain of Salisbury, it is the most magnificent of stone circles. When I first saw a picture of this magnificent and awe-inspiring site in *National Geographic* I was blown away. I started reading serious research along with wild speculative materials trying to learn the what, where and why of it all. Of course, there are lots of competing hypotheses, each the product of the author's own views. Now I have the chance to get my own read on what they are all about.

We discover that this Kenmare Stone Circle is actually in a park-like setting and is surrounded by a ring of tall evergreens, not the bucolic setting I envisioned. Fifteen really big boulders are positioned to form a magnificent oval rather than circle and it is wide, maybe 50 feet at its widest part. The boulders are not the tall, vertical stones, reaching to the sky I had imagined.

And I am surprised by the big, flat sideways boulder in the center that is like an altar. It is actually sitting on smaller stones that create a base. I read ahead of time that that makes it officially a dolmen—a configuration of three vertical stones and a flat horizontal cap stone which looks like a table. In fact, some call it a giant's table. I think I am right in saying dolmens are unique to Ireland.

Truthfully, if not for my Internet research, I wouldn't have even noticed, because the capstone itself is so commanding and the stones below it are barely noticeable.

I turn to Mark to say, "These stones are nowhere near the size of those at Stonehenge and nowhere near as intimate as the stone circle in the sweet watercolor I have at home. What do you think?" I ask him.

"It really gives the impression of an outdoor chapel. And, yep, it is quite different from any of the other pictures you have been showing me. By the way, that reminds me, I want to hear more about your watercolor now that we are here in Ireland. Maybe over dinner?" As he speaks a blackbird dips in and out of the space above the circle and continues punctuating the silence we have just broken.

"Is this an act of welcome, I wonder; a good omen, I hope," I ponder aloud. "Mind if I lead us in a short prayer in response to that thought?" he asks. "Please do."

So, we position ourselves on opposite sides of the altar stone and clasp hands. He begins:

5

Mother/Father God, Source of All that is sacred and holy

Bless us and our trip as we stand within this magnificent monument

May we learn from the wisdom of those who came before us

May we carry forth the connection to Nature and to the Universe they understood.

As the psalmist proclaimed so long ago:

The Heavens declare the Glory of God and the Firmament showeth his handiwork.

I come around to embrace him. I am so moved that he gets it. That he gets his own sense of meaning here. No words pass between us. None are needed.

He then leaves the circle while I remain at its center. I begin to go around the inside of the circle three times. I have read the Ancients are thought to have done this and I know modern pagans do it now days. Each time around the circle, I experience it differently. First, my circumnavigation creates a sense of framing the space. On the second go round, I feel myself inside the space. The third time, I feel suspended in time, if only for a moment. I then move back to the center, where I stop at the altar.

Much as Mark just did, I stop to honor all who came before and I ask that I be given an opportunity to learn the wisdom of the stones. I don't know where that last request came from or what I even mean by it, but I am moved to put it out there.

As I move to the center, a spot on the altar stone catches my eye. It is a circular growth of lichen that looks like a labyrinth. I call to Mark to come get a good picture of it with his camera. I am struck by how it is like a natural logo, a symbol. Both a stone circle and labyrinth invite a similar ritual and message. I am intrigued by it for some unexplainable reason.

Mark, though, offers a brilliant comment: "People began creating labyrinths since before recorded time to symbolize life's journey. Christians carried the tradition forward. Think of the floor of medieval Chartres Cathedral in France or Grace Episcopal in San Francisco. Seeing you make the round of the circle makes me wonder which came first; a stone circle or labyrinth. Indeed, it is powerful to think of rituals that connect one's own journey to the path of the sun, moon and stars. And then to have this natural symbol growing on the rock. Wow, Abby, you have really brought us to a sacred place. Thank you," he adds as he kisses me on the cheek.

He then moves out of the center to take some more pictures, even wanders out of the circle to get some wider shots. I stay and move behind the altar stone, placing my hands on it, closing my eyes as I try to soak in the feel of this stone that has witnessed so much. I have heard that the stones can speak. I try to listen. But I guess that is just a myth because nothing comes. After some time, I notice Mark seems antsy to go. I am ready, too, I guess, although I feel strangely incomplete as we leave.

A great meal, a first round of traditional Irish music and a couple of glasses of wine prepare us for bed. We fall asleep in one another's arms almost upon hitting the bed. I never really thought about the fact that the stone circle was somehow disappointing in the flurry of so many other things going on. I guess that is why Mark's observation and questions surprised me.

• • •

Now here he comes back from his errands and I still have no answer to why the circle felt flat to me.

"Hey, Abs. Fancy meeting you here. I got our maps. Still OK sitting here for another cup of coffee?"

"Sure. I have been sitting here running through our experience at the stone circle yesterday and trying to figure out what bothers me about it."

"By the way, the woman at the tourist office says locals refer to it as The Shrubberies. She expressed their pride in its restoration."

"Maybe that's what bothers me. It is so well-groomed. I thought there would be kind of a raw/earthy feel. You know: energy, awe, maybe even a sense of magic. But it felt flat, like walking through a well-tended but kind of sterile garden. And with all the big evergreens, there is no way you could watch the sun rise or set on the horizon."

"Those are really good points. Guess it depends on what you were expecting. Me, I'm just the guy choosing to escort his goddess to the circles," he chuckles. I stick my tongue out in playful protest.

"And I did enjoy my chat with that nun who shared the circle with us. She greeted me in Irish. Fahl-cheh, I think it was. I'm sure I just butchered the pronunciation, but you know the word I am after."

"Yeah, *Fáilte* is welcome. You know, like the famous *Céad Míle Fáilte* (kayd MEE-luh FAH-cheh): 'A Hundred Thousand Welcomes'."

"That's a mouthful. I will have to practice it a bit—you know, to show my respect for the country and all. I pick up the idioms quickly but am terrible with foreign languages."

"Well, that's why you're traveling with a teacher. Retired or not, once a teacher always a teacher," I joke.

His retort: "That's not what attracts me to you, you know."

I love feeling attractive and wanted again after many years on my own with only casual dating, and not much of that. "Hopefully, we will learn a lot more phrases as we go. I have been told one of the great things about Ireland is that you aren't expected to speak the native tongue, but people are patient and encouraging when you do. And all the signs are in English and Irish so that will help us at least recognize the words. But . . .what? Back up a bit." I am flabbergasted when the rest of his statement sinks in. "What nun are you talking about? I don't remember a nun."

"Sure, you do. Remember when you called me to that center stone to take a picture of that spiral-shaped patch of lichen that looked like a piece of art? Then you stayed and meditated while I went out to go around the outer circle taking some video. She came along then. She is visiting the convent up the hill. I think she said she is from Limerick."

"Too bad I missed her."

"Oh, but you didn't! She went up to you in the center of the circle and said something to you."

"No way!"

"But you had to see her. I remember loving the image of her in partial habit and you in jeans, both seekers but so different in lifestyle. I remember thinking it would be fun to listen to you share your perspectives with one another. I may even have it here on a video snippet. Here, let's have a look".

Sure enough, there we were. "I can't believe I don't remember her at all. What is she saying?"

"Looks like she is giving you a blessing. Good thing, I moved in at that point to get pictures from another angle. I think we can hear her if I turn it way up. Wow—*May ye find yourself amidst the stones.* That is quite something. And that seems to be all she said. You still don't remember?"

"No...I don't," I practically stutter.

"I wonder why she chose you and if the blessing is just a general thing she does? Or was she was moved to say it to you alone? And if so, why? I mean as she and I talked, she just sounded like any woman religious on retreat. She said her order has a house right around here that she was visiting." He ponders all this aloud almost as incredulous as I am.

"I'm not sure which idea is weirder-that she came up to me, a complete stranger, or that she singled me out. And, of course, the bigger question, is how could I forget all about it?" I say, dazed by the revelation.

"You must have been deep in mediation to forget."

"Yeah..."

"Well, we were pretty jet-lagged and bone-tired from the trip over. And I think that short nap we took was worse than if we had just stayed up."

"Hmm."

"Besides, we were both a bit overwhelmed yesterday—landing in a new country, heading out on a month's adventure with no reservations, traveling together for the first time. At first, I thought it was just the driving on the other side of the road, but it was a lot for each of us."

"Yeah."

"Abby, are you OK? This seems to have really thrown you."

"It is a lot to take in. It leaves me feeling very disconnected from myself and I don't like the feeling at all," I say honestly.

"I guess it would spook me too. It is just that I saw and spoke to her and she was so perfectly normal that it is easier for me to dismiss it as your being distracted. Now that we are rested and off to the countryside, I bet you will be your usual self and not miss a trick!"

I shake my head. He's right about the overwhelming feeling. And I hope he is also right that when I am rested and into a travel routine, all will be normal. And, then, I am hopeful we will be able to relax. He surly needs it. It has been a hard year for him. Retiring early to care for his wife and then being there all the way to witnessing her death.

For me this year of retirement has meant a sense of freedom, something I have never felt before. It still has been a radical change for me. Bringing up two boys virtually alone on a teacher's salary meant I worked summers and I led a pretty hectic and intense life. Now I have time for myself, a new relationship and this incredible trip. Here I am at fifty-six years old, finally getting to Europe, and with a great guy. I don't want anything to mess that up.

"Are you OK for us to head out? Before long, this place will need the table for the lunch crowd. The woman at the tourist office says there is an old cemetery with a famine plot at the ruins of an early monastery just south of town on our route. I would like to stop."

"Sure. I am getting antsy anyway. And truthfully, I would like a reason to stop thinking about the nun."

"It's not like she said anything bad or scary. She actually gave you a blessing as I see it. You were just tired and had come out of a deep meditation," he says soothingly. "And the blessing is a nice sentiment, not like you were accosted by a banshee, spewing black magic."

"Black magic? Where did that come from?" I ask, a bit sharply.

"I have no idea," he says, laughing at himself for the comment. "I don't even really know what banshees are. Some kind of Irish spirit is all I know. Just trying to lighten things up."

"No worries, I am OK with it. You are probably right. She was just a nun with a lovely blessing and I was too distracted to remember. Although I wonder why she thinks I need to find myself. I think of myself as well-adjusted, but is there something I am missing?"

"You certainly seem to know yourself from my perspective," he says giving my hand a squeeze. "I wouldn't be here with you otherwise."

"Thanks for that," I smile. "So, let's get going. As charming as this town is, we have lots more to see."

"I passed an amazing bakery down the street when I went for maps. Let's drop by and get some goodies for the road."

"We have barely finished breakfast. How can you even think of food?" I laugh, as I nod in agreement. "And what about your lighthouses? When will we get to your lighthouses?"

"It looks like a day or two until we begin seeing them. But I didn't forget, and glad you didn't forget either that our mission is to visit them all. My personal goal is to view and take a picture of every single lighthouse in Cork, then make a calendar for all my old Navy buddies before our reunion."

"Let's get started then since there are a zillion or so, right?"

"Seventy in Ireland, but you will be glad to know, not all of them in Cork. Besides we are not yet in Cork; the next 20 to 30 miles are still part of County Kerry. You get to see more stone circles before we hit lighthouse country."

• • •

So we choose from a host of tea cakes and "biscuits" each looking yummier than the last. The irony of stopping at the famine plot with full bellies is not lost on us. We find the cemetery as soon as we cross the bridge over the Kenmare River. Our first visit is to the ruins of St. Finian's monastery. Not much left but they seem to give Mark the same sense of awe I get from the stones. And I also feel the sacredness of the site.

We then move to the famine plot. It is a sober and gut-wrenching experience. So many lives lost. It reminds me a lot of visiting Gettysburg. But worse: here also lie women, children and entire families who were simply trying to eke out a living in peace.

We pay our respects and Mark leads us in a beautiful prayer for a world where all people have food and shelter and no group denies another the basic needs of survival.

I never saw myself with a minister, but I appreciate his sensitivity as well as his ability to keep life in perspective. Wow. We pull ourselves together and move on.

Impulsively, Mark pulls into the Kenmare pier just to look out at the water and feel its cleansing energy. We get out to walk and to breathe in the salt-water-filled air off the bay and to take in the magnificent view.

"Remind me the names of what we are looking at, please?" I ask.

"They call this the Kenmare River, but it looks like a regular bay to me. It separates the Ivernagh Peninsula to the north (the famous Ring of Kerry) from the Beara Peninsula to the south. Imagine putting your left hand out, palm facing toward you. Kenmare River, this bay, is the space between your index and middle finger. Your middle finger is the Ivernagh Peninsula. Your index finger is the Beara Peninsula where we are headed. Then on the far side of the Beara is a bigger bay, Bantry Bay. Think of that as the space between your index finger and your thumb. Then the thumb represents the mainland southern coast of County Cork. Basically, that's where we will be traveling—along the coast from Kenmare, around Beara north and south and then on to the mainland coast of southwest Cork."

"So we are standing at the bottom of the "V" my two fingers make. OK, then. If I get confused as we travel around, I can just stick my hand out to reorient myself. That is very cool. You should have been a teacher, Mark. That is a great way to remember it."

"Glad to be of service. And I am glad you agreed to come to the Beara Peninsula rather than wanting to travel to the better-known Ring of Kerry."

"Well, Beara is where *Ondine* was filmed, right? And my stone circles are here too, right?" I ask to confirm.

"Yep, this southwest area has more stone circles and lighthouses than any other place in Ireland, and it is less touristy. Shall we continue on?"

"Absolutely." In a few minutes I add, "So here we are on the Beara Peninsula. Our first foray into the Irish countryside," I announce to the world as Mark makes the right-hand turn away from the main road that leads down to Glengarriff. I am proud of myself for following the new map that Mark got specifically of the area. And the names are even beginning to feel familiar as I read them.

"I'm so grateful to be doing this. We are going to have a wonderful adventure, I have no doubt. Just keep watching how close I am to the edge of the road for me. It's so hard to gauge distances to my left. Thankfully, this road is not narrow like the streets of Kenmare. And you're also keeping track on the map, right? I looked over the road map this morning, but it takes so much concentration to drive on the left that I could end up passing up the stuff you want to see."

"No chance of that," I say with confidence. "I am on it when it comes to reading road signs even though not so great with general geography. I used to take road trips with my dad."

"Tell me more about your dad. You don't talk much about him," Mark asks.

"Don't I? I think about him a lot—associations like the one I just made, stuff we did together, things he taught me. He brought sunshine to my life."

"And the grandmother you lived with was his mother, right?" he indicates he wishes to hear more.

"Yes, and she was stern and cold and so unlike him. For a long time, I thought it was because she resented having to raise me. She was nicer to Dad, but still cold and distant. I came to realize she didn't single me out. She was just a bitter, unhappy and uptight woman. I never knew my grandfather but pictured him as a loving, cheerful guy like my dad. He was the one with Irish roots, though Grandmother never shared much about that. I think she was embarrassed that his people were second generation and lived in poverty. I sorely wish that Dad had lived long enough for us to have come to Ireland on a trip. As I said, we talked about doing it after I graduated college. But then, he died suddenly. He wasn't even there to walk me down the aisle.

"I really never thought I would get here until you began talking about your desire to visit Irish lighthouses."

"You were telling me about your mom and the watercolor of the stone circle yesterday. I would love to hear more."

"Not much to tell. I think I remember her, but, as I said, I wonder if it was just Dad speaking about her and trying to keep her memory alive for me. I do know she came from an Irish background too. Sometimes, I would imagine her coming to me at night, tucking me in, looking like Glinda, the Good Fairy in *The Wizard of Oz*. But, as you can guess, Grandmother put an end to that—calling it silly fantasy and forbidding me to talk about it, especially to Dad. She also refused to let Dad hang the watercolor I told you about in my bedroom."

"That is downright mean. What reason did she give?" he asks.

"Didn't match the décor; translation, not highbrow enough. Plus, I don't think she ever liked my mother."

"Hmm. So, it sounds like the watercolor has a charged and meaningful history. Tell me more," Mark encourages me to continue.

"I think I told you it feels like the only thing I have of hers that is truly mine. Dad says she bought it for my nursery the day they found out she was pregnant. It's of a small stone circle out in a field. I'll show it to you next time we stop. I have a picture of it on my phone. Dad said he assumes the sheep in it caught my mom's attention. He tells me that sheep were the theme for my nursery. I can't believe I didn't tell you all this before."

I stop for a breath, then continue. "After my mom died, we moved to Grandmother's house. Grandmother refused to let him put it up on the walls in my bedroom. But he kept it. When I got my first apartment, he brought it to me. There was so much going on that at the time I didn't ask him much about it. I had just moved in, had just started teaching, and had just begun dating Hal. We put it up in the hallway of my apartment, but I never got the full story. Then, Dad died suddenly. It was one of the many things I wished we had talked more about. And then there were things we had planned to do together, like come to Ireland. We always said we would make a trip over here after I graduated college. I still miss him terribly," I say wistfully.

"I am sorry you didn't get that opportunity, Abs. I truly am," he says quietly.

"Thanks," I tear up as I say that. "It has been twenty-five years since I lost my dad, but some days his loss still pains me. He was such a great guy. He was on the road all the time, so I was basically brought up by my grandmother. But my childhood was defined by the times he was home and we were together. His love made up for my grandmother's lack of love. So, it worked out."

"Still sounds sad and lonely at times. You must have missed not having a mom. I am so grateful Lizzie lived to see Cheryl grow up. But also sad to think Lydia will never know her grandmother. Lizzie would have been such a great grandmother."

"Loss is never easy, is it?" I say quietly. After a few minutes in the silence of our individual thought, I add, "Did I mention that on the flight over I kept getting images and thoughts of my mother and a vague message to connect with my past? Also, pictures of the watercolor kept popping up."

"No, but given what you just told me, it isn't surprising. I hadn't realized the connections stone circles have to your mom."

"Truthfully, I don't think I realized it either until now. Maybe that is also part of the answer to why the Kenmare Circle didn't wow me. It did not feel anything like my watercolor."

Switching gears, I notice that we have been driving along with no view of the water for what seems like ages and I am feeling very closed in. Instead of sharing that, I blurt out, "What's with all these trees? I thought the English cut them all down for ships, and that Ireland was all carpets of green and purples with no trees at all. I can't see the water at all. This looks just like home. Are you sure we are going right?" My voice sounds shrill even to me.

"We have to be right. I'm positive I took the first right turn out of town; this has to be the coast road. Give it a few more minutes to open up. Admittedly, I was so focused on my driving and thinking about what you were sharing, I barely noticed the lack of scenery, but we have to be on the right road."

"You're right. Don't know what is making me so impatient."

"Yeah, that's not like you. Perhaps it is talking about your family? We don't have to if you don't want to," he offers.

"No, that's OK. I just think I am anxious to see the stuff we came to see, the picture I have in my mind."

"Did you ever read William Least Heat-Moon's *Blue Highways*? He takes a cross country trip and only drives on secondary roads—the blue lines on maps. He goes to towns with interesting names that are off the beaten path. I feel we have begun a similar adventure. And I have every reason to believe it is going to be awesome."

"I am sure you are right," I say in a calmer tone. "So, what about your folks? I know they had you late in life and both died when you were in seminary, but did they ever talk about travel? Did they have an interest in Ireland or lighthouses?"

"Well, the store occupied their time. We took a couple of weeks each summer while Dad's assistant ran things, but we drove. Mom hated the idea of flying. I don't think either of them ever imagined anything as exotic as going abroad. Ah, there's a sign for a marina ahead. Let's stop and look out at the water. Let it still us, like back at the pier. We don't need to be in a hurry. Let's savor all the firsts we are experiencing."

"Like first time on the wrong side of the road," I add with a smile in my voice. He has a way of bringing me around and out of myself I realize as we park and walk over toward the shore. "Now, this is the Ireland that I expected to see."

"It really is beautiful," he says as he takes deep breaths. "And for now, we have sun. Guess I better get some pictures while we have all this sun. From what they say, in ten minutes it could turn to rain."

"I guess that's why Ireland has so many rainbows. I can't wait to see one," I say enthusiastically.

He smiles, hesitates and then asks, "You're glad to be here then?"

The questioning look in his eye suddenly makes me realize that he is again asking are we OK together. After all this is our first trip together, to a place he knew I had wanted to go all my life and yet until now I have been moody in ways he had not seen before. Poor guy. So, I reply with assurance. "Yes. I am very glad to be here, to be with you and I know the trip is going to be fantastic."

"I'm glad too."

We look around, take in what we think to be oyster farms and walk up the hill to the restaurant across the road for a quick cup of coffee and a bathroom break.

"Oh, before we go, I want to show you the picture of my watercolor," I say as I pull out my smartphone.

"I'll be. It's delightful: sheep, stone circle and a beautiful depiction of the Irish countryside. No wonder you were anxious to visit Ireland to experience it all firsthand.

CHAPTER TWO

S o, our next stop is Uragh Stone Circle. I just have this feeling I am going to love it," I say brimming with anticipation.

And sure enough, we see the sign we need in just a few minutes. We turn off to the left, down a narrow road. The road narrows even more, curving first to the right toward the bluest of lakes and then away toward sheep-grazing fields of variegated greens. Twisting and turning, we soon see water again. It is breathtakingly beautiful.

This, this is the Ireland we have crossed the ocean to see. This is a dream come true. Traveling with Mark makes it even better. He is the best thing that has happened to me in a long, long time. I try to take it all in, to be in the moment and to hold the moment long enough to capture it in memory. How wonderful to finally be here. How wonderful to soak in the power of this place. I am finally in Ireland. Oh my!

"So which way, Abs? Both lanes look equally narrow. I thought we were trying to get to the west side of that lake, but now I can't tell. What does the map say?" Mark asks with a bit of tension in his voice.

"Not sure. According to this one map, it looks as if we have to go left some more before going right but…I'm not sure," I reply as I balance the three maps in my lap. Then I add, "It is all so beautiful, I guess we can't really make a mistake."

"As long as we don't meet someone coming from the other direction. As it is now, I'd have to back up about a half mile to get to a place wide enough for them to pass. I was prepared for driving on the left but these lanes are something else…"

"Thanks for doing this…I know this stone circle quest is my passion, not yours."

"No problem, just remember how self-sacrificing I'm being when we are going by cable car over to Dursey Island to see one of my lighthouses," he says laughing, as he bears right and continues along at a snail's pace. Then he adds, "I sure hope you aren't disappointed here like in Kenmare."

I start to say something about the cable car when I see a cattle gate. "Look, bearing off to the right over there. I think that is the lane we want."

"Better be, I am ready to stretch my legs. Glad to have a small car but the knees are not used to it. And we're pressing our luck not meeting any cars."

Mark pulls up to the gate—one of those livestock gates with rollers making up the road surface to keep the sheep from crossing. He jumps out in the mist which has just begun to creep over the surface of the land, stretches like a cat just waking from a nap and opens the gate.

As he comes back to the car, I realize someone will need to close the gate, so I hop out and soak in the view while he drives through. "Wow, it is so gorgeous," I say as we continue. Just as we both wonder aloud if we are on the right road, a sign appears.

"Praise be, an actual sign," Mark sighs. "And look, there is off-road parking up ahead."

"And the sun is peeking out again. This is going to be great. But let's wear our rain gear just in case the circle is further up this path than it looks," I say as we prepare to hike up to Uragh, one of the stone circles I starred as a "must see".

We arrive and are surrounded by rolling hills spotted with sheep, and an irregularly-shaped lake that blends the greens and blues of Ireland in picture-perfect beauty. There is even an incredibly appealing waterfall in the distance that at home I would be drawn to in a heartbeat. But here, it is all about the stones. They draw me in a powerful and unexplainable way.

I keep moving up the hill and then here we are. The circle is smaller than I expected. But it is all that I imagined and more. I immediately love it, absolutely love it. It consists of five small stones and one larger alignment stone. The stones are only a few feet apart. And right in the middle is a ewe and her two lambs lying in the grassy circle as if they own the place! And they have bright teal blue swatches of dye across their behinds. Too cute! We walk forward slowly so as not to disturb them and get a few good pictures before the lambs scamper off, followed by their mama.

Still silent, we smile at one another and approach slowly. Now, this is what I imagined! Actually, it is even better than I imagined. I have no words, and I always have words. I walk to the opening and hold my hand out for Mark to join me.

"Let's do a small ritual of appreciation and set our intention as we enter," I whisper.

"Whatever you want, Abs," he says, giving my hand a squeeze.

So I begin with my version of a Celtic blessing:

May we experience the beauty of this circle,

Earth, sky and water coming together in perfect harmony.

May we experience the energy of these stones waking us to Mystery and Miracle.

May we experience the oneness of all sentient beings.

"And may Mother/Father God bless us on this adventure," adds Mark.

I tear up. We have been talking a lot about theology (mostly him talking) and spirituality (mostly me talking). I knew he could talk abstractly about the Feminine Face of God, but I didn't know he would experience the awe of what I call the goddess energy. He doesn't call it that, but the terms don't matter, especially here. What's so great is that he gets it.

I walk three times around the circle, clockwise as in the ancient tradition I copied when in Kenmare. I quietly chant, "the earth, the air, the fire, the water," as I go. On the third go-round, I stop at each stone and just feel its vibration. I find that some stones give off more energy than others do. That energy builds as I complete the circle. I am again speechless. I stand in the middle, turning, turning in all directions. The Native American words come to me: *Beauty before me, beauty behind me.* Mark has been taking a video of "my antics", as he lovingly calls them, from above. Now he joins me inside the circle. "Do you know the hymn *Find a Stillness?*" he asks as he begins singing.

I join in: "Let it carry me..." And carry me it does. I am transported. I feel such an outpouring of love, such a sense of peace, such a feeling of Oneness with the Universe. Now, this is what drew me to the stone circles. This is what I sought but did not have the words to express. I am so grateful, I could burst.

We remain silent together until Mark says, "We both were feeling it, weren't we? What a powerful connection. Wow." After another lengthy silence, he begins taking pictures from each cardinal direction looking outward. "I know it is foolish to even try to capture this, but I can't help myself," he chuckles as he snaps away.

"You are right, it is foolish, but I love that you feel the impulse to try," I exclaim.

Then, he moves out of the circle and up the hill to take more pictures. "Abs, this is much more like your watercolor than Kenmare, but I can't quite get an angle that matches."

The thought itself give me chills. It finally sinks in that the watercolor is central to the pull I feel to these stones. I repeat the thought to Mark.

"Yep," he says with a smile. He then leaves me with my thoughts for a while before joining me back in the center of the circle. "You know," he says haltingly, "now I get why you said those stones in Kenmare fell flat of your expectations. This place...it is spectacular. As powerful as any cathedral I have ever visited. I don't know if ancient peoples chose it for some esoteric or religious reason or just because of the natural beauty of the setting, but wow!"

"So I can drag you to the next 26 of these places on my list?" I exaggerate to make a joke.

"You can drag me anywhere, kiddo," he says smiling at his corny reply as he pulls me to him. No other man could get away with calling me kiddo, I think to myself, as we embrace.

"This is certainly an unexpected aspect of stone circles," I murmur as he pulls me closer.

After we part, Mark whispers, "I'll be back in a few minutes. Just going to the top of that knoll." Mark says this abruptly. He hesitantly adds, "You know, to get a bird's eye view. Be back shortly."

I sit leaning against the tallest stone for a few minutes of further silence. Not sure what is going on with him, but a little time alone feels right to me and I assume to him as well. But his decision to take a walk has turned my thoughts to our relationship. Interesting that he stopped the embrace where he did. He still is tentative and unpredictable at times. But it is already obvious to me that getting away from the curious, prying eyes of our small town was a brilliant idea. Already our relationship has gone to a new level. He is so more at ease and spontaneous here.

This trip came about as a way of dealing with our reluctance to commit to one another. What if we weren't really good together 24/7? Neither of us wants to take the risk of answering to everybody if we start living together and it doesn't work out. And marriage? Not sure that I ever want that again. When I think about my marriage to Hal, I want no part of a second marriage. When I wonder if maybe it could be different, I then think about the fact that I have been living on my own since the kids left for college, divorced longer than I was married, and I just get cold feet.

Mark may be even more reluctant to commit (a big relief actually). While I fear being too long on my own to change, he is newly widowed and has had too little time on his own. He wants some time and space to adjust; to find his way as he terms it, and to explore his new status as a minister emeritus.

The stones call me back from my reverie about our relationship. It is as if they are beings wanting—demanding—my attention. I sense them individually and collectively. This time as I touch each one, I get a different emotional connection: Joy, Love, Peace, Strength, Roots; and at the big one, Oneness.

As I move to the center again, a phrase begins to run through my mind: *your story lies amidst the stones*. I have no idea where it is coming from or what it means. I just keep hearing: *you will find your story amidst the stones*.

Trying to take this in, on one hand, and on the other hand wanting to shake off the weirdness of it, I go outside the circle and up a knoll opposite Mark to pick buttercups. Asking the sheep to step aside, I gather a bunch and go back to the center of the circle. "Did I tell you about the buttercups?" I ask Mark as he returns to the center as well. Getting a shake of the head, I continue, "On her deathbed, my friend Judy, you know, from my circle group, and I talked about gathering buttercups as children. I told her that if I found buttercups at sacred sites here in Ireland, I would perform a ritual for peace and love in her memory." I pause to wipe tears from my eyes.

"Will you join me? Please include Lizzie, if you would like," I add, giving him half the bunch of flowers. As I let the first petal fall, I begin:

> *Let us remember and honor our loved ones who stood with us, who supported us, who brought joy and gladness to our lives.*
>
> *May they be in a place of peace and love.*
>
> *Judy, this petal is for you, Dad this second one is for you, and Mom, this for you.*

"Beautiful, Abs. And this one is for you, Lizzie, and Mom and Dad, for you, Here, in this piece of Heaven on Earth, it helps to imagine them at peace. Here in this circle, I am so aware of the Presence of God, of Spirit, or Universal Source."

"Yes, and of the cycle of life, the cycle of the seasons and of time-out-of-time, time eternal as celebrated by our Celtic ancestors." I add, "Blessed Be."

"Amen."

After a few minutes of silence, he breaks in: "Hey, Abs, it looks like the rain is coming. Mind if we leave and try to get back to the main road before a downpour?"

"I could stay here forever. I get this amazing sense of warmth and peace and safety. But you're right, let's try to beat the rain."

"Just one second," I say, returning to thank the stones for this amazing experience.

"OK, Abs, but hurry up," Mark says with impatience.

I slowly back out of the circle, with tears in my eyes. I take it all in, a final time; filled with awe and wonder. Then, I start down the path to take Mark's hand. The downpour begins as we run back to the car, slipping and sliding as we go. Luckily, the lane is empty and we make it back to the main road without incident.

• • •

There isn't much on the main road, but we find a gas station, get a cup of coffee and sit for a bit, enjoying some of our bakery items. Ireland and rain. We anticipated lots of rain, after all, this is Ireland. So, we savor this moment too. The car heater counteracts the piercing dampness.

After a while, we decide it is time to move on. We allow as to how we really aren't ready to venture on for another outing in the rain. So we decide to check in to a B&B to wait it out.

Besides, our online research isn't matching road signs very well and there is no cell service. We decide to take the next brown sign that says B&B and find a place, ask our hosts about the area, and get our bearings. We also want to ask them more about the term "Beara Way." Sometimes it seems to mean the major ring road around the peninsula. Other times it seems to be a lane higher up into the mountain foothills, then again a road closer to the coast. Then, it seems to mean the bike trail, and then just a walking path. Each map is different. It is really frustrating to try to figure it all out. Even directions to the stone circles seem to vary from map to map. I remark to Mark that the island needs an AAA with a Cracker Jack map division.

We see one of the brown arrow signs that we have been looking for, so we turn off the main road and head up along the ridge, following along until we see a farmhouse with brightly colored fuchsia bushes all around the gate. Their colors pop even in the rain and the variety of colors intrigues us: lots of hues of purple and violet and an almost rusty red that we don't see at home. And there is a welcoming sign—the classic *Céad míle fáilte*. Smoke is coming out the chimney and it looks ever so inviting. A no-brainer. We stop.

"Bring yourselves in out of the wet now. Welcome. Is it a bed you'll be looking for, is it? Me name is Eileen and you are very welcome here," she says in a fast tongue as she practically pulls us into her hallway.

"Yes, we would like a room for a couple of nights, if you have it. And I am Mark and this is Abagail." I add, "Call me Abby, please. What a lovely home."

After settling on price and doing the signing in, Eileen directs us to a room at the top of the stairs. It is spacious and bright in spite of the drizzle outside. "Now, sort yourselves whilst I put the kettle on. Are you experiencing the jet lag still? You can have a drop of tea and then perhaps you will want a wee nap 'til the rain blows over. Later afternoon, it'll be lovely again. Himself will be back and it is he that can direct you to all the sites around t'ese parts."

We take tea as they say and we also take her advice about the nap, snuggling in under the down and quickly falling fast asleep in one another's arms. I wake first and just lie thinking about how lucky I am to have found this man. I think he is a keeper, as my friend Karen used to say.

Jimmy is at the table and ready to meet, greet and direct us when we emerge from our cozy new nest. "Ardgroom then, is it? Then for your supper you can take the road back past us to Teddy O'Sullivan's, just down to the ring road and a wee bit east, Kilmackillogue in Lauragh, it is, so you remember passing it? Great mussels they have there too. And tonight there would be a session—that's when the lads gather for traditional Irish music—*trad* we call it."

"As fer the particulars of your stone circles now, I don't rightly know. Never went there meself. There is one up and behind us a ways, a bit of a walk from here called Shronebirrane. But as fer those in Ardgroom now, we never took the time to visit. But you will not miss it if you follow the road off toward the sea. Now then, there may even be one of those brown Beara Way signs. Would be before the pub, mind you."

"That reminds us, what actually is the Beara Way?" Mark asks.

"You needn't bother bein' fussed about that now. 'Tis just a branding the tourist people use to get visitors here instead of goin' round the Ring of Kerry. The idea is the walking trail, the bike trail and the ring road all can get ye all around the peninsula with views of the coast and a good number of ancient stones along the way. Ye may cut through the mountains and across the peninsula here at Healy Pass—one of the most beautiful drives ye will ever find here in Ireland or anywhere ye go. Another road cuts through further out toward the ocean."

"And the brown signs?" I ask.

"Information for the tourists. Ye will find places of interest, lodging and pathways marked well in these parts," he replies.

"That is really helpful, Jimmy. Thanks now. By the way, do we need a key to the front door if we come in late?" asks Mark.

"We will be leaving it open for ye to midnight. Now, Teddy closes before then so no bother. Oh, now, you might want to stop off at another of those circles coming back into Lauragh…called Cashelkeelty. Higher up a wee bit it is, so you get a full view. Car park as well."

I am thrilled to think all of them are so near. The sun begins to come back out as we prepare to take off. Eileen pipes in: "Sure, you'll be needing some 'wellies' to slog through the fields in the damp," as she scurries off to get them for us. Wellies it seems are rubber boots of a particular kind.

Jimmy and Mark talk a bit more, while I get our things from upstairs. We thank Jimmy for the info and Eileen for the boots before heading out for the next part of our adventure, glad to be rested and dry.

We enjoy the ride, but the easy-to-find sign alludes us. Is the post office/gas station/café building considered Ardgroom? Or is this turn further down by the pub a better bet? Doubling back, we find our way and then see a place to park, a place to dip our wellies in disinfectant to protect the sheep at the gate and a path to our destination.

The setting is lovely: Shades of blue upon blue to the north as the bay waters glisten and shadows begin to fall over the mountains of Dingle on the far shore; shades of green and purple as the two Beara mountain ranges rise into the blue, blue sky to the south. It's the scene I expected to see when we first left Kenmare. Postcard perfect. And we both remark how quickly the weather changes in these parts. We are almost on the Atlantic coast so I guess fast moving systems are to be expected.

The stones themselves are not as magnificent as those at Uragh. They are thinner and taller, and there are no sheep to greet us. But Mark and I enter hand in hand as before. Without speaking, I walk around the circle, touching each stone as I go. Mark stands in the center, taking a 360 degree picture.

"I sense the energy build as I go around, but the missing stone and the general look and feel of the place kind of scatters the energy in some ways. Kenmare seemed too manicured, but this seems neglected, Uragh was small, but it had an intimacy and power that was charming."

"You sound like Goldilocks tasting her porridge," Mark teases.

"Seriously," I say with a laugh, "what do you think?"

"I don't know. The idea of these places is new to me. I haven't read up on them like you have but this does feel different. I sense a hard life lived by those who came here. Let's take a few minutes in silent prayer and then see what more we get in the way of an intuitive sense of the place." After a few moments, he asks, "What are you sensing?"

"That *déjà vu* feeling that I have been here before; that somehow this entire expanse of land sloping down to the bay was inhabited by ancient peoples who lived in clans in small settlements and then met together as a larger community for ceremonies. Not sure if they were driven off, or perhaps they moved on. But, somehow, I get the feeling that the true purpose of these places was lost. What do you get?" I throw it back to him.

"Just that it was a hard life but that how they worshiped or came together here in ritual is what sustained them. It really is something to imagine back to those times." Then he adds, "On to the next?"

"As soon as I gather some buttercups for the center of the circle."

"Of course. Let's repeat the ritual at every stop. It's lovely." As we finish, he adds, "Shall we just hike over the field? Doubt we can park any closer and we can follow that family of hikers in the distance who seem to know what they are doing and where they are going. They must have a hiking map."

The second circle seems of the same period, though the stones are thinner with more jagged top ends. The view looking down to the bay is even lovelier given the changes to the sky this time of day. We enter it in reverence and we walk the circle, once together, and then I go another two times while Mark takes a video. Mark makes a quick remark about wondering who will show up in this video, but I choose not to respond and keep walking. Maybe I am on overload, but I don't feel very connected. Again, we leave buttercups and then sit silently. Although Mark is being quiet, I sense that he is ready to leave and I allow that thought to keep me from going deep into my own silence. No message comes.

Then, as we begin to walk away, I fall forward onto my knees, breaking my fall with my hands.

"Abs! Are you OK?

"Yes, damp and jarred but luckily I landed on grass not rock."

"Maybe the wellies are too big. You sure went down fast. Here, let me help you back up. For a minute there, you looked like a Muslim praying to Mecca."

"Glad the grass was my prayer rug," I quip, as I rub my left knee and then elbow and wait for him to come over to help me up. "Actually, let's just stay here for a while."

"Sure, no rush," he offers amiably, giving me his arm. "I would sit down with you Abs, but the ground is too damp for either of us. Why don't you stand up and lean against me for a while. Better than sitting on that wet grass. And of all the stones around, there isn't one that will work as a chair.'

"This sounds crazy, but I feel as if I was tripped. And I keep getting this phrase repeating in my head: *Listen to the stones, listen to the Ancient Ones.*"

"You are not crazy, but I don't know about all this; it stretches my credulity."

"I can appreciate that it is a stretch. It's one for me too. Thank you for staying with me and supporting me," I whisper. "I think I am being told not to leave. I think I am to remember to take time at each of these circles, not to judge them by their beauty but just to listen. The trouble is I don't know how—not sure how to listen better or what to listen for…"

"The Quaker 'still voice within' always made a lot of sense to me. We find ourselves by listening to ourselves. It may be as simple as that. Profound, but simple."

"Maybe. Or maybe I am supposed to somehow intuit the lives of others from the past by my own connections with the stones. Or maybe I was here before, in a past life. I just don't know."

"There again, that seems a stretch to me, but I agree these are places of mystery and wonder. Ireland has produced many mystics you know, in modern times and down through the ages. Now that we are here, I can see how the land adds to one's ability to connect with the Divine, with Spirit, or even with the Otherworld as they called it. But, for now, what do you say we get you back to the car so you can dry out? If you feel compelled to come back, we can do it another day."

I remain stubbornly fixed where I am for a bit longer. When nothing more comes, I agree to move on. In the car on the way back, we pass near two more stone circles (Cashellkeely and Drombohilly), within walking distance according to my map. I want to go to them and I want to know why there are so many concentrated in this small area. What were they really for? What is this connection I feel? My stumble was some sort of symbol or signal, but for the life of me I don't get it. Be more humble? Surrender? No going forward or back until I listen? Though tempted to stop and pursue these gnawing questions at these not-yet-visited circles, I decide not to suggest we stop again. Enough for today.

Mark comments on how starved he is and I agree. So we head to the pub for mussels, beer, and what Jimmy called "the *craic*". We still are a bit uncertain to its meaning so we translate it in our minds to "a good time out with friends". After his vague explanation of the Beara Way, we didn't even bother for a definition of *craic*. Jimmy is right about the mussels though; all the food is delicious. But it seems Jimmy was wrong about there being live music. Instead, we listen to a small group of regulars speaking Irish as the bar. That in itself is great entertainment.

"Sounds like we have some Americans visitors, do we not?" asks one of the older gentlemen. Mark answers, "Yes, indeed, we are from the Finger Lakes area of New York."

"Aye, New York, me nephew is with the police there in Brooklyn."

Mark tries to explain the Upstate versus New York City differences but it falls on deaf ears. Then some of the other guys tell us about relatives and friends they know in the states and ask if we might know them. I guess it is hard to imagine the size of the U.S., even though two or three of them have visited—Texas, Louisiana and New York City. What different views of America the three of them have. And what a wonderful glimpse of Ireland we are getting, and it is only the beginning of our trip.

We decide to drive out to the end of the peninsula and go to Dursey Island tomorrow so Mark can have his turn, getting a view of the first lighthouse on his list. I am dreading the cable car but since it doesn't go up a mountain, just straight across to the island, I am hopeful it is not too big a deal. I want to be a good sport about it. But that's to worry about tomorrow. Today has been a very full day. With a final drink, we bid the guys at the bar a goodnight and head back to our B&B.

Mark is out like a light. But I keep going over my experiences and reactions to the stone circles. What drew me to them to begin with? What are they all about? What messages am I missing? And what's the connection to my watercolor?

During the night sometime, somehow the thought comes that I am to listen to the stories, to the dark stories as well as the light ones—to my own story, to not just the happy parts, but the hard parts, too. I sit up, worried that honoring this call might interfere with the anticipated fun of this trip; worse yet, that it might interfere with my relationship with Mark. I like to think I am open to learning about myself, but the timing sucks.

CHAPTER THREE

I wake to find that Mark is not in the bed nor is he in the room. A sudden feeling of panic, of being all alone sweeps over me, and surprises me. I don't want to think I have become dependent on him. I chalk it up to the fact I have never been so far away from home.

Looking out the window, I see him in the yard, the garden as the Irish call it. He is peacefully reading. Good. We both need our own down time and he is taking it as he needs it. I pull out my journal and start capturing a bit of what has happened since we arrived at Shannon. But I can't concentrate and I am starved. I dress quickly and find Mark ready to go to breakfast too.

"Coffee or tea now? Aye, two coffees and will it be full Irish now? And will it be fer the both of you?" Eileen asks in the quick Cork accent we are just beginning to understand.

We have read of the famed Irish breakfast and the hotel buffet yesterday in Kenmare looked amazing. It seems prudent to ask for details here.

"Full Irish in Cork is your porridge, your eggs, rashers, sausage, black and white puddings and tomato. Some also offer beans. If ye would like I could offer them as well."

"Wow, and what are rashers?" I ask.

"'Would be like your American bacon or the Canadians say 'tis like their bacon even more. And as fer ye puddings, ye know they are sausages? The black being a blood sausage. The Irish sausage now is lighter and has more meal. 'Tis what ye find in bangers and mash, don't ye know."

We go for the full breakfast this time, just for the experience of it all, even though it sounds like way too much food. I plan to give my black pudding to Mark because it sounds disgusting, but he is up for trying it.

Jimmy comes in to the house moving slowly, speaking in almost a drawl, in contrast to his wife's fast pace. "Mornin' to ye, now. Sleep well now, did ye?"

Seeing our nods, he continues "There will be no Dursey Island for ye today. The winds have picked up fierce and the cable car will not be runnin' I would fear."

"Gosh, it is so sunny and bright, I never thought about being held back from going there today. What a shame," Mark says with obvious disappointment.

"Aye, well now, your sandwiches are already made and it's a lovely day for exploring around these parts. You can still enjoy a picnic by the water and have a grand day altogether," chirps Eileen as she brings our plates to the table.

We are so busy eating and then so stuffed that we forgo going through our pile of tourist materials and maps Mark collected. Instead, we are going to play the day by ear. We take a short walk around the grounds of this lovely farmhouse and Jimmy takes us to see the new calf born just last week. He also points us in the direction of a neighbor's donkey which we see before starting out. I love donkeys. Sadly though, Jimmy explains that they are often abandoned these days, now that they are no longer used in farming. We vow to ourselves that we will send a donation to one of the donkey rescue funds as we say goodbye to the cute little guy begging us for food, even though he looks well cared for.

As we get into the car, Mark asks "Do you remember the turn off to the old coast road we passed yesterday morning right after Uragh when the rain started? Let's go back to that. It should follow along the coast and give us a view across the bay to Dingle like we saw from a distance at the Ardgroom stone circles and that you were looking for when we left Kenmare."

In agreement, we travel back to the Old Kenmare Road and the sign to Taoist. Taoist we discover consists of just four corners with one building that combines a post office and small store. We are surprised because there was a book on Eileen's table with the title *Taoist*. Plus, she spoke about it as we would speak of a sizable village back in the States. We learn from the clerk that the name refers to the parish and the parish is quite large. I love learning about stuff like this and no one makes me feel foolish when I ask, which makes it fun.

We only meet one car and see two wonderful elderly women sitting sunning themselves on a bench with their dog. "Not much seems to be going on in Taoist," Mark remarks as we wave at the ladies, and leave Taoist with more chocolate, some chewing gum and water for the road.

We come to the coastal road as we start wondering if we had made the correct turn. We had. The views are stunning, with the one in front of us surpassed when rounding another corner. While on the inland side of the road, the rhododendron splashes of purple adorn the roadside, sturdy in the strong wind that roils the bay.

"These bushes remind me that Eileen mentioned some gardens around here that people come from all over Ireland to see," Mark recalls.

"I kinda prefer the out in the open, seeing the natural flora and fauna myself. What about you?" I reply.

"Agreed. Let's just...Oh my gosh, I think we are at Kilcatherine. I thought it was the other side of Eyeries, but this is it!" he exclaims as he pulls into a small parking area along the road.

We have come across the noted 7th century monastic site with the ruins of a 12th or 13th century church and a stone cemetery that dates back to the early Celtic Church. It is a quintessentially Celtic sacred site. And we have the whole place to ourselves. Fantastic!

"Will you join me in prayer as we enter?" Knowing full well that I will, he begins:

Mother/Father God who appears to us in many shapes and forms,

Grace us with your blessing as we enter this sacred place.

Help us to understand your word down through the ages.

Guide us as we work to restore balance to the world, to honor nature and live by Christ's teachings.

Thank you for the privilege of walking on this Holy ground and

May we continue to evoke the spirit of St. Catherine as we travel this sacred landscape.

"May it be so," I add.

It's hard to describe what makes ruins beautiful and inspiring, rather than bleak and depressing. After all, they are remnants of stone, indicating a place of beauty has been left to fall in disrepair or intentionally destroyed. What remains has not been purposely placed for aesthetic effect. Quite the opposite is the case. Yet, there is a natural beauty and a kind of balance that is often beautiful. Such is the case here. Instead of seeing the shell of what once was, we see a magnificent representation of what has been. I love the arched windows and door frames.

Mark knows the historical ages represented by the different shapes of the arches. He can distinguish early church ruins from Norman and later influences. I just enjoy framing views of the bay through the window spaces as I try to capture the perfect picture. With the north wall of the church almost totally missing, there are lots of photo angles that capture my attention. There also is an energy to the place that pulls me to it. Not anywhere as strong for me as at Uragh, but still palpable.

"Abs, over here. Look, here is the altar, and here's a small cupboard or storage area for the relics. And look up there. That's the stone called the Cat's Head. It's supposedly cat-like and represents the church's namesake St. Catherine, *Caithinghearn*, 'The Cat Goddess'. What do you think? Does it look like a cat to you?"

"Not really, but it is not a typical woman's face. Fascinating. Do you know anything about this Cat Goddess legend?"

"Well, I wish we had cell service so I could bring up the info, but I do remember some of what I read on the plane. The main thing is that she was a figure, who like Brigit, bridged the pagan and early Christian culture. One legend has the Hag of Beara stealing a Bible from *Caithinghearn* and the saint striking the Hag with her staff, turning the pagan goddess into stone."

"So the story goes from embracing the pagan representations to cutting them down," I protest.

"Certainly, that story does. But what I love about the place is that I not only can feel Christ's presence; I also can feel the presence of the Divine Feminine that I have only come to know more recently. This is what I love about early Celtic Christianity. Here it is! We are here and it feels like coming home to a place I did not realize I longed to find. It is truly awesome."

I identify with the sentiment about finding something I had not realized I sought. Tears come to us both as we stand together in silent gratitude. The wind whistling through the site is the only sound we hear.

Finally, Mark says, "Let's walk on through the crosses. The tall one over there is reportedly one of the oldest in Ireland. The circle of the Celtic cross, you know, represents your stone circle, the idea of wholeness and the cycles of life, seasons and celestial movement you honor. Later, let's say Roman times, brought the crucifix."

"Oh, of course. That's why I find the Celtic cross so compelling and yet so soothing."

"Yep."

We wind our way between stones and grave sites as we look at all the crosses and headstones. Finally, we reach the big one, a Celtic High Cross. It is just a few inches shorter than me. Standing next to it, I can't help but feel a similarity to the standing stones we have been visiting. Each sacred. Each a statement of a culture's connection to earth and sky, to the Mother Earth and to the transcendent Sky.

We also notice a grassy mound a little ways away which proves to be the remains of a holy well and more ancient burial markers. Water as source. All the elements present. No doubt, this was a pagan site before a church was built.

Again, we fall into silence. Finally, Mark breaks the quietude. "The harmony, the balance, the profound simplicity. I feel so blessed to be here. You know, we have always talked about my fascination with *Ondine*, but I think it is the Celtic part that is meaning the most to me. The Celtic spirit, the Celtic Church ruins, the ancient stones, all the Celtic aspects just move me beyond measure. They stir up my Scottish roots and make me want to visit Scotland and all the Celtic nations, not just Ireland."

"I know that Ireland, Scotland, and parts of England are Celtic but there are more?" I ask.

"Yep. Let's see, Besides those you mentioned, there are Wales, Isle of Man, Brittany, which is part of France, and the part of Spain called Galicia. Oh, and the English part is called Cornwall. Wish I could remember the Gaelic names but I can only think of Eire right now."

"Well, I am game for going whenever you say. Even if there were no stone circles, I still would want to come." I squeeze his hand as we continue to stand amid the stones of the church cemetery.

• • •

It is quite a while before we feel like moving. Finally, we head back to the car, where we turn our focus to the bay. We just sit, staring out at the choppy water and kind of regrouping. Skellig is just across the bay and a closer distance to us than it has been all day. We add that to our next-time list too. Mark reminding me that Skellig Michael, the ancient island monastery where Star Wars was shot, and the Skellig Lighthouse are just beyond our view.

I feel full, but also spent. It was such a powerful experience. I think even more so for Mark. After a while he breaks the silence, "OK, shall we move on?" I nod; and we continue down our magical coast road.

Around a curve and down the beach less than a half mile away, I notice another parking area and a family grouped down by the water. "According to the map, this must be Coulagh Bay. It's a gorgeous view, but those people seem to be looking at something specific. What do you think we've come across this time?" I ask Mark, as I point to the shore.

He instinctively pulls in to the parking area and remarks, "Don't know what they are doing; it can't compare to where we have just been, but let's have a look."

We actually have stumbled upon the Hag of Beara, the stone version. It is on my must-see list, but I am surprised to find it so close to Kilcatherine. The rock itself is not nearly as large or imposing as I had imagined, and it is at first rather indistinct amid an already rocky coastline.

Mark asks, "Is this big chunk of rock down a rocky slope closer to the water but not at the edge what we have come to see?"

"I think so, but let's read the sign before we head down the rocky part. Not what I expected, but I think that this is it, all of it."

Cailleach (Hag) is the name for the crone phase of the Celtic triple goddess. She represents not only the strength and wisdom of the third stage of life but winter. Some Celtic goddesses were local but this one was both local and also known in other Celtic lands, particularly Scotland. Here, the local goddess, Cailleach Beara, was said to be a protector and shape-shifter who carried rocks in her apron which she would use to build shelter for the people but would also hurl at enemies.

We make our way down the rocky path toward the shore and then see the rock more clearly. I am struck by the number of *clooties* (pieces of cloth and other tokens) offered to the goddess, that have been left by countless visitors. I search my pockets and find only a tiny heart-shaped stone I had picked up at Ardgroom circle. It seems appropriate that I leave it here, as somehow all of these places are connected in a sacred landscape. The landscape and the seascape emit powerful energy and appear to hold the stories of an ancient people connected to the land. I am greedy to see more, hear more, and feel more.

Mark offers, "I do wish our smartphones worked out here. I had this earmarked on Google too. The legend I recall has it that this rock which rises out of the bay represents the fossilized remains of the face of the Cailleach Beara awaiting her husband Manannan, God of the Sea, to return to her. I kind of get that—she sure is looking out to sea from one of the most beautiful bays imaginable. And the harmony here of water, earth and sky—that represents the original Celtic trinity. The fierceness and power of the sea meeting the sturdy, solid rock of earth…"

His beautiful image of the Celtic trinity goes totally over my head as I vehemently react to the part about this Great Goddess waiting for her man: "Whoa there, waiting for her man, right, like Tammy Wynette, huh!"

"Hey, don't jump on me. I am just the messenger. Back up a bit and cool down. Where did that fire and fury come from?"

"I'm not sure," I say sheepishly. "I often get frustrated that women's stories get distorted, minimized, appropriated and all. But I am shaking with emotion and can't account for why."

"Do you think I am so sexist that I would expect you—or any woman—to be waiting patiently at the shore for me to come in and out as I like?" with a hint of both challenge and hurt in his voice.

"No, no. I wouldn't be here with you and we wouldn't be able to do all of this together if I did. Sorry to spew at you about it. I really don't know why it bothers me so much. It isn't that such slights in history—or even in modern times—are new to me. But I felt gripped by rage and indignation."

"The legend of St. Catherine, our favorite Cat Goddess, turning her to stone probably didn't help," he quips, trying to lighten my mood. "I really am sorry for jumping on you. But I don't think that I can be easily teased out of the rage I am feeling at the moment," I reply.

"The term Fierce Feminine is trending these days. Looks like the Hag of Beara could be its archetype. Maybe, you are to become a leader of the movement," he speculates. "But beware that Tammy Wynette line brought Hilary Clinton a lot of enemies," he teases.

"I sure am fired up and feeling the Hag's power."

"I have to say though that I believe she could be waiting for her man without being subservient or less than him. Cannot equals want each other?" he asks.

"That is a very rational statement, but injustice is not rational nor are the norms that have developed about how men and society in general treat women. I need some space to just be with this place for a while. I am going to take a walk down to the water's edge, if I can navigate the rocks."

"I take it you don't want help or companionship at the moment. I have an idea. I am going up and across the road to collect buttercups, I will bring them back and we can do our ritual after you have had your space. I don't want us to leave a beautiful place like this with tension between us," he states with certainty and he heads back up the path toward the car.

I pick my way across the rocks but watching my footing doesn't give me a chance to let off steam. I go back up the path and then walk parallel to the shore, letting the earth ground me as I appeal to the Hag for guidance. Feeling calmer, I sit and try to absorb the power of the place, of her message of sovereignty and all its complexities. The fierceness of the wind contrasting with the exquisite beauty of the place strikes me most of all. As I meander back to the rock, there Mark is. Just waiting patiently.

"Feel better?" Mark asks as he hands me buttercups. I nod and we do our ritual of gratitude for life and those we have loved and who have loved us.

We are all the way back to the car before I actually answer his question. "Yeah, thanks. I do feel better now. You know, it is not lost on me that you were sitting waiting for me. Thanks." I give his hand a squeeze and he quietly nods. Smart man, to not start talking. No mansplaining from this guy! We just sit a bit longer in silence.

"You know, I thought I wanted to visit the site to lift up 'hag' as a word of honor again and to reflect on my own aging. But the experience has been so much more. The stone itself isn't what I imagined. But the place is powerful and represents so much that has been almost lost in women's lives, in all our lives. It is the notion of sovereignty that was lifted up to me."

"More than just lifted up, Abs. Not sure what all it was for you, but more than just lifted up. Your reaction was fierce," Mark remarks, "and, rightly so in my opinion. This concept of sovereignty is really the challenge of the day, not just for women, or men and women in relationship, but communities and governments, culturally and globally, it is at the heart of all our struggles. Even with God. How do we live from our own sense of self, be complete and yet be part of the Oneness. I admire you for tuning into that today and for your tenacity in staying with it. I have been sitting here thinking a lot about it thanks to you giving me a nudge."

"I feel like my nudge was more of a jolt. This surge of anger and power overcame me. In fact, it was really disconcerting. And, yes, this sovereignty thing is a hard thing to unpack, isn't it?"

"Yep. But I hazard to say The Hag would be proud of us," he jokes as he starts the car up.

"This is breathtaking. Is it the cove we saw in *Ondine*? The one that left us drooling and starting to plan our trip?" I ask.

"Ha! This time it is you who brings up *Ondine*. I wonder just how many times we will be reminded of that night we watched the video and decided to come to Ireland? I don't think this is the cove in the movie but I am not sure. I do know the major cove featured in the movie is nearer Castletownbere. I have it earmarked. But there was filming in Eyeries, so maybe. That coast guard station in the distance for instance sure looks familiar."

"I have had a feeling of being familiar with everything we have done so far, in an eerie way," I quip.

"Hmm, suggestive of past lives more than movie watching, isn't it?"

"I didn't know you believed in past lives. Do you?"

"Not saying I do, but then the Universe is Mystery and Miracle. Shall we walk for a while?" I agree as he pulls over into a parking spot.

"Hey, see that huge standing stone up there? Want to climb up? I think it is the ancient Ogham Stone I read about. What if I get the picnic stuff and blanket Eileen packed for us and we head up there?" Again, I am in agreement and so we hike up amid stone and grassy patches. The view upon our arrival is beyond description.

As we reach the stone, we realize it is the tallest we have encountered: almost three times Mark's six foot, three inch frame. It also is the first time we have seen ogham, the early Celtic writing which consists of marks, both straight and slanted on either side of a straight line. "Did you know that ogham "letters" represent trees, which were sacred to the Druids?" I ask Mark as he places the blanket on a fairly flat surface nearby.

"I did read that and, guess what? I have that earmarked too. I would love to study it, especially now that we're seeing it in real time. Fascinating."

Reading from a map of the area he brought along, he continues, "OK, this will get us oriented. Still don't get how Kilcatherine and the Hag of Beara can be considered west of Eyeries, but maybe the early blurb I read was incorrect. For sure, we were looking out at Coulagh Bay and this little hamlet is Ballycrovane.

And this is the Ogham Stone cited. But it doesn't say anything about the inscription: *Son of Deich the descendant of Turainn*. Another legend to look up."

Then he grumbles, "That's the trouble with researching this stuff beforehand. It is hard to relate to it from an armchair at home. And bookmarking doesn't help if there is no cell service. On other trips, I have come to rely on Google, but I still can't get cell service around here. We'll have to look it up later. Anyway, this place is too special to muddy up with facts and details."

"Agreed. Let's just sit here for a while. It is all I imagined and more. Let's just listen to the birds. Soak it all in," I respond dreamily.

"And dig into Eileen's sandwiches," Mark adds with a sheepish grin.

We finish the sandwiches and the flask of tea Eileen so graciously provided for us.

Then we lie still, looking at the clouds and listening to the sounds of the sea. The wind is still fierce and as it pounds against the rocks. I daydream about The Cailleach and Manannan coming together in love. First, I see her morphing into a *selkie* or *ondine*, as I guess mermaids are called here, and swimming out to merge with the sea. Then, the scene changes as they shape-shift back into human form and swim into this little harbor below.

"Penny for your thoughts?" asks Mark.

"Imagining the Cailleach and Manannan coming together," I say still partially in dreamtime. Then add, without filter, "Have you ever made love at the beach?"

Mark gives an awkward laugh, "Not within a minister's repertoire, at least not this minister's. Have you?"

"It's always been a fantasy of mine."

"This isn't the beach, but there isn't a soul anywhere around…"

I give a nod and we give ourselves over to the pounding sea below…

• • •

"Well, was it what you imagined?"

"The ground was a little lumpy," I say laughing. "But yes…perhaps better than I had imagined."

"We'll just have to find a quiet sandy beach and try that too."

I nod and add "But this place is so perfect, even without a sandy beach. If there was a cottage on this very spot I would want to buy it. I can't imagine a lovelier place to live."

"Yeah, it is really beautiful. I could watch the clouds and the waves all day, maybe every day."

Dark clouds blow in fast from the west. "Looks like Dursey may have had a storm as well as high winds. Glad we weren't over there today."

I realize the shadow of the clouds is really amping up my anxiety. "Do you think it is all just too ideal?" I ask.

"I hope to never find beauty and balance too ideal, but if you mean does the notion of living on this hillside sound too ideal, yep. I mean I need to engage in service of some kind, not just retire into fantasy land. Is that what you are talking about?"

"Not sure what all I am talking about. I know this last year has been one of a kind of freedom, joy and ease I don't think I have ever had. Yet, I am drawn to these stones. While I experience awe and beauty, I am also encountering unknown forces and fearful feelings. Like a big shadow is looming over me."

"What's that expression about the brightest flame casting the darkest shadow? Your flame is getting brighter, Abs, seeing your shadow is just part of that, as I see it."

"I hope that's it…"

"Let's walk for a bit, explore the remains of the coast guard station and then go see those brightly painted row houses in Eyeries that so attracted us online."

As we approach the remains of the coast guard station and try to find safe footing to get down to the wall, Mark recalls what he has read "I am remembering that this was a British station they filled with munitions. During the 1920s, the IRA exploded them all. This is what's left. Talk about darkness where there is beauty, huh?"

"Yeah. Wow."

"Is that a well over there? Think we can get to it without breaking our necks? I would like to say a prayer." We get closer and Mark leads us in a short prayer:

Water of Life, Source of Life,

You of the deep well, the babbling brook, the calm and the raging seas

Help us live in peace and harmony with one another.

Help us appreciate this blue-green planet and the lives of all beings upon it.

Amen.

We decide to get the car and drive into Eyeries rather than hike over. The colors of the houses and shops are just as vivid as in the website pictures but not a thing is open, not even a place for tea or coffee. So we start back. We pass by the stone circles of yesterday without even discussing whether or not to stop. I think we both are feeling we have had enough for one day. We want to get back, shower and go to dinner early.

The views of the mountains and Glenmore Lake from the patio of Josie's Lakeview House are supposed to be spectacular. A comfy seat and a glass of wine sounds like a perfect end to a perfect day. Plus, as Eileen told us, "Go when you have the weather, ye never know when it will turn." The dark clouds have indeed blown off across the bay and the sun is bright again.

Once we are refreshed and ready to go, Jimmy gives us directions. "Irish directions," Mark quips when we are on the road and clearly out of hearing range. "They all say 'just down the road a piece and ye can't miss it.' I know we turned south as we were supposed to do, but I think I missed the left turn that can't be missed. We clearly are headed down the Healy Pass."

"I think you are right and it is beautiful. In fact, it is drop-dead gorgeous, and the light this time of day makes it even better. Let's just drive on a bit more if you are OK driving on this winding, narrow road."

"Yep, and glad you are comfortable with my driving; 'cuz I see no place to turn around."

"I would love a drone right now to capture this view. The road actually makes what seems like a perfect horseshoe."

"Yeah, it is amazing. There's something white and man-made ahead, not sure what yet. See it?"

"Now I do. It's a cross and other statuary. A crucifix actually. This is the first time we have seen that. All the other crosses I have noticed have been Celtic. Wonder what's up with that?" I ask him.

"The modern Roman Catholic stamp on the territory. Let's stop and read the sign as well as take some pictures when we turn around. The light is so beautiful," Mark says as he stops for pictures over the valley.

"On another day, I might find the cross and the statues impressive. But, today, we have been so delightfully steeped in all things Celtic, that the modernity of it leaves me cold," I announce as I look downhill along the road. "There's a little shop. It looks open. Shall we walk down?"

What a treat. Mountain Cabin it is called. We meet the owner, Donal Sullivan and he tells us about the area. We discover all sorts of books, including an archaeological map *The Stone Circles of Cork*, another *The Antiquities of the Beara Peninsula* and a book of modern poetry called *The Hag of Beara*, all of which I am delighted to buy.

"Hey, Abs, come here. Listen to this passage:

> Whatever legend you believe in, the Hag of Beara in many ways has come to represent *Mna na Eireann*—the women of Ireland—due to her power, fertility, and strength. Surely she will rise to help nurture Ireland once again."

"I think we need this one too!" I say with excitement.

We easily see the sign to Josie's on the way back for a fabulous dinner. Someone in the airport lounge had first mentioned the place to us. Then some folks back in Kenmare mentioned it. And, of course, Eileen promoted it as well. It seems Josie's is an institution. Josie is also is a real woman who takes great pride in both her property and her food. She greets us and invites us to wait on the back terrace until our table is ready. She is demure and understated in manner, but I imagine the Fierce Feminine embodied in this almost-legendary restaurateur.

The wait is not a hardship but a real treat. The views of the lake tucked between mountains feel more intimate sitting on the terrace than they did driving down the pass. Perhaps, it is the closer proximity to the lake. After a day spent looking out to a rough sea, the tranquility of the lake is soothing. And the grounds offer a peak at Irish gardening customs as well as provide a blaze of color over the tastefully landscaped site.

It is only the evening chill that convinces us to go inside where the warmth of the fire awaits. When the still beautiful views out the window fade as the sun sets, Josie herself lights the candle on our table. What a beautiful setting for our first romantic dinner in Ireland.

CHAPTER FOUR

"W hat is it about the first cup of coffee in the morning? I'm a bear until it's in my hand," Mark, ever so thoughtful, grumbles in a whisper so as not to be heard beyond our table.

I start to tell him he never is that fierce and maybe make a pun on bear in Beara, when Eileen enters the room and comes straight over to our table. "You'll be havin' a full Irish breakfast this mornin'. Ye have the weather fer Dursey today. Mind, go now when the winds are down," she says in a tone somewhere between authoritative and scolding.

"Thanks for that advice, Eileen. We were contemplating doing just that. So a full Irish breakfast for me then, but hold the puddings…and what about you, Abs?" he responds energetically.

I nod agreement and, I swear, Eileen is the Celtic equivalent of a whirling dervish. "So glad she didn't ask again about those puddings…I just can't even look at the black pudding…all that blood, even though I can't see it, I know it's there; and the white looks like suet for birds, nicely browned though…"

"Yep. Easier to just say we're trying to keep our cholesterol levels down. Though hard to say with a straight face when eating two eggs, bacon and sausages," Mark replies as he slathers his brown bread with famed Irish butter.

"Good thing we have a long walk to see your lighthouse when we get to Dursey," I quip, giving him a mock look of disapproval. "Here we are on one island, and we need to take a cable car to get to another island. Then the thing you really want to see is on an even smaller island off the coast of island number two. It's like nesting dolls, only spread out."

"What?" Mark asks in a very confused voice.

It is only then that I realize how crazed I have gotten over the cable car ride I have agreed to take.

As if on cue, Eileen reappears at our table, saying, "If it's the lighthouse way off on the wee island you want to see, I hear from some Yanks here last week that a lad with a donkey cart has set up a wee enterprise as you get off the cable car. You may have the idea of walking, but time is your enemy for getting to the fer end and back this time of year. The cable car's hours get longer in June but fer now, you would be rushed."

We nod in appreciation, mouths still full, while she refills our coffee. We hear her "for" and her "far" as the same word but are developing an ear for her accent. She continues, "And I will make ye a wee lunch and be reminding you to fill your water bottles. You will find no shops or services on the island, even in these days of wee kiosks all over the countryside. Mind now, be prepared."

We thank her profusely. Then with very full tummies, we pack up for all-weather conditions, and are off down to the ring road.

• • •

We head west for Allihies, the last village on the peninsula, where the map tells us to turn down the road to the Dursey cable car. I am more nervous about the ride across the water than I want to admit, but I try not to think about it. The drive is so beautiful; I am able to tuck the fear away. We pass through Ardgroom and pass by the turn for our blissful cove in Eyeries on our way to the furthest point west. Somewhere before Ardgroom we enter County Cork. I meant to take note of the border but missed the sign again. It is no different from going county to county in New York, but here the county names are used as major designators.

"I read that the Anam Cara Writing Center is just beyond Eyeries. Will you start looking for it?" my handsome driver asks.

"Sure, but what is it? I never heard of it and it is not on my map." I hate not knowing things.

"It's on that little map of galleries and such. You have read John O' Donahue, haven't you? The place is named for his best-seller, *Anam Cara,* which means "soul friend." The man writes the most beautiful and insightful prose about Celtic spirituality and the heart-centeredness of the Irish spirit. I think he was from County Clare, so we will have to ask why the center is here and if he founded it."

"Do we have time to stop?"

"Not really. Plus, the brochure says by appointment only, but I thought we would just drive in to try to get a sense of the place. You will LOVE his work. He has a way of talking about God and including the Divine Feminine that just is so natural and true sounding. I used the book as the basis of a men's small group ministry at church. If I say so myself, it was one of our best offerings ever."

"The place looks inviting. It would be great, if we had a week to dedicate to writing. Let's add it to our list of next-time items."

We continue to talk about writing, journaling, and how we would like to capture the beauty and soulfulness all around us. It keeps my mind off the dreaded cable car ride. Instead I start thinking about my stone circle experiences. I realize I really need to carve out some time to journal. So much is happening and some of it is lost on me because it is overwhelming and simply too much to take in. I don't want to lose it, but I also don't want it to take over the trip.

Mark pipes up with his own query, "I wonder if I would have liked being a monk? You know the contemplative life, the life of a mystic, a life of prayer? What if I had chosen that instead of choosing congregational ministry?"

"Had you become a monk, who would travel with me to Ireland?" I ask.

"Good point, look what I would have missed," he replies. "Now, if we go way back, monasteries in Ireland were co-ed. We could both have lived a life of contemplation. Together."

"Maybe we did," I tease.

"Now that's an interesting thought," he muses on the idea.

We drive through the charming little village of Allihies, noting the beautiful beach on the right and the renowned vermilion-colored O'Neill's Bar and Restaurant on the left. Without words, with just a nod, we tag it as the place for dinner on our return. Mark lets me out to take pictures while he goes to get gas and cash. The diesel engine really goes far on a tank, but he is a careful guy. Besides, he wants to get some extra cash for the boy with the donkey cart. ATMs are a scarcity on Beara.

When he returns to pick me up, I convince him we have time to stroll the beach for a few minutes. This beautiful small village at the tip of the Beara Peninsula is a treasure and I want us to savor it a bit more before driving on. And, if honest with myself, I am procrastinating too.

The road out to the cable car is narrow and longer than I expected. I am beginning to feel guilty that my wish to stay at the beach might cause us to miss the cable car. My apprehension skyrockets. I really do not like cable cars. I rode one up in the Adirondacks, not to ski, but in the fall to see the leaves with the boys when they were young, and I could not wait to get off. It was excruciating getting back on to go back down. But I had no choice.

Now here I am doing what I vowed never to do again. But this one goes straight across, not up and down a mountain so I am hoping it will be tamer.

I don't have a lot of fears—fear of falling and fear of drowning at sea are the two biggies. I don't know where they came from and I have just avoided doing activities that involve either, which has not a problem until now. Both fears are blocks to going to lighthouses with Mark.

We arrive and things move fast. Parking is easy. The cable car is already on the mainland. Two other people, who look like locals, are waiting to step on. We meet Paddy the cable car operator who is charming and upbeat, urging us to the cable car platform since the car is about to leave. No sheep or cattle, Paddy tells us, though he reminds us they would get first preference. All very smooth and easy—except for the fact I do not want to go.

That is even before I see that the gondola is nothing but a custom-made wooden box, brightly painted and inspiring even less confidence than an Adirondack ski lift. While the starting platform and the disembarking platform on the other side sit on flat land, the car travels very high over the water. Trellis-like towers spike up out of the water to hold the cables and we are expected to travel across the roaring sea below.

"Oh my God! This is so much worse than I expected. Mark, I don't think I can do it."

"You'll be fine, Abs. Trust me."

"Trust you? What the hell does trusting you have to do with it? If that cable snaps, you will end up drowning in that roiling sea as fast as I do. This is really too much. Nope. Not doing it."

"Really? I mean, if you really can't, OK, but are you sure? How about taking some deep, deep breaths and then taking my arm? You can close your eyes and hold on to me all the way across if you want."

"Ach, now, lass. Ye will be in good hands. We've had no troubles here. And the day is calm," adds Paddy.

"Thanks, but I think what I want is to just wait in the car with a book. Mark, you go ahead without me. Take lots of pictures. I will be here when you come back."

"Abs, don't you think you will kick yourself later if you opt out? It is a calm day. Come on, deep breaths."

I give him a wicked look, but I relent; and we board. I notice Paddy has the good sense not to ask Mark for money while the focus is on getting me aboard. The other two passengers slip on and take seats on one side. Mark and I step on next and take the other side, looking straight at them. I am mortified now that they are witnessing my panic.

Paddy gives a warning and we are off. Before closing my eyes, I see the prayer mounted on the wall and the bottle of Holy water displayed next to it. "Not funny," I whisper to Mark as I bury my eyes in his shoulder.

He talks soothingly to me, describing the beauty around us but not coaxing me to look. The rocking, dangling feeling of the cable car has me sweating and counting the minutes until we get to the other side. I begin to zone out and am only vaguely aware of the conversation that pursues.

"Americans, are ye?" asks the local man. "Do you see the dolphins there by the fishing boat? Would ye be having those now in America?"

"Thanks for pointing them out. They are beautiful and so playful. Are they looking for fish?" Mark asks politely.

"Playing just, I imagine," replies the man.

"Yes, we do have dolphins in America, but not where we live. I have only seen them a few times in my life. They're amazing."

I am not even tempted to look. I am caught up in a day dream, a nightmare of a harrowing storm at sea.

"We are coming to the platform, Abs. Expect a bit of a noise and a bump as we reach land."

"Thank, God," I say as I try to snap out of the dream of drowning. The ten-minute ride has seemed like an eternity, but we reach the platform the wooden platform, then grass under foot ground me. I am ever so thankful, but still reeling from the experience of the crossing.

When I seem stable again, Mark rushes ahead to engage the boy with the cart. Then he returns to pay the cable car operator. I pet the donkey to calm myself as I stand by the rickety cart we will be traveling in the length of the island. But I have no complaints. The wheels may not be rubber, but they are wheels rolling solidly along the road. Much preferred to dangling in the air over water in a tiny wooden box.

For a while we are all silent. Me, to center myself. Mark, to take it all in. Who knows about the boy? Finally, the boy, named Colin, asks, "Will you be wanting stops or is it straight out to the end fer ye?"

"Straight out to the best view of the little islands beyond if you don't mind. I read you can see Bull, Cow and Calf Islands from the end. And I am especially interested in the lighthouse and the ruins of the old lighthouse. Do you know much about them?" Mark replies.

"I just came out West here a fortnight ago, so I am no expert. I can take you to the right places but as for telling you much about the places, I am not much use. I do know that there is a fourth wee island—Heifer it is called, a wee extra surprise for those expecting just the three."

"We can't wait. As for the stops, I am thinking we will go straight out, picnic about an hour and then make stops on the return as time allows. Does that work for you, Colin?" Mark asks.

I hear their conversation, but on another level I am still caught up in the internal drama of the crossing. I had felt I was on a long, treacherous sea voyage. Then, I had the sense that I was back at the Hag of Beara Rock. I imagined I was

41

the Hag connecting with her Sea God husband. Then, my boat was dashed on the rocks. Damn, Ireland certainly is bringing out an imagination I never knew I possessed.

When the cable car reached land, the dream stopped, but I still felt foggy. What the hell is happening to me? I never zone out like this.

Thankfully, the views are all not only beautiful but tranquil. With a few deep breaths, I ease myself away from the scary sea images. Instead, I focus on the vista before me; rugged, untamed beauty. So far, once we left the cable car parking lot, we have seen no one, only sheep and cattle and birds. I guess a few people still live here but I cannot imagine it. Even if there was an alternative to cable car or boat, I would not want the isolation of living on an island. At least not one small enough that I would realize it was an island every waking moment.

The birds are amazing. I read that this is a bird sanctuary, but bird identification is not in my wheelhouse. Yet, it is fun to watch them soaring and diving and making patterns in the sky. Colin says the big white sea-birds with dark wings are gannets. He says we will get to see them dive like missiles into the sea when we get to the end of the road. He also points out their yellow heads as they fly by.

When we do get to the other side of the island, the smaller islands come into view. At first, we simply enjoy the view. Then Colin speaks up: "Now I'll be pointing out each island by name and telling you where to find the angle that gives best advantage to seeing the shape for which each island is named. Then, most folks, I am finding, want a wee walk and a picnic before returning to the cable car. If you have no questions to ask of me, I will be asking where you would like me to drop you off. I will leave you be for a while and pick you up wherever you decide to end your walk."

"That sounds great, and what about you? Would you like to join us for a picnic?" Mark asks.

"No, now, I will be grand on me own. I have a sack here of eats and I can pass the time with no problem. So, you just tell me when to meet back up."

We arrange for him to meet us at the appointed lay-by in one hour. No cell service way out here so we agree to the plan, knowing he will come looking for us if something goes wrong.

At first, we just take in the vista. Far to the north, we see Skellig in the distance and imagine the monks walking up their winding stone path of steps leading to its monastic settlement. We've added it to the list of next-time visits. To the south, we see the mouth of Bantry Bay with Bere Island asserting itself in the middle. With his binoculars, Mark sees fishing boats and another of the lighthouses on his list. He is in his glory.

Yet, he expresses a bit of disappointment that we are so far away. "So many of the pictures I looked at were from the sea or helicopter. I didn't realize how limited views were from land. Now, I wish I had that drone you were talking about when we were at Healy Pass. Even better, I wish I could get out there in a boat, go through the arch of rock and all."

"Maybe there is a boat out of Castletownbere that you can take. Let's ask when we get over there."

"You wouldn't mind, Abs?"

"I would mind going very much, but I wouldn't mind a bit if you want to go on your own. Small boats and open sea don't agree with me."

"Well, I might look into it then."

We separate for a bit—my wanting just to take in the energy, his wanting to identify everything for his lighthouse notebook. It reminds me that I haven't written more than a couple of paragraphs in my journal since we arrived. I see and feel so much, want to capture every sentiment and thought, but then arrive back at the B&B exhausted.

It has been a long time since I have traveled with a man I care about, and so my pattern of journaling before bed or writing morning notes has been interrupted. Pleasantly so. I am not complaining. Mark is a treasure and he is a delight to travel with. He really handled my freak out at the cable car well. I sit in gratitude, once again forgoing my journal to just bask in the moment

We rejoin to walk further, hand-in-hand, experiencing the breeze off the sea, listening to the roar of the waves hitting rock, and seeing the spray generating around these fascinating islands named for cattle. In between dashing wave action, we can actually see into and through the Calf Island arch or is it tunnel?

"I would love to get up close to those islands and get around to where you can actually see the Bull Island lighthouse," Mark says wistfully.

"Seriously? I know you said that a few minutes ago but it looks so much rougher from here. Would you really want to be bounced around out there at sea?" I bite my tongue from adding all sorts of judgmental and cautionary warnings going through my head.

"Oh, definitely. Remember that lighthouse tour I saw online? As wonderful as all this is, I keep wishing I had found it in time for us to coordinate with the guy's tour."

"Yeah, I would have taken a few days to wander around my stone circles while you went out on your own for that. I'm sorry you will miss that piece of the Beara experience." (What I don't tell him is that I was able to book us two nights in a lighthouse keeper's cottage at Galley Head. It is a surprise and so far I have kept it that way.) Then I add, "I thought we were looking at a lighthouse?"

"No, those are just the remnants of an old lighthouse on Calf Rock. It was made of cast iron, very trendy in the mid-1800s. But after fifteen years or so, it was destroyed in a storm. I think I remember reading that six men lost their lives trying to save the lighthouse keeper. Can't imagine being out in a storm that powerful.

The new lighthouse went up at Bull Rock. They say the light from Bull Rock can be seen for miles, but we would need a boat to get round to the backside of the island to actually see the lighthouse."

"That makes sense, since it is meant to help ships not us land-loving tourists," I state the obvious.

We leave thoughts of disasters at sea and head back to meet Colin. He is just putting away paints as we approach.

"May we see your canvasses?" I ask.

"Indeed, you may. 'Tis good light today for capturing the shapes of the islands," replies Colin.

"They are wonderful," I exclaim, examining not just the one he is completing but his stash of earlier paintings. We marvel at how good they are. They are all watercolor depictions of the four little islands; the canvases stretched over boards about twelve inches long by four inches high. Each scene is slightly different, but all capture the seascape beautifully.

"So, is this how you spend your time waiting for your riders?" Mark questions Colin as I continue to utter words of praise. "Beautiful and very enterprising," he adds.

"Aye, you see I've been painting and selling them for a fortnight now. I have found the rhythm of it."

We hop aboard. Then choose our favorite. Mark and Colin come to an agreement about price which prompts Mark to begin a running conversation with the boy about his background, his hopes and dreams, and then his troubles. The long and short of it is that the boy was living the life of a gang member in Limerick City. His father sent him here to his grandparents for the summer to "get himself right again". He is not to return until he has repaid his grandparents for his room and board and has 500 euros to repay his father for bailing him out of trouble in Limerick.

Mark gets the boy to open up and affirms the good in the kid. I hear him say "You know, it is hard to be a boy growing up in a tough city neighborhood when you have the heart of a poet and an artist." He says it with such empathy that for a moment I am thinking he grew up in some urban setting even though I know he lived a Father-Knows-Best small-town life as a child. I am impressed by the bond he creates in such a short time. He always knows what to say and takes the time to say it. Finally, I say "Guys, I hate to interrupt, but is that a ring fort? And do we have time to stop?"

"Aye to both questions, Missus," says Colin as he steers the cart to the ring fort. The two of them continue chatting, if it can be said that a teenager chats.

More accurate to say Mark continues to coax answers out of the boy. I go over to, around, and then into the ring fort. The name ring fort, of course, suggests a military defensive structure, but I get a sense of community from inside the circle. People lived here. Maybe it is even a fairy ring. I chuckle to myself when I think of adding fairy connections to the confounding experiences I am already having at the stone circles. And at that moment, I get a sense that there are entities maybe or guides or perhaps fairies present and that they are affirming me and encouraging me to connect with the stones. There are no words and I cannot explain where the notion comes from. It is just a knowing I have. I think back to the nun's blessing and I wonder what more is to come.

The guys are ready to move on. I perform my little buttercup ritual and back away from this place noting it as a place of memory and meaning. Later down the road we make another short stop at the ruins of O'Sullivan's castle. Colin tells us he is an O'Sullivan and gives us a short history of their clan. I show polite interest, but this is not the story that appeals to me. I want to know more about the ancient peoples of the stone circles and ring forts. Somehow, I sense that my own story lies within the story of the Ancient Ones. But I am too preoccupied by my dread of the return on the cable car to give any of it much more thought.

"Here you are now," announces Colin as he pulls up to the cable car dock. There is no need for a ticket booth on this side, but there are some benches in a small waiting area. I am so anxious that I barely say goodbye to Colin. Mark talks with him as I pace around. I think he gives the kid a generous tip and takes a picture of him holding the canvas next to his donkey and cart. At the moment I could care less, but I know when we get home my anxiety will be gone and I will love having the picture. Oops, what am I thinking? Mark is buying the picture. It will go to his house.

Before I can give that idea any thought, Paddy arrives with the cable car; I feel D-Day upon me. Poor Mark has to balance the canvas we bought and me as well as we board. At least this time I know what to expect and even open my eyes occasionally, looking out but not down. I will survive, I keep telling myself.

"Mark, thank you for your patience and calm presence when I freaked out," I say in all sincerity and gratitude as we head to the car.

"No worries, Abs. We all have our fears and sore points. You would do the same for me. Let's go get you a drink, perhaps a stiff Jameson?"

"Ha-ha. That might have helped earlier. Now I will go for a nice glass of wine, and I'll treat you to a pint...or two."

With a final symbolic wave to Paddy and Dursey, we head back to Allihies. Noting the copper mine shaft to our right, and the gorgeous views all around, we welcome a visit to the charming little town and a pint of O'Neill's finest.

• • •

The pub is rocking though it still seems early. At first we don't see any seats but then someone yells out, "Would this be more Yanks I see comin' in now? And would you be likin' to join us?"

We nod and move toward the group, when the spokesman continues, "Meet our Yank cousin Jack Sullivan, his wife Cindy, me brothers Ian, Liam and Sean. And meself, Arthur. We are all Sullivans and we welcome you to the Beara."

"We thank you very much," says Mark as he introduces us to the group and we take seats among them. Cindy gives me this welcoming and grateful look as if she is pleased to have another woman and assuming I will be her BFF—at least for the evening.

"The young man with the cart of Dursey said he was an O'Sullivan. Would he be a cousin," I ask.

"There are the Sullivans and the O'Sullivans and a very long story to tell about it all that goes way back. I canna do it justice at the moment, since me mind is more on the football on the telly and the conversations at hand. Ye see it is long and complicated. Ye only need to know that Sullivans, with or without the O, and the McCarthys make up the most of Beara. Most everyone is related to one or the other or both." With that answer, Arthur turns back to his brothers at the bar, "Is that not right, lads?"

"Aye, Arthur, whatever you say, we are in agreement. Now let us watch the telly in peace. Is that not why we are away here for the night?" quips one of the other Sullivans.

Cindy ignores them all and chats away to me. She tells me she and Jack are staying here with relatives before going on to Cork City. She reports everyone is always friendly, with or without the Guinness. Big trays of pizza fill the table, and dinner seems like a second thought to drinking.

"I just ordered Irish stew for myself. No way, Honey, that I am coming all the way from Tennessee to eat pizza in Ireland, leastwise not the first week we are here," she announces with this big, hearty laugh. "The specials are on the board there, Honey. When you are ready, just get the bartender's attention. The more formal restaurant is upstairs.

"And I am learning that waiters here don't bug you about ordering more or bringing your bill until you ask. You could sit here all night sipping beer if you wanted. No one would say a word, it's so laid back and friendly. Even a popular, well-known place like this doesn't rush you. This is our third time here with various relatives since we arrived. If we got no further than here, the trip would still be worth every penny. It's great *craic* as they say."

I have really never understood the lure of a pub or the meaning of a good *craic* until tonight. Good food, good company, lots of laughs, the beer flowing and then the music starting, taking us through moods of joy, of sorrow and back again to joy. That, we learn, is the *craic*.

Mark and I order the lamb special and he squeezes in next to me long enough to eat. Then he is back to the bar. Cindy introduces me to sticky toffee pudding, her favorite dessert. No better bonding than wine and dessert in my way of thinking.

At one point, Jack and Mark get talking about lighthouses. Next thing I know, it is arranged that Mark and Jack will join Sean, the Sullivan cousin who has a fishing boat and is willing to take them around to the lighthouse at Bull Rock and the others around Castletownbere. Mark then brings up *Ondine*, (no surprise there!) and the guys begin telling tales of the making of the movie, drinking with Colin Farrell and people they know who were extras in the film. I just smile to myself, wondering if we would even be here in Ireland had we not watched that video together.

Before the night ends, Cindy and I agree to meet up at a place called Jack Patrick's for coffee the morning the guys meet the Sullivan boat. The plan is set for Castletownbere, Berehaven Harbour, two days from now. That fits beautifully with our plan. It was our next stop anyway and now Mark will get his boat ride out to the little islands.

I mention a bit about my passion for stone circles and start telling Cindy where we have been and where the others are that we plan to visit.

"Honey, these stone circles are all new to me, and it's hard to hear and concentrate here. Tell me all about them when we meet up. I did watch that *Outlander* series on TV where the gal goes back in time and meets a man in a kilt in old-time Scotland. But I didn't know there were stone circles like that here in Ireland. Do you think we can find a guy in a kilt if we go? I have always wanted to ask what they wear underneath," she laughs that hearty laugh of hers. "And if we don't find a guy like that in real time, maybe we can conjure one up or ask the fairies for help. I am game to try."

I don't directly respond to her because I assume she is joking, but I begin to think to myself she might be able to help me get an explanation of what is going on at the circles. Worth a try anyway and fun to have company at the very least.

We finally say good night having exchanged cell phone numbers and after having a final round for the road. As much as we love staying with Eileen and Jimmy, we are wishing that our B&B was here in Allihies tonight. It seems a lot longer going back than it did coming out.

CHAPTER FIVE

I feel a little sad as we say goodbye to Eileen and Jimmy and move on to Castletownbere. They have been so warm and welcoming. Eileen has even called ahead to a cousin to assure us a good room in a B&B in town center, where we can easily walk to dinner and the pubs.

It is so strange to think about sharing someone's home, eating their food, seeing their family pictures on the wall and all without really knowing them. It is so contradictory to know them so little and then have such affection for them. Add to that the fact that they are folks we probably will never see again, and it is even stranger.

We say, "Cheerio," to Eileen at the front door and then walk up the lane to Jimmy. He leans against his shovel while he tells us a final story of the Beara. It is about the origins of Healy Pass, called the Famine Road in the 19th century. The story reminds me of the Civilian Conservation Corps we had in the U.S. during the Depression, but I bite my tongue. As delightful as he is, I am anxious to get going. We make one more stop to give our first and favorite donkey a carrot, given us by Eileen. His bray is our final goodbye to this sweet place—a real Celtic experience.

We decide to combine a long walk with visits to the stone circles we bypassed earlier. I think Mark has become just as intrigued by them as I have. Well, that's wishful thinking, but at least he's quite interested.

"We really haven't officially walked The Beara Way trail until now. It sure beats trying to find the road and the signs by car," Mark observes as he finds a place to park.

"And I absolutely love this map Mr. Sullivan sold us. The Cashelkeelty Stone Circle is coming up soon. Meantime, these woods are magical. Do you think there are fairies in there?"

"I'm not going to hazard a guess. I don't even know if you are teasing or serious. I only know that so far, traveling with you has been an adventure and we're only a few days in. I can't imagine what's next."

"Well, I am getting that *déjà vu* feeling again. There is *something* about the stones that draws me, and it is as if someone is trying to speak to me. There is this stirring of deep memory that I can't quite put my finger on. "

"Maybe it's a book you read and have kind of forgotten. Was it that *Outlander* series? Doesn't that woman get transported back in time when she visits a stone circle?"

"Yes, I read those and yes, she does; but it isn't that. It is more about a voice trying to make a personal connection. I can't explain. Sometimes I think it is the Hag of Beara herself wanting to get my attention. Other times, it feels like a different voice, or entity, trying to come through. And as hard as I try, I can't get any further than that. I have never experienced anything like it, not even in my dreams. In fact, I seldom remember my dreams. But that seems to be changing on this trip. Oh, well, let's not keep talking about it. Let's just soak in this glorious day. You can help me figure it out later. Ireland has so much more to offer and the weather is so good, let's not miss a minute of it, not here nor in Castletownbere."

After walking a while in silence, we come to our next destination. Mark notes, "I'm struck by how this site seems to have been used by modern visitors more than the others. See that small circle of stones someone has recently made into a fire pit?"

"How odd to think that is maybe weeks old and the big circle is centuries old. Of course, it is right along the Beara Way, probably hikers stopped, folks who might never have heard of stone circles until they arrived. I wonder if the stones tried to speak to them?"

Mark quips back, "I doubt it, Abs. Somehow and for some reason, you are the Chosen One."

"Hmpf," I remark as we stand at the opening to the ancient stone circle. "I am struck by how each of the stone circles differ and yet I can tell they are part of a whole. I feel like this whole stretch of land from mountain to bay is part of a group of communities that were really connected to each other, and all were so much more connected to universal forces than we can imagine. What was it all about? Is it directly connected to the Hag of Beara? How does it connect to other Celtic places, like Stonehenge or Orkney or the Callanish Stones in Scotland?"

"I don't know, but it sure has aroused my interest in this time and these places. I am embarrassed to say I kind of lumped all pagan things together and labeled them primitive before this trip," Mark admits.

"Yeah, I mean we learned in school that civilization evolved slowly, blah, blah blah. But all this says to me that there were civilizations before us that knew things we don't give them credit for knowing," I add as I turn my attention back to the stones themselves. "Shall we enter together, and will you join me in a ritual again?"

He nods in agreement.

I begin:

> Ancient Ones, we come in gratitude and awe of all that has come before. You remind us to live in right relationship with all that is.
>
> You remind us that We Are One, each part of the great circle of life. Cailleach, we seek your wisdom as we move into our own third stage of life. Bless us with your knowing and your strength.
>
> Teach us a deeper understanding of sovereignty for us as individuals and for our living together.

Chills overcome me and I feel lightheaded. "That is really weird. I had formulated the first line of those words before beginning, but I don't know where the rest came from."

"Abs, are you OK?" Mark asks as he puts his arms around me.

"Yeah, yeah. Not sure what happened, but yeah, I'm OK. I just got a chill.

"What happened?"

"Don't know. I suddenly felt this surge of energy go through my body. It was as if someone—something—was coming into my body and talking through me. I have never experienced anything so strange in my life. I didn't feel in danger particularly. It was just weird. I don't know what to make of it."

"Let's go get you hydrated. In all the British and Irish mysteries, they always offer tea with lots of sugar to the person in crisis. How about we get you some?" he says with strained levity. Then adds "I was beginning to feel you were being taken away, like the woman in *Outlanders,* and I only read one of the books."

"Hardly. But I can't leave just yet. I need to listen to the Cailleach," I say with a renewed thrust of energy. "Let me just have a few minutes to collect myself. I feel like I am close to really connecting with the stones, maybe the Hag herself. I don't want to lose the chance. Please stop pacing. I know you are concerned but it is distracting. I need to calm myself and get centered again."

"OK. If that is what you really want."

"You know, it felt like my words came from somewhere, someone else. Beforehand, the words of invocation came easily but they felt like my own. This felt like it wasn't me, that it was another entity coming through my voice. Did you ever have that feeling when you were preaching?"

"You mean did God ever take over and speak directly through me? Not really. But I have felt prompted to speak and enabled to speak by Him at times. Not to the point of almost fainting though like you just experienced. Abby, all this has me worried. I am not sure you should be playing around with whatever these forces are. Not sure at all."

"I just got a chill and felt a little wobbly. I didn't feel in danger or in harm's way, just momentarily overpowered," I respond.

"Well, just take it slowly," he suggests.

"Let's do a buttercup ritual and add on a gratitude round. My energy will be restored if I focus on my blessings. Will you lead it this time?" I ask.

He does, and it is a joyful and meaningful experience similar to our time at Uragh.

"I feel better already," I say.

We sit for a while longer and begin to speculate on the lives of the people who lived here in ancient times. We ask ourselves about how Ancients used the stones, what powers they possessed, what beliefs they held. We have no answers but we both have a sense that the picture of these folks as primitive peasants misses something big. The ability to connect with the stars and align with the sun and moon had to have significance beyond knowing the seasons. I then add "You know, I have also read and seen on TV speculations that the builders of Stonehenge and the other Neolithic sites in the British Isles may have used sound frequency and vibrational energy as tools. I even read a theory about crystals being used to cut stone as well as to manipulate light."

"It is amazing and mysterious. I wouldn't even begin to speculate. I suppose if someone from a different century saw just one of our smartphones and speculated about its use and how it was made, they would be just as stymied as we are. What I do agree with is that while these stones look primitive, more was going on than we realize," Mark says thoughtfully.

I ask again for a message:

> Ancient Ones, please help me to hear you.
>
> Assist me in knowing how to listen to your message.
>
> Give me the information and the insights I need to do your bidding.
>
> Help me to understand what you want from me.

Nothing comes. I sit down with my back against the tallest stone in the group as Mark continues to stand near the portal. We are both silent, but Mark's fidgeting is distracting me once again, perhaps diffusing the energy. I decide to say something although I don't know how to ask him to leave me alone when he has been so supportive. I feel like I am in one of those early assertive training classes . Why can't I just ask for what I want and need?

Finally, I just say what I am experiencing as if that is a monumental decision and a fantastic insight. I just simply say, "Mark, I am distracted by your fidgeting. Would you mind leaving the circle for a while so I can try again to make connection?"

"I'm worried about you, Abby. But, OK, I will take a walk," he says as he leaves me on my own in the circle.

It is quite some time before I feel anything stir within me. I ask for guidance and assistance in opening to that which, that who, is trying to reach me. "Please," I ask out loud now, "Help me to know how to listen to your message. I just don't know how."

All of a sudden, I become lightheaded again. I have been leaning back against the tall portal stone and now find I need it to hold me up, to steady me.

"Abs, you look white as a ghost. Are you OK? What's going on?" Mark's words punctuate the silence as he reenters the circle and kneels down beside me.

"This time I am feeling a little faint," I say with a forced smile as I take his hand and hold it between my own. "No need to worry though. I just think I have to adjust somehow to taking it all in. You know, I am like a kid learning to ride a bike. Still a little wobbly."

"I think we should call it a day here," Mark says with authority.

"OK. I admit this last hour or so has been exhausting. There is something about the intensity of my interaction with the stones that is out of balance. But you're right; Let's leave it for now."

• • •

At the little café, Mark suggests I add lots of sugar to my tea. I pass on that, but I do drink down a bottle of water and get some chocolate.

"Want to talk about it?" asks Mark with concern on his face.

"I really don't know what to say. People talk about out-of-body experiences, but I felt the stones' presence so it wasn't that; I wasn't really in a trance, I don't think; but time did seem suspended. And it felt like a different me took over the last lines of the opening words I gave. And, then, when at the end I asked to be told how to listen, I felt like too much power was coming at me. I felt overwhelmed, but not threatened or scared. It was kind of eerie."

"Well, I think we should lay off stone circles for a while. Let's just head back to Lauragh and enjoy the scenic turns of Healy Pass. Then we can have a good stiff drink and supper in Castletownbere."

"There is more about sovereignty that I am supposed to hear. I hate to leave before it comes to me. After all, this is the sacred landscape of the Hag of Beara and St. Catherine. I don't want to give up just because I got a little woozy."

"Maybe the message will come to you when you relax away from the intensity. Besides, there is a lot more of Beara to see."

"Maybe. There is a notable stone circle near Castletownbere, but only the one that I know of. Let's at least check out Shronebirrane. We have seen the sign so many times and it looks like the lane right off the highway goes up to it. It won't take long."

"I can't believe you are asking for more, but it's your decision. When we get to the sign, if you still want to, we will. But let's get some more water before we go."

Shronebirrane seemed to be in a wooded area away from the road, but when we get up the lane, we see it is quite near a fairly modern house. No one is around for us to ask permission, so we decide to walk on over to the circle. Quite a few stones seem to be missing and the overall feeling or vibration is disappointing.

But, as I touch the tallest of the stones, the feeling of disappointment turns to one of deep, deep sadness.

"I feel like something heart-wrenching happened here—maybe when some stones were removed. Maybe early on when Ancient Ones actually were here, but it feels deeply disturbing," I say to Mark.

"Ah, perhaps that symbolizes the attack on Irish sovereignty and on women's sovereignty that you have been talking about."

"Yeah, maybe, and maybe that's the story I am asked to hear," I say as I begin to weep.

"OK, we are out of here! I don't know about you, but I have had enough. Let's move on!" Mark says with more impatience than I have ever seen him exhibit.

I nod reluctantly, and we get into the car and make our way to Healy Pass.

The views along this renowned alpine stretch of road are different in the light of mid-day. We stop at what feels like the heart-center of Beara as well as its geographic center. We stop to absorb it all in peaceful silence. Then we both try to capture its essence on film, knowing it is a fool's attempt and laughing at ourselves as we take one more picture of Beara and then another. Finally and reluctantly, we get back in the car and continue down through the Cara Mountains until we begin to see the waters of Bantry Bay and the big island smack dab in the middle called Bere. I remember Mark's illustration that my index finger represents the peninsula, the bay the space between it and my thumb and my thumb is the maintain coast of County Cork. That helps me get a sense of where we are.

"So we are looking down at the south side of the peninsula now and seeing mainland Cork on the far side of the bay, right?" I say more to anchor myself than to seek confirmation.

"That's right, Abs. And after we visit Castletownbere at the mouth of the bay, we will travel back around to Bantry and on from there to the lighthouses that dot the coast. I am so excited to see them," Mark adds.

This southern side of Beara is more rugged, yet equally breathtaking. Bantry Bay is huge and, from some angles, Bere Island with its high hills looks as though it is actually the opposite peninsula. As with my first sight of Dursey Island, I am struck by all these interesting smaller islands off the big island of Ireland. Mark reminds me that there is a lighthouse and several points of interest on Bere Island. We agree to put it on our must-see list, especially when I am assured there is a good-sized ferry that goes over and at least one pub. We continue our descent, coming to a sign for Beara Way that strikes us both.

"That is the longest ten miles I have ever driven: twisty, winding, harrowing and breathtaking beautiful. I am so grateful we had good weather. We lucked out that we chose to go top to bottom rather than go bottom to top. I think you see more coming down. And I love the way it felt as though we were driving right into the sea." Mark says as he pulls over one last time.

"So we are coming to the southern loop now, right? The Beara Way walking trail and the Ring of Beara road."

"Yep. And we are completely in County Cork now. On the north shore we were sometimes in Kerry and sometimes in Cork," Mark reminds me. He muses, adding "It would be fun to get out and to walk a bit of it, but I am really anxious to get to Castletownbere."

"Right, your lighthouses await us. You really have only gotten to see the one, and that was from quite a distance. Let's keep going and get into town as quickly as possible so we can get settled and then go exploring."

"Yep, but I am not sure I can hold off lunch much longer. After these huge breakfasts, I keep saying I won't need any lunch, but I'm starved. Let's see if there is a place to get a sandwich and then truck on to Castletownbere."

There is just one place to stop after we turn right onto the coastal ring road. We get subs, munchies and ice teas, and then take them up the road to a lay-by where we can look out at a rocky little island. The views across the bay are gorgeous. Good choice. The seals are playful and amuse us. I have only seen seals playing like this at the zoo so it is a real treat. Mark mentions how much his granddaughter Lydia loves seals and speculates on when she will be old enough to appreciate a big trip like this.

We have spoken so little about home or our families these last few days. I feel as though we have been in suspended animation, so totally removed from everyday life. And every time I do think about Mark's family, a shadow of doubt crosses my mind. Things are certainly great with Mark here, but will they be when we return to everyday life?

As we near Castletownbere, we decide to explore what looks like sea access in to a former navy boatyard. We find this is called Pontoon Pier, which I had incorrectly pictured as a floating dock with a few yachts.

"This is great! I love being down at the water and what a good perspective on Berehaven Harbour," Mark exclaims as he pulls off to the side for a better view.

"Hey, look, there is a ferry loading up over there. I think it goes out to Bere Island. Want to hop on?" I ask excitedly.

"We don't have a reservation and they only take a couple of cars. I thought we would make a day of it later in the week."

"But the weather today is magnificent and we have been looking across at the island for the last two hours. Why not hop on as walking passengers and then just turn around and come back on the return trip? Maybe, we will even get views of the *Ondine* lighthouse."

"I thought you didn't want to go out on a boat to see it?

"I don't want to go out in a sailboat or one of those motorized rubber raft things, but a ferry is solid and there is no wind today. I would love to go out on the water."

"OK, then. Let's make a run for it before the guy pulls up the gate."

We just make it and find ourselves to be the only Americans on board. School kids and shoppers mainly, and the two cars belong to Brits. A local guy points out what we are seeing and puts names to it all. Sadly though, we won't be going by the cove most featured in the *Ondine* movie. Our new friend suggests when we disembark we look for a fellow named Kevin who sometimes gives car tours to the lighthouse and Martello towers. His advice comes in the form of a question: "Aye, ye have the weather today now, don't ye?" It's a powerful motivator, convincing us to have a longer look today rather than wait.

The luck of the Irish, as we Americans say, is with us. For ten euros, Kevin takes us to see Roancarrig Lighthouse and the "wee" islet and cove. Yes, it was used for scenes in *Ondine*. And it is as breathtaking as we expected it to be. Sadly, but no surprise when we remember the movie, you can only get there by boat. Mark will probably get a better look tomorrow, but we both are thrilled to see it from here.

Next, Kevin drives us as far as he can up to the Ardnakinna lighthouse. He explains that there has been a beacon at the site since the mid-1800s but that it was only converted to a lighthouse in 1965. It is solid and white like a typical lighthouse, I guess. I am somewhat disappointed that it seems quite ordinary and the hill it is on is not at all dramatic. Mark is disappointed we do not have time to hike up for a closer look. But the views from here are stunning. We have not numbed to the beauty of mountain, hill and dale in harmony with sea and sky. Kevin points out Sheep's Head, Mizen Head and Dursey Island from differing vantage points. Mark is in heaven. He asks a dozen more questions about the lighthouse and its workings while I just soak in the quiet, peaceful surroundings.

Kevin then takes us on to a Martello tower, a round, chunky stone fort built by the British about the same time as the beacon. He says there were four such towers built on the island although only two remain. On our way back to the ferry, I see the tall standing stone that looks like it was the original sentinel and guardian of the island. Kevin zips us over to have a quick look and still gets us back to the ferry for the next boat back. The singular stone speaks to me but nowhere near as strongly as the stone circles. Probably a good thing. Standing stones are so plentiful we would go bonkers trying to see them all.

"That was exhilarating. I love being on the water. Did you enjoy it, Abs?"

"I really did. What a beautiful bay and what a beautiful afternoon."

"I can't wait to see the rest of the town. Shall we check in and then walk around?"

"Sounds great to me!"

Eileen's directions are perfect. We park, go in and register with a polite young school girl. No fuss. After I freshen up a bit and we partially unpack, we take our jackets and head down to the main street. Mark has to check out the Coast Guard Station, the lifeboat and the fishing wharf. I am surprised that they are all dead center of the town and one block over from the main commercial street. Fishing and shipping are clearly big enterprises here.

"This is a fairly new rescue boat. A beauty, isn't it? I could spend hours standing here and then getting pictures from every angle. Stop me when you have had enough," Mark says as he takes in the waterfront.

"Enough," I say after a while. "Or at least let's wrap it up. We can come back, but I am curious to see more of the town."

"Sure. No problem, Abs. I'm with you and there sure is more to see." We begin walking and he continues to be thrilled with everything he sees.

"Wow, and how cool to recognize so many things from the movie. And look, the fish market. It is closed now but will be abuzz with activity in the morning. I read that this is one of the top three international fishing ports. I love the contrast of the homey market town with the huge barges, giant fishing boats and one-man fishing boats and then fancy personal yachts. Oh, I downloaded *Ondine* to my tablet. Want to watch it tonight, comparing it to the real thing?"

"If you mean compare it to the street and shops and scenery, sure. But if you are looking for your own mermaid or Celtic *selkie*, I'm not so sure. I might get jealous," I say jokingly.

"No worries there. You have more than enough mystery and Otherworldliness in you for me: witness you at the stone circles."

"Ha." What else can I say?

"Ready for dinner? Why don't we go into McCarthy's here, have dinner and listen to the first set? But, first, let's take a selfie here at the front door."

"OK, but why here?" I want to know.

"You don't recognize the place from the cover of the book, *McCarthy's Bar*?"

"Never read it, but tell me about it once we are seated and I have a glass of wine in front of me."

We take the pictures, find a seat and order. "Guinness for me, please, and the lady will have a red wine. And then in a while we would like a food menu," Mark says before turning to me to continue his explanation of the book.

"The book is an irreverent memoir of sorts. This Brit named McCarthy, who has Irish roots, decides to take a pilgrimage of sorts to Ireland with the intention of stopping at every pub named McCarthy's. He comes in to Cork by ferry and travels up the west coast. He tells the story of coming here to this bar and being royally welcomed. Seems they have an after-hours party, too, and all his drinking is on the house. He is outrageously funny."

"So did you plot out our route to include all the McCarthys he visited?" I ask.

"I didn't, but I could. It does sound like fun. Want to?"

"Sure. The Irish say there is magic in threes—so we can say our triple focus is lighthouses, stone circles and pubs. Sounds like the quintessential Irish vacation." I am thoughtful for a moment. Then add, "I am finding I have given very little thought to what is going on at home. Is it just that I am so caught up in the stones, or are you feeling removed from it all as well?"

"Except for thinking of Lydia and the zoo earlier this afternoon, not much thought of home at all. You know, I said I very much wanted to try to live in the moment, overcome my grief and unplug from my parish life. That part isn't new, but I am surprised at how easy it is here. I am not even trying, it is just happening."

"Everyone says there is something magical about Ireland. Even without my stone circle experiences, I would have to agree. Thank you for sharing it with me. All of it."

"My pleasure, Abs. My pleasure indeed."

• • •

Our evening is not raucous, but the wine is welcome, the fish beyond fresh, the music wonderful—just as we had imagined as we sat in snowy Upstate New York planning it all back in February. I marvel at how far and how quickly our relationship has progressed. And I get a kick out of getting to know more of the many facets of this outwardly reserved man.

Our night ends with the viewing of *Ondine*. It's a clever movie, mixing a modern love story with the romantic myth of a *selkie*, who brings love and hope to a broken man and his ailing daughter. Of course, we are more captivated than ever by the scenery of Beara and the scenes of the town we now are visiting. Plus, we continue to marvel that we are here in Ireland mainly because we watched it that snowy winter's evening that seems so long ago. What fun.

"I can't believe my good fortune," I say to Mark as he turns his tablet off and turns to me.

"Me neither."

CHAPTER SIX

Mark has already showered and dressed by the time I wake. "Top of the mornin', Abs. Sorry if I woke you," he bends to give me a kiss. "I'm going down to see if I can rustle up some coffee, take it to the parlor and FaceTime my girls. Stick your head in to signal me when you are ready for breakfast."

I groan and try to joke, "I read the Irish never say 'top of the morning' but then again we are Americans so 'top of the morning' back at you."

I am having trouble getting going this morning. Lots of dreaming has left me foggy. By the time I get downstairs, Mark has finished talking to his daughter and is reading. He gives me a warm embrace as we head into the dining room. Everyone is pleasant enough, but this B&B is much more impersonal than Eileen and Jimmy's place. The proprietress, Maggie, pops out to ask if everything is OK, but disappears just as fast as she came in.

I choose scrambled eggs and what has to be the freshest salmon I have ever tasted. Mark goes with the full Irish since the details of where he will be at lunch time are vague. As we dive into the food, he fills me in on news from home and tells me how cute his granddaughter was in trying to figure out what it means to fly to Ireland. His exuberance about the call and the upcoming sailing trip is infectious. I finally am wide awake and ready for the new day.

As we finish, Mark gets quiet. "Abs, thank you," he says tenderly.

"For what?"

"For understanding about my daughter and for not making a fuss about my going off for the day without you."

"Just because we are in relationship doesn't mean we don't have our own lives to lead. I want you to follow your passions, just as I want you to give space for me to follow mine. I may not know all I need to know about sovereignty, but I do know that. And thank you too. You have been really supportive about the stone circle stuff, and the cable car freak out and my not wanting to go out on the rough seas."

"Yeah, so we are good then. Got to rush. Bye."

Mark heads off to meet Jack, while I sit a bit longer, savoring the moment. Clearly, Mark appreciates the fact we give one another space for independent activities as much as I do. It's not about permission nor submission. Just like hearing that the Hag of Beara waits for her man, I cringe at the thought that we lose ourselves in partnership. No. We don't have to lose ourselves. I guess that's at the heart of sovereignty. Wholeness. Opening to another without becoming less whole in the process. Maybe, just maybe, I have found a guy who gets that. Ha. Maybe I have reached a level of maturity where I get that too. Now there is an idea!

The young girl clearing tables is making more noise cleaning up than warranted. I look around to see I am the only one left in the dining room. Time to go.

Back upstairs in the room, I pick up my journal. There has been so much to see and to adjust to that I have neglected writing. Private, quiet time gets traded off for the delight of intimacy. No complaint, just an observation.

I start by trying to recap my experiences with the stones:

> Kenmare - The nun I don't remember seeing: "May ye find yourself amidst the stones."
>
> Uragh - I feel so at home, so at-one with the Universe and I hear: "Your story lies amidst the stones."
>
> Ardgroom - I get pushed to my knees and told: "Listen to the stones, listen to the Ancient Ones."

I add the word sovereignty to the list too.

SOVEREIGNTY

The messages about sovereignty are actually getting through to me and making sense in spite of all the drama of yesterday when I felt overwhelmed by the energies coming in. I just need to learn how to receive the information.

Glancing at the wall clock, I realize that I better get started in case the rendezvous place Cindy has chosen is much of a walk. I pop my journal into my backpack and head down to the main street. Once again, I need to put aside my attempt to figure this out. Time to meet Cindy.

• • •

First thing I notice is the corner market: Murphy's SuperValu underwent a name change to P O'Sullivan's in the movie. I bet Jack's family knows the story behind that! And then I also notice Harrington's, the shop that had been transformed into a clothing store in the film. Might be fun to pop in later to get a souvenir for Mark's birthday. I also make note that the library is just across the parking area. Maybe I will have time to get more of the local take on the Hag of Beara. I wonder if the librarian plays the librarian in the movie. That would be fun to hear about. Drat it. Even without Mark here I can't get the movie out of my head. I laugh out loud as I walk down the street.

Jack Patrick's Bakery and Restaurant is a little way beyond McCarthy's, on that side of the street, so I cross over and snap another picture or two. When I arrive, I have to pass a scrumptious looking bakery case to get to the tables toward the back. I choose a view of the street, order a cappuccino and pull my journal out while waiting for Cindy. I wonder what her insights will be on my stone circle experiences. She seemed interested enough, but might not be when she hears what has been happening.

"Hey, Honey, how are you?" Cindy asks, entering the café with great flourish and enthusiasm. I have noticed that her Tennessee accent comes through when she is excited and wonder how much more noticeable it must be to the two Irish women staffing the restaurant.

"I am having a wonderful time and am so pleased you suggested we get together," I reply, going on to ask in turn how things are going for her.

"Honey, the Sullivans are wonderful, just wonderful people. But, Honey, there are so many of them. And they all want Jack and me to visit them. And the great aunties serve us tea all the time. One day I had sticky toffee pudding three times because they all heard I liked it. And I am gonna float away in tea. I tell you, you have saved my life today. It's great to have an excuse to get away."

"Maybe you actually would like to go off on your own for the day," I say with a laugh but in a way that I hope allows her to make that choice if she wishes.

"No way, an American girls outing with a cappuccino start is exactly what I want and need. And maybe one of those meringues in the bakery. Want one too?"

"No, thanks, I just had a big breakfast. So do you have anything that you particularly want to see or do today? And when are we expected to meet up with the guys?"

"I have nothing in mind but the stone circle we talked about. And then play it by ear. We have invited a bunch of the Sullivan cousins to a gathering over near Adrigole, kind of like a tailgate party. Just to thank them for all they have done for us. You are invited. The guys will get Mark there if we want to hang out all day. There's decent cell service here in town so they will call when they get back."

She takes a sip of coffee, then continues, "But first let's talk for a bit. How long have you and Mark been a couple? I know from our pub talk what brought you to Ireland, but how's it going?"

Deep breath on my part. It's easy to forget how hard it is to do the let's-get- acquainted stuff. "Well, let's see. We met not quite a year ago at an adult ed class, but things didn't heat up until right after Christmas. Mark lost his wife not that long ago. And me, well, I had stopped looking for a serious relationship ages ago. The idea of the trip came up when we were watching *Ondine*. Mark may have already told you that story. We both were oohing and aahing over the scenery, loving the accents and saying how great a trip to Ireland would be. Anyway, we also saw it as a way to explore our relationship away from prying eyes. He's a widowed minister and both he and his wife were beloved by the church he served. He may have just retired, but they hold him dear and the women all keep a fierce eye on him. In fact, he often jokes that he's flooded with casseroles when he's home."

Cindy's laugh warms the place. "So you spirited him away!"

"Hardly, Mark isn't one to be led and he takes things slowly. Truth be told, I think that was part of the appeal. I'm reluctant to commit and don't want to be pushed into anything I will regret."

"I'm curious. What adult ed class hooks people up these days?" she quips.

"Ha-ha. Would you believe 'Humor: How to Create Humor in Every Day Life'? The teacher was an English prof who studied humor and wit in literature. I didn't notice Mark until about half way through. His quiet way grew on me when we did small group work. So many of the guys were trying to be hot shots."

"Well, that's a new one. Good for you. But, Honey, do you realize that you told me all that without using the M-word once? Jack and I have been married 25 years this fall. It's not always been easy, but it is good, girl, good."

"You certainly don't miss a thing and say your mind. You are right. I am a bit phobic about marriage. Once burned and all that," I admit.

"Letting go of past hurts ain't easy. Good for you for getting into the game again."

"Yeah, and finding how to avoid slipping into the roles and patterns of the 'game'. But, for today, I would like to ask your help in sorting out what's going on with me and the stones."

"Going on with the stones? I don't get what you mean."

Over a second cappuccino and a scone, I try to recap what has been going on.

"Wow, that is somethin' else. Something is going on, but this ancient stuff is all Greek to me. I really never heard tell of it before. Now, like, I sometimes have seen my grandmother…you know, like, watching over me and giving me a look that says watch out. And my aunt who died young—her message usually is 'go for it', but that's been it. I have had a few psychic readings. I also have friends who do healing—some into Reiki, others into crystals. But having ancient stones speak to you, now that's a new one."

"When I woke today, I imagined us meeting for a quick coffee and then heading out to Derreenataggart, you know, the stone circle. I am surprised at how long we—I—have talked and how important it has been for me. But if you are still up for it, I say we go out there now," I say with pleasure.

"Sure, my car is right nearby. Let's do it."

Luckily, Derreenataggart Stone Circle is just a mile or two north of us and the directions are pretty straight forward. I explain what I know about stone circles, especially those here on Beara. This one is supposed to be one of the best examples of a recumbent stone circle, one with a horizontal slab stone aligned to the cycle of the moon.

I see the standing stone at Knockaneroe. "This is where we are to turn," I tell Cindy. A short distance down the road, a brown heritage sign tells us we have arrived. There is easy parking and easy access. Unfortunately, the roadside trees now block the view of the bay. In times past, I bet there was a clear view like the circles we visited on the north shore.

The circle is silent, awaiting our visit. One of the portal stones is about eight feet high, the other has been broken off. I suggest we enter between them and do a blessing in the center. Cindy nods.

So I begin:

> *Ancient Ones, thank you for creating this sacred place.*
>
> *We seek your wisdom and support as we attune ourselves to the elements of earth, of air, of fire, and of water that were so present in past rituals at this place and remain so central to our being here today.*
>
> *We seek to align ourselves with the sun and moon and stars as you did so long ago.*
>
> *We seek to live in harmony and Oneness.*

"Beautiful. Did you write that or just memorize it?" Cindy asks.

"Neither, the words just came to me," I say. "It has happened before. Words just coming to me like that. Last time I felt so overcome that I felt faint. Today it feels quite natural."

"Hmm," is all Cindy says before following me as I go round the circle touching each of the stones and trying to connect with their vibration. She begins humming an Enya song as we progress around a second, and then third time. I feel a building of energy as we go. No particular message or vibration of an individual stone this time, but definitely a feeling of their collective power.

We each lean against one of the nine stones left standing and remain silent. Three other stones have fallen over, and there's a gap where three others used to be. The circle still is very powerful even with these gaps. As hard as I try, no messages come; no clarification of what is going on for me or why I am drawn here. I look to see how Cindy is doing and see her staring out to the west, past the gap in the circle.

"I can feel the power, Honey. I think though that they only want to talk to you. They really aren't interested in me. I sense they are trying to work with you, waiting as you gradually adjust to it so you can become a receiver. In channeling, I have heard people say that spirits need to adjust intensity so humans can receive the message. Maybe that's what's going on for you. You are adjusting; yeah, I think you just are meant to stay with it," she says drawing out that Southern drawl as she tries to make sense of what she is receiving herself.

"OK, but how do I do it? And when you say 'they', what do you mean?" I ask in frustration.

"Good question, Honey, but one I can't answer. It's just what I experience and how it comes to me. I guess I say 'they' 'cuz I can't fathom who-is-who in the spirit world. Like, I have always felt comfortable talking to God and connecting with those who have passed, but never thought of connections from way back like this Hag of yours."

"I see what you mean. And I appreciate your support. Mark is a bit fearful that I will be sent back in time or something that has him sending out protective vibes and rushing us away when things get tense. On one hand, I have felt safe with him and grateful that he is supporting me. On the other, I feel I need to open up more and his uneasiness misdirects me."

"Everything happens in perfect time, Honey, and the help we need comes when we need it. Maybe I am meant to help you move into your next stage of exploration."

"Hmm. That would be terrific. By the way, I have started doing this buttercup ritual, to honor the memory of my friend who passed last year and to just show gratitude for life in general. Would you like to join me this time?" Upon her nod, I explain further and we leave the circle to collect buttercups.

As we finish, Cindy clears her throat and speaks quietly "Honey, I am surprised how much that got to me. It grabbed my heart and gave it a big squeeze. Thank you, glad we did it. It has got me thinkin' about my granny and about my blessings in general."

We both sit quietly, deep in our own thoughts.

"Abby? Do you see her over there?" Cindy whispers.

"See who?"

"The woman who has been staring at you."

"What are you talking about? I don't see anybody."

"Honey, she is right there." Cindy points across the circle. She is dressed in a whitish-gray gown. Not like a prom gown, more like a night gown. I guess it is just a simple peasant dress—old time, rough material—like medieval times. She has this stick—walking stick maybe. I think it may be a shepherd's hook, like in the pictures of Jesus as a shepherd."

"So, she is just staring at us?"

"She has started pounding her stick into the ground. Like she is hell-bent—I mean determined to get me to do something…"

"I don't see anything. What does she want?"

"I'm to get your attention. She is frustrated with you. She says you tried harder to reach the Hag of Beara than you are trying now. She wants to talk to you. She wants your attention. She's really agitated that she can't reach you."

"I'm frustrated too. How do I do it? I don't even know who she is. What am I supposed to do?" I ask in desperation.

"I don't know. She just wants you to listen…something about a story…*listen and tell the story* or maybe it is stories," Cindy says and then pauses for a bit. "Let me see if she can say more about how to help you hear her." Another pause and then Cindy shakes her head and adds, "She just keeps saying 'Listen' and she is very emphatic about it."

"Does she want me to tell the story of the Hag of Beara and teach people about sovereignty?" I ask.

"She is shaking her head no and beating her stick up and down into the ground. I get the impression you are not wrong about the Hag part, but she wants you to hear a different story from her. One that is even more connected to the two of you." After a long pause, Cindy wearily adds, "That's all I get."

"What story then? Who is she and how are we connected?"

"Beats me. That's all I keep getting. Then she just gives me that look again and now she is disappearing." Cindy shakes her head.

"You mean like the evil eye kind of look?" I ask with concern.

"No. She loves you, puts up with me, and is just upset that she has to go through me."

"Wow. This is crazy. I don't get it. Why can't I see her?" I say with agitation.

"I don't know. She's gone."

"Are you alright?" I inquire.

"Yeah, she is a strong presence but not at all threatening. She just isn't interested in talking with me. She wants your attention. Are you OK?" When I nod, she continues, "If so, I am going to walk a bit. Take your time. See if you get anything when I step away. Maybe you will be able to make connection now that you have a description of her and can visualize who is trying to connect with you."

"OK. But first, has anything like this ever happened to you before? How do you do it?" I ask.

"As I think I told you, I have had family come to me, and some friends and neighbors. They just wanted me to know they were OK and that they have my back from up in Heaven. But this is different. This lady in her robe surprised the hell out of me, but as I told you, she is just anxious to talk with you and I happen to be her best shot at reaching you."

"But I still am wondering how you do it. And, of course, wondering even more, how I can do it."

"I really don't know how it happens. Maybe, if you try deep, deep breaths and stay very still. You know, like if you were trying to get a butterfly to land on your arm. Be patient and see what happens," Cindy advises.

I nod, then try to calm myself, but still I see nothing. It is so frustrating. I can feel the power of the stone I am leaning against. My body feels all tingling and I feel a warm sensation on my back. Perhaps, a sign of encouragement? But nothing else comes. Am I trying too hard or is this all nonsense?

I don't know…but the urge to soak in the energy of this circle is palpable. I feel like I would like to just stay here all day, all night until sunrise. I do sit for quite a while until my thoughts are interrupted by birds squawking and soaring around. Cindy must have walked too close to a nest or something and flushed them out.

I give up for now. So I wave to her that I am ready to go. But I stop to ask the shepherdess not to give up on me and to help me learn to connect with her as I back out of the circle. I am full of gratitude, but also frustrated.

"Well, I am curious to know. Did the shepherdess come through to you after I left? Were you able to connect?" Cindy asks.

"No. I tried, but the only thing I was getting is vibrational energy from the stones. It's not like I don't want to connect and I don't consciously feel afraid. So am I somehow blocking her or am I just never going to be able to see entities like you see them?" I hear myself whining as I ask.

"I don't know, Honey. But I think you may be trying too hard. Ease up, just let it come. Or maybe somebody in your childhood shamed you or scolded you for having an imaginary friend. I have heard it said that we cut off our ability to see fairies that way. And that it often happens in childhood when our parents tell us to grow up. You know, the whole Peter Pan story, seeing Tinkerbell and all that.

"Perhaps…"

"You know, I don't feel much like going back into town right now and expect you feel the same. Let's drive along the ring road and go to the Zen center. There will be great views of the Atlantic from there and a combination tea and book shop I hear."

"You are kidding. A Zen center here in rural Ireland?"

"Trust me, Honey, not as strange as what I just experienced. Holy moly!"

• • •

The beauty and silence of the meditation center are exactly what I need. It is such fun to see palm trees blowing in the breeze, sit out under the protection of a giant Buddha statue and watch the dolphins play in the distance. Mark and Jack are out there somewhere too.

Cindy gets restless before me so she goes over to the shop while I sit sipping tea and wondering what is going on. I feel like such a failure. I don't think I am afraid, I don't think I am blocking connection to Spirit, but here I am days into an experience that makes no sense.

"I can take you back to town if you want, but I have a suggestion. Come to the waterfall out in Adrigole and stop at the art gallery along the way. Jack won't want to go. If we have time, there is a walk cousin Katie says I would love and it sounds right up your alley. Standing stones and such. We'll have to come back to town, I want to pick up food and beer at the last minute. They shouldn't be left in the car all afternoon. The extra trip back won't be that bad and it should be worth it."

"Sounds great. I like the idea of checking out a grocery store here just to see what is different."

"Actually, I will call Katie and ask her to call the guys. She's at work. We might not have cell service out at the waterfall."

We stop and Cindy whirls through the store picking up snacks, ordering a bunch of things from the deli and paying for them now so we can just load them up and get going when we return.

"Hey, what's this with your name? Have I been saying it wrong?" I ask, as I pick up the credit card receipt that dropped off the counter. "CynDee" pops off the page and takes me by surprise. I have been thinking of her as Cindy and somehow this spelling seems so different.

"Oh, I don't pay any attention to it any more. My mama named me CynDee. At home, we go strong on the "Dee" part, but it makes no never mind to me. Momma wanted me to have flair. Ha-ha. Beware what you wish for. I grew up with flair that's for sure. Little did she know that I would grow up to be 5'9" and busty. Not sure if my name created my personality or vice versa but I took up flair with gusto. Named my beauty salon Hair with Flair and am known for bold and fanciful styling. I'm gonna write a book someday—*Secrets of a Makeover Queen*."

"I'll be," I chuckle.

"So my family called me Dee or DeeDee when I was a kid. But as I matured, so to speak, the name was too much like a porn star's. We dropped it back to Dee, but I kept the CynDee spelling for Momma's sake. Now, Jack's the only one who calls me DeeDee, privately, sexy-like."

"So do you prefer CynDee or Dee?" I ask.

"CynDee is good. My family still calls me Dee, but most everyone else knows me as CynDee. And, of course, the spelling doesn't matter until somethin' official comes up." With little prompting, she continues as we drive along, "My family name is Burke, Anglo-Irish I think, but in these parts better just to go with Sullivan. Not much into history and genealogical stuff anyway. My family goes back eons in the States. Doesn't really matter to me where they came from. I think of my hometown as shaping me more than where we came from generations ago."

She muses aloud, "I'm not that connected to Ireland. The stuff we did today stirs me more than the clannish stuff. I'm just along for the ride and to be at Jack's side—the dutiful wife role which I only can do for so long. I made Jack promise me we will go to Cork City after this. Some shopping and night life…that's more my style. I work hard and I play hard. Dancin' helps me let off steam and in between I just pretty much take things as they come…here's the gallery now."

The gallery isn't open. We easily find the lane back to the waterfall. I am glad not to be driving because the road is so narrow that bushes scratch the side of the car. I hate the thought of meeting a car coming toward us. CynDee—I think the name differently now that I have seen the spelling and heard the story—doesn't seem to mind, but I can't imagine having to back up if we meet someone coming from the opposite direction. The place is worth it though. It is the tall, skinny stream of water Mark and I saw as we came down Healy Pass, and it is enchanting. And, of course, up close the stream of water is wider than it looked from afar. The sounds alone are mesmerizing and the play of light fascinating. For the first time, I see fairy-like images dancing in sunbeams. We sit for a while in silence until we run out of time. We return to town to pick up the food and beer and come back to Sullivan's Mile, the beach site for the picnic.

• • •

A lane just beyond the turn up Healy Pass takes us down to the shore and to our meeting place. We begin to set up when Mark arrives with Jack. The other guys are right behind them. Their wives and the others dribble in from jobs and various places on Beara. Somehow, Jack and I find ourselves alone working on set up. "Glad to have this time with you, Jack. I feel like I really got to know CynDee today but you are still a mystery," I say in a light, playful way.

"Now, 'mystery', that's a word I have never been called before," he quips.

"Straightforward guy, huh? Like the Tom Hank's version of Sully? Were you ever called 'Sully'?" I ask.

"Nope, that was my dad. He was killed in 'Nam. I was only two. He was a river patrol boat skipper killed by a sniper attack. I understand he loved to sail; instead he had to motor through the jungle in the ugliest war ever."

He continues, "My stepdad never asked that us kids take his name; he was a good guy, good to my mom and good to us kids too. But I could see the hurt in his eyes when as a teenager I wanted to be called 'Sully'. I gave it up within a couple of days. Just didn't seem fair to him, you know."

He pauses and then continues, "But, now, I want to get to know the Sullivans and the O'Sullivans. You know, hear their stories. My grandfather's people came from the Beara here. They left when the copper mines closed, seeking mining jobs in the U.S. Then at the end of WWII my grandfather visited here and married a third or fourth cousin. So I am actually connected to two branches of the clan. Their Irish-American wedding was a big deal. The guys you met at the pub and the folks that will be here tonight are actually second or third cousins, but they treat me like a long-lost brother."

Mark comes back to see if we need help and pipes in, "I can attest to that. The guys today clearly showed they think the world of him."

"CynDee was saying today that the whole family has been amazingly hospitable," I note.

"Yeah."

"So, did you go in the Navy like your dad?" I ask.

"Tried to, but a college football injury kept me out. Had a ROTC scholarship and everything but was put out of commission junior year. Fluke thing, but what can you do?" He then asks me, "Did CynDee tell you about this place and why we chose to have the thank-you picnic here?"

"She was just about to when you guys arrived."

"This mile long stretch of beach was named for the Sullivan Brothers. Five Americans killed together during WWII. There was a big ceremony wherein this stretch of beach was named Sullivan's Mile. The U.S. Navy sent in a destroyer named for the brothers that sailed right down the harbor to here."

He continues, "The story was made into a movie with Frank Sinatra. Sad case. The upshot of it is that these five brothers from Iowa join the Navy and insist on serving together. It was against Navy policy to put brothers on the same ship, in case it went down, but the Navy relented. Then their boat was torpedoed in the South Pacific and all five died."

"Oh my. What a tragedy, but how does this stretch of beach fit in? You said they were killed in the South Pacific," I ask confused.

"Their grandfather was from here. An Irish-American just like my grandfather."

Sean arrives as Jack is telling the story and takes over. "Aye, 'twas in the summer of 2003, when we were after celebrating the 400th anniversary of O'Sullivan Beara's historic march from Beara to County Leitrim. We Irish are always finding ways to lure our American cousins home again, you know. And for peaceable people, we always seem to be coming upon the anniversary of another battle."

That sparks more cousins to come over and jump in. Lots of fun and conversation ensue. Finally, I find an opening to ask about stone circles, but there is not much response or interest. One elderly uncle says, "Sure, don't I have enough stones in me own yard?" And a middle-aged woman offers, "A lot of superstitious rubbish, that."

Then, CynDee comes to the rescue and drags me over some of Jack's cousins who are very into the legends and perhaps even believers of the Old Religion. They tell us more stories of the Hag of Beara as we sit out looking at Bere Island in the middle of the peninsula with the mountains behind us. I am loving every moment.

One of the group, Sean's wife Katie, actually grew up with the woman who wrote the poetry book named for the Hag that I bought back on the Healy Pass. (And, of course, these Sullivans know and are distantly related to the store owner and doesn't he live right on the main road above us.) "Aye, she teaches at Uni in Cork these days. Important that these stories not be lost but are brought back to life in modern ways if you ask me. Right timing in my way of thinking…need stories of strong women, I was coming into me own when Mary Robinson became president of Ireland. Powerful role model, she was. And look at the peace that came."

Maureen, the solicitor in the family, adds "Powerful women were important within the church but also the wider culture. Sovereignty for women goes way back you know. Brehon Law predates English law. Women could own land, be judges. It was based on restorative justice principles not punitive ones. No capital punishment, you know. Before the Romans and the Normans came and tried to wipe out Celtic culture. Here in Ireland we pretty much carried on with Celtic ways. Until Cromwell came through, and then there was the Famine after it. England did a number on us then and the old ways were hard to uphold."

"I have a friend up in Galway who runs workshops on all this, you know," adds Katie. "Will you be going there? Sure, I can text you her group's website."

"Sadly, not this trip. But do send it. I hope to come back. Plus, winters are long in Upstate New York. I have a list of things to check out online already."

Mary jumps in, "CynDee tells me you two are talking to the Ancient Ones at the stones, now. Let's hear more about that, if you will. Now, me, 'tis in the gardens where I speak to the divas and fairies. They guide me in the planting and the growing, as they did me granny. Best to have them on your side. But never have connected with the Ancient Ones. Do tell."

"So you believe in all this?" asks another cousin.

"I do when it comes to plantin' and growin'. Hard to tell about the rest, but then sure you would not want to ignore or cross them now, would ye?"

Maureen offers, "I have always been a John O' Donahue fan…Celtic spirituality and nature. To actually talk to the stones is a big stretch for me, but then again, right above us, up there on the Beara Way, is an amazing small dolmen. I do sense some magical feeling when I visit there, I must say."

"A small gateway, now, isn't it? Abby, we Irish have an expression 'the mountain behind the mountain', you know, meaning away in the Otherworld. Driving along here in the West, it is easy to imagine the Ancients believing in gods and goddesses, spirits and fairies beyond their own world."

"Aye, and we have another expression the 'thin places' meaning where the veil between worlds can be lifted or seen through. For some that means you can connect with the Otherworld, for others it means you can touch the hand of God. Same thing in my way of thinking."

Just then Mark, Jack and Sean join us. Mark and I haven't had a chance to hear about one another's day, but he clearly has been riding high on the experience. I have seldom seen him so excited.

He reports, "Jack's uncle just gave us a rundown on the best Cork lighthouses to visit by car and also told us the story of the lifeboat rescue teams. He is a volunteer, actually. And, Abby, did you know that fifteen miles out to sea from the Cork shoreline is the main sea route from Europe to America? No wonder, there are so many lighthouses. I read it, but only now that we are here do I get the full impact. Things are so much closer together than in the U.S."

"Your man sure does have a passion for lighthouses," one of the women observes.

"He sure does." Somehow the expression "your man" doesn't grate with me here in Ireland as it would in the States.

Eventually, the party moves on to Murphy's back in Castletownbere. We leave our car up at the B&B and join the group for a rousing night of fun and great *trad* music—"great *craic*" as they say. Sleep comes easy after all the beer and loud music.

Then, I wake suddenly as the words 'come back' seep into my consciousness. By the time I go off to the bathroom, the feeling of connection I had is totally gone, but I still remember. The words come again as kind of a whisper. Of course, I know immediately what it means: come back to the circle. I lay still asking myself not if, but when should I go. I am so tempted to go back to sleep and think about it later. But I am too restless. I have to go now to be there at sunrise. As one of the women said last evening, there are "thin places" and there are thin or in-between times when connection to the Otherworld is most possible. Sunrise at a stone circle hopefully offers a great possibility for me to connect with the shepherd woman. At the very least, it will be a sign of my willingness to reach out to her.

I quietly put on last night's clothes, write a note to Mark from the bathroom, find the car keys and slip out. He stirs, but luckily does not wake. I drive up a sleepy Main Street, where the only activity is at the docks, and on to the dark road back to the circle.

• • •

I wait a bit until the early morning light is gracing the field and the stones of the circle are appearing out of the dark. I grab my backpack, lock the car and cross to the site as the sun makes itself known. There's an eerie peacefulness about the place. Yet, I feel this surge of energy overtake me and quicken my heartbeat as I enter the circle. Strange familiarity is mixed with awe and wonder.

It feels like being at Grandmother's lake house during a mesmerizing summer storm. My mother would come to me then. She would soothe me and sing to me and tell me not to be afraid. But Grandmother stopped all that. She scolded me. Told me I was silly and to never speak of such foolishness again. A flood of tears come as I remember all of this. It is so real and so raw.

And a message does come through, not as a voice per se, but, nonetheless, words come: *Listen, you are not foolish to listen. Listen. You will find yourself in your own story…in all the stories.*

Nothing more comes, but the sense of liberation I feel is overwhelming. I sit for what seems like an eternity, regaining my equilibrium and then I stand. I dance. I kiss each stone. I sing out in gratitude, to my mother, to the shepherd woman who has been trying so hard to connect to me and to the wise Cailleach who brought me the strength to stand up against my grandmother's admonitions. I sing "I Am Woman" or at least the parts I remember at the top of my voice.

There are buttercups all around so I pick some and bring them to the center of the circle. Saying more words of gratitude, I leave them as I have been doing since day one of the trip. I have a sense that Judy and my mom are cheering from the other side. It is a strong sense of connection not just a notion.

I have released the block! I have made connection. My new buttercup ritual has an added meaning now that I can connect with my mom again. The image of the small, dainty wildflower, growing in bunches and popping up to welcome spring is a gentle, but powerful one. I may not be able to see the shepherdess or any guides or loved ones, but I can feel their energy. I know they guide me and support me. What a blessing.

I never connect with the shepherdess, but actually feel like she was behind this morning's experience. I shed a tear of gratitude. All is well, as Mark would remind me if he were here. All is well.

I promise the shepherdess that she does indeed have my attention; I feel confident we will connect in the future, and that I will commit to listening and telling the story she has for me. I am not sure how we will connect, nor do I know what I am to do with the stories, but I know now that I am on the path to find out. And that this morning has been the beginning of the realization of the nun's blessing: *May ye find yourself amidst the stones.*

• • •

Mark is still in bed when I get back. Sleepily, he asks, "What's up, buttercup?"

"Buttercup?" I repeat incredulously.

"Yeah, that's what we always said to Cheryl when she was a little girl. Not sure, why it popped up. Just felt like saying it. Why? Does it offend you? Too childish or something?"

"No, not at all. It's just that I went to the stone circle and did the buttercup ritual, and it kind of freaked me out when you said the word. That's all," I respond.

"That's how come you are dressed? What's up with that?" he asks.

"I woke early and was drawn back to yesterday's stone circle. I want to tell you all about it. It all was amazing. And I want to hear all about the boat trip."

"Let's say we get breakfast and then just come back to the room and have a lazy morning catching up with each other," I suggest.

"Sounds perfect, I will slip on my jeans so we can go right down to get coffee. Then we can maybe shower together when we come back?" he asks with an impish grin.

The salmon is even better that yesterday, if that is possible. Back in the room, our quiet morning of making love and sharing seems all the richer for us having been apart for the day yesterday.

Fish for breakfast, fish for lunch and fish again for dinner. Given that this is arguably Ireland's best fishing village, it is imperative. In between meals, we walk the town. We watch the fisherman unload the last of their morning's catch and the barges unload cargo. Mark makes some short videos based on scenes from *Ondine* and we stop by the library.

Back at the B&B, we watch Mark's great video clips of his sailing adventure, take naps and answer emails. I finally get to chat with older son Brian who has been off on a canoe trip with buddies. Seems neither of my boys needs me any longer. I raised them to be independent. Hopefully, they also will learn to trust in love and sharing life with another. Sadly, that isn't something I was able to model for them.

Then it is back to Murphy's and McCarthy's for pints and music to celebrate our last night on Beara. We remember to bring over and now pin up a picture postcard of Rochester, New York's Lilac Festival and one of the Susan B. Anthony House to join with zillions of others who wanted to say "we are here" and Mark buys a t-shirt. Then, we settle in to a corner table to listen to music. It is Saturday night and the *craic* is even more robust than the other pub nights we have experienced.

Some guys come in to collect for The Royal National Lifeboat Institution (RNLI). Of course, Mark engages them in conversation while he pulls out his wallet. I am amazed to hear that Ireland is connected to anything with the name "royal" after all the English have done over here. But with the noise level and general fun-loving nature of the night, I save my questions and comments for another time. The guys go on to say that collections are made in pubs all over Ireland every Saturday night. They ask if we have noticed "the wee wooden lifeboats" by the cash registers during the week. They explain that the lifeboat rescue fund is the largest charity in Ireland and that it helps save lives at sea around the coasts of the UK, the Republic of Ireland, the Channel Islands and the Isle of Man. It is heartwarming to see the passion and pride they have for their volunteer work. Makes me think of my dad and the volunteer firefighters in my hometown.

In spite of the fun we are having, we miss Jack and CynDee and the whole Sullivan clan. Last night, it never occurred to us that we might never see any of them again. We vow to call tomorrow before we leave Castletownbere to thank everyone once again. We raise a final glass in celebration. *Sláinte!*

We have learned to say cheers in Irish; "good health" actually and to reply "good health to you as well". For the first time, tonight the words slide off our tongues: *Sláinte. Sláinte agad-sa.*

CHAPTER SEVEN

S aying goodbye to Castletownbere and via cell phone to the Sullivans, we move on toward mainland Cork intending to hug the coast, viewing lighthouses along the way. We have come to love Beara and the people we have met here. The pang of sadness I felt leaving Eileen and Jimmy on the north shore is minuscule compared to saying goodbye to CynDee and Jack, especially CynDee, who was so instrumental in my connecting with the stones. The Sullivan family added so much to our experience of Beara. Mark talks about his sailing trip all the way to Adrigole where our last goodbye is to the seals.

We make one stop on the way to Glengarriff. I want to see the dolmen that the Sullivan cousin mentioned Friday night. From my archaeological map it appears to be one of the few in County Cork. For unknown reasons this area, so full of stone circles, has almost no dolmens. Mark likes the idea of walking a section of the southern loop of the Beara Way, as a test to see if it should be on our list of return places.

We drive up the Healy Pass to find the lane paralleling the coast road, right above Sullivan's Mile. We park and walk from there. It is terrific to look down to our picnic site and to look over at Bere Island from this vantage point. We now know what we are looking at and have meaningful memories of all of it. Mark especially is pleased since he had not had the freedom to have a leisurely look while driving down the alpine turns of Healy Pass. After a short hike, we see the dolmen sign.

"OK, I bite. What's a dolmen?" Mark asks.

"Well, it a kind of passage tomb made of stones in the shape of a three-legged table with a capstone top. Some call it a giant's table, in fact. And some think it was an altar of sorts. Another interpretation is that it was a gateway to the Otherworld, the Celts name for what some call the Dreamtime. Officially, the altar stone back in Kenmare was one, but the legs were so short that they seemed more of a foundation."

"Interesting. So, instead of worrying that you'll go through a stone circle into another century, I have to watch that you don't slip through a star gate, huh?"

"Or into the land of fairies," I retort.

As we get ourselves over a stile in the farmer's field and into the grassy knoll where the dolmen is situated, it becomes clear that this is a very small one. No skipping through it as I had imagined I would do. I crawl through and say a little ditty about wanting to meet the fairies, but mostly in jest. Mark is too large to go through and seems glad of it. It has a nice gentle energy, but no voices come. In fact, it has a totally different vibe than the circles. Not sure how they differ, but I think they do. Were they actually used as gateways to another dimension? Were the stone circles more about ceremony on the earth plane? I only know that I feel playful here and serious at the stone circles. And as for standing stones, I really am at a loss. They are everywhere. Sometimes they seem like directional signs or placeholders, other times like sentinels or guardians. It is all too much to comprehend.

The scenery is ruggedly beautiful with the water of the bay gleaming in the distance. "My favorite part," Mark says, as we hoof it back to the car, "was going over the stile. I had read about stiles in Victorian novels, but never experienced one. Never a dull moment with you, that's for sure."

We stop in Glengarriff for lunch at a café with a lovely outside area. This is a charming little village that seems made for visitors, including bus groups. Luckily, the only one in town is pulling away as we park. I can also imagine Irish folks out for a Sunday drive or taking a long weekend stopping here. But at the moment it is quiet. The proprietor tells us that most Wild Atlantic Way tour buses stop here but skip the Beara Peninsula, going for the Ring of Kerry. I am so glad we chose Beara, and Mark agrees.

We find a great store with wonderful woolens. While Mark is shopping for a sweater for himself, I slip a really neat flannel Grandfather shirt into the pile of Christmas gifts I am getting. It seems like something Colin Farrell wore or might have worn in *Ondine*. Mark will love it.

"Hey, Abby, will you help me pick out some jewelry for Cheryl and little Lydia? Lizzie always did the shopping for such things. Last year was our first Christmas without her and I just got them all gift cards. I picked out a hat for my son-in-law, but I want to get my girls something special."

While we pick out jewelry for his daughter and granddaughter, he asks, "Do you want something for yourself?"

"Nothing speaks to me, but thanks, I would love to find something as a memento. Let's keep looking. By the way, the sweaters are too itchy and too warm for me, but that is very handsome on you. And it's your color. I hope you're going to get it."

"Yep, I think I will. Then let's finish off our gift list with some of these scarves. They're beautiful and won't take up much room."

"Good idea. I already chose one for each of the boys, but let's look at the list. They will make great Christmas presents."

Bonane Heritage Park is about mid-way between Glengarriff and Kenmore and proves to be a harrowing but beautiful drive with the mountain peninsula we have just enjoyed to one side and a steep drop off into a green inland valley on the other. The park itself offers us a sample of what we have seen and introduces us to some archaeological things that are new to us.

"So, it says here that a *crannog* was a very early lake house. Given that it is made of thatch, this one clearly has to be a replica. The brochure says the rest of the stuff is all real. The timeline covered ranges from the stone and bronze ages, up to the famine times in the 1800s.

"This little pond with the *crannog* is so sweet and the views so beautiful. I wonder if it was a sweet life or a harsh one back in the day? It looks idyllic, but the dampness here in winter would be hard to take."

"Seems pretty similar to Native American lodges at home and New York is much colder. Though I am not suggesting any of it would be easy. I like my creature comforts." As we start up the path to the ring fort, Mark further observes, "This must have been a place of regional significance, the size and the way it overlooks the whole peninsula. It seems much more complex than anything we have seen so far. In a way it is quite isolated so far inland, which I assume protected it from invasion. Yet, it also is at a crossroads. I assume it was a gathering place for people from the peninsulas and the mainland. This stuff makes me so curious to know how ancient people lived and worshipped."

"Agreed. I get a strong sense of it as a gathering place, but I am dying to know more about the rituals and purpose. Mind if I go ahead for some quiet time at the circle while you check out the other stuff?"

"No problem. I will just follow the path outlined on the brochure. I want to see this stone with holes, called a *bullaun* stone. When you think of how hard it would be to bore a hole through a boulder, you have to ask, why? And how? I also want to take some time at the famine ruin. We were kind of in a hurry in Kenmare. I want to spend more time at this one in prayer, honoring those who passed and forgiving those who contributed to the problem. There was such suffering and anguish. Anyway, if you are deep in meditation when I get to the stone circle, I will quietly have a look and then move on. There is a place called the Druid Walk further on. I am fascinated by the Druids. This is the first place to even mention them. I am curious to see what it's like. You can find me there, communing with the wizards and fairies."

"Doubt you'll be doing that, but thanks. See you." I give him a quick kiss and am off.

The stones of the circle are massive, but not high. There is an altar stone in the middle. In fact, it looks much like the Kenmare stone circle, only this one is in perfect harmony with nature. I read that it aligns to the moon; but, of course, mid-day that isn't anything I get to experience. I wonder about its connection to the Hag of Beara and to the stone circles of the peninsula. Did the Ancient Ones meet at different places for each change of seasons? Did one community honor one god or goddess over another?

We know that the Celtic calendar is based on the turn of the seasons. Stone alignments to the solstices and the equinoxes abound. We have learned that the holidays that lay in between were often connected to moon cycles. Stone circles must have held great power and meaning for people to build these things and then to travel great distances to partake in festivals and ceremonies at various sites. "Curiouser and curiouser," as Alice would say.

I bring all those questions with me as I approach the circle. I take a few deep breaths to clear my head and to release any blocks that might cause me to resist listening to the stones. I remember CynDee's advice to relax and not try so hard. I bring my attention down from my head to my heart. I take some more deep breaths. I stand and tune into my senses and inner knowing. The feeling that I have been here before is stronger than at previous places. The imperative to "listen" comes in stronger too. I hope I will be able to hear more today.

The opening words come to me more easily than ever before and my voice is strong as I offer them out loud:

> *Ancient Ones, Great Mother, voice of the shepherdess, I humbly come before you.*
>
> *I now understand that these stones hold the memories and the stories I am meant to hear.*
>
> *I have come to listen to your message.*
>
> *Please make yourselves known to me.*

I round the stones three times and then sit with my back against the center stone looking out across the mountains of Beara. We are just a few miles from Kenmare, so I reflect on the circles we have traveled: our stops, the energies and the messages I have received.

What else am I to hear? How am I to serve? A word association riff pops into my head as I say the word "serve". It takes me to thoughts of the Holy Grail and Percival asking: "Who does the grail serve?" To Percival piercing the veil? To the message of the Fisher King? To us all recognizing our own wounds and showing compassion to the woundedness of others, showing compassion for the world? Is this the story I am to tell? It certainly is a mighty one, an important one.

But it is a story that has already been told down through the ages. What could I add? Would there be benefit in writing it from a feminine or feminist perspective?

Listen…and trust that the way will be made clear.

The message doesn't come as a being or entity talking to me, but it is the strongest and clearest of all the messages I have received. This time it doesn't leave me lightheaded. I feel I have finally begun to truly connect. I also realize that, even though I am not seeing an entity or channeling it like CynDee can do, I am receiving messages. I know to be OK with that and to relax into it. "Don't push the river; just be in flow with the Universe." I chuckle as I think about how long that has been a mantra for me. To date, it has been a key to my finding myself. As the nun's blessing offered, I am indeed *finding myself amidst the stones.* Wow. Amen and Blessed Be.

I just sit with all this for a bit, then take out my journal. I want to write before I forget. There is so much to consider, so much swirling around in my mind. Then, a voice comes:

Listen with your heart. It is only with the heart that you can truly see.

Of course! That is the central message of the Grail legend, the heart of it, if you will: Love and Compassion. No one can find the castle, no one can find the Grail otherwise. It's only when I breathe through my heart and get out of my head that I hear these messages. We are all meant to be heart-centered beings. We are meant to connect with each other in a circle of Love. We are meant to connect with the elements and the directions with Love. These circle rituals that have been handed down through the ages remain to remind us of this truth.

I feel full of love and yet my energy is spent. I focus on my breathing again and bring my breath to my heart. My energy comes back. I then ask the stones if there is more for me to hear today while I am here at this place. I wait in silence, but nothing more seems to come. I wait a bit longer, then I thank the stones and leave with this feeling of exuberance and joy, anxious to tell Mark all I've experienced and get his thoughts. I am glad to be with him in all this.

The Druid's Walk holds its own energy, its own kind of magic. I try to take it all in. There is so much here to integrate with what I just experienced. This Druid link is not something I have explored to date but I get its importance, not just to the Grail story but to keeping the mysteries alive. As I walk deeper into the woods, I see an image of a wizard in a long, purple robe with black pointed hat sitting on a stump along the path. His hands circle a deep blue sphere with specks of light shining through it, like stars in the night. In just a flash, he is gone, but there sits Mark.

Whoa! I was already wondering where to start filling Mark in on all that happened. Now, this. What on earth is it about? I make a quick decision to keep quiet for a bit first to see what has been going on with Mark.

"Abby, you look radiant. Come join me. I have been communing with the trees. The only place that has felt to me like this is Kilcatherine. Wow. It is so peaceful, yet there is a depth here that is beautiful. And there is a magic in the stillness, like the trees are speaking to me. One of the 'thin places' the Sullivans were talking about, at least for me," Mark says quietly and reverently.

"So, the trees are speaking to you like the stones speak to me?" I ask this incredulously. I haven't begun to process the Druid image and now this.

"Not literally, but I do feel connected. I have been thinking about the role the Druids played in bridging the Old Religion with early Christianity. They say that many became Christian monks. The fanciful animal figures from Celtic art in the Book of Kells had always puzzled me until I realized this. And Merlin: he was as important a bridge from pagan to Christian cultures as was Brigid. This is grabbing me. Making me realize that I, too, am here to learn about the balance of the Divine, both male and female; Mother/Father God. I often say the words. Indeed, my intellect believes in this Divine Balance but this, this experience, is about getting it viscerally. Whew. Sorry to blast you with all that, Abs. How were your stones?"

"No need to be sorry, that is wonderful. I love it. And it is really mind blowing when you consider how it fits in with what I was receiving at the stone circle while you were getting all this." I fill him in and then add, "Merlin, wizard and some say Druid, was at the heart of the King Arthur legends and the Avalon connection too. It really is coming together in my mind. As you say, it is about restoring balance."

"Yep. Whether it is a Jungian thing of connecting to the collective unconsciousness or something else, I don't know. However, I do believe it is a message to take notice and to work toward restoration and balance. And, of course, here we are on a Druid forest walk. What better place to contemplate the Grail story and tie it in to your shepherdess and your stone circles."

"There is one more piece I want to share with you, Mark," I say a bit nervously.

"OK…what is it?"

"As I came up the path, I saw a wizard, maybe even Merlin himself, sitting on this stump," I offer.

"This stump?" he asks incredulously.

"Yes, and then in a flash the image was gone and you were sitting here," I reveal.

"No way. That is too weird—a trick of the imagination or of the light coming through the trees. I don't even know what to say or think about it. Let's walk for a bit," he says, shaking his head as we begin to walk down the winding Druid Walk toward the site exit.

We both remain lost in our own thoughts and fantasies on the way back to Glengarriff.

• • •

"Let's stop at Molly Gallivan's Cottage," I say. "You know, that charming thatched place we saw on the way up and said was too touristy. I am thinking we could use a little grounding and lightening up at the same time. It looks like the perfect place for that."

Yes, it is touristy, very touristy, but then again, we are tourists. It's fun, it's crammed with souvenirs and items that tell the story of farming in a simpler time. The views of the valley are spectacular and seem to stretch forever. The tall wooden statue of a monk looking over the valley gives us pause. Soon—after bathrooms, snacks and picture taking—we are refreshed and ready to move on.

Back in Glengarriff, we stop at the pier for a long view of Bantry Bay with Beara now to our north. Garnish Island looks inviting, but we decide we don't have the time to take the ferry out to its renowned gardens today. We also by-pass Bamboo Park, but we take notice of the lush, tropical plant life that is the product of the Gulf Stream's warm breezes and the importing of exotics by the wealthy Lord Bantry. We are anxious to get on to Bantry itself where we will stay the next few nights. Sean Sullivan told us his favorite band is playing tonight at one of the hotels and we don't want to miss it.

This time as in Kenmare, we stay in a hotel. This one we found on TripAdvisor. It isn't the one where the band is playing, but it is nearby. We have found that the key to an evening of *Ol, Ceol agus Craic*, the new Irish phrase we have learned for drink, music and fun, is not having to drive afterwards. So, this works perfectly. And the anonymity is kind of nice. Neither of us feels like small talk after such an intense day.

We lose ourselves into the sensory delights of a rich meal, wonderful music and a coming together that is both tender and heated.

We have a lazy morning, both lingering in bed later than any day so far. We opt to wander the streets in search of a café like the one in Kenmare, where we can skip the full Irish and where we can get cappuccinos and linger further, this time over a newspaper.

Bantry proves to be a lively town that has a commercial and tourist mix that is quite different from any place we have visited thus far. I still never know what is considered a town, a village, a city, a hamlet or crossroads. At home, I would call this a small city. The lovely harbor and park suggest Lord Bantry's old money at work, while the bustle of traffic and commerce suggest a practical market town keeping pace with changing times. It is fun people watching while we plot separate paths for the remainder of the morning.

I intend to arrive at our meeting place for lunch early so I can get a glass of wine and take some time to reflect and journal on my dreams. A lot of things are coming to me during the night. Then, I start a busy day and they are gone. There is so much going on. The stones are saying: *listen*. But I have to admit I don't take the time to listen and reflect; too busy doing to just be. That has been my standard pattern. I used to blame it on the job, the kids, all the commitments I had. Here I am on vacation and I still run the pattern of operating in a perpetual state of doing over being. I really want to change that about myself. Mark is a good influence in this regard. He seems to know how to just hang out and be in the moment better than I.

I'm torn. It is so exciting to be here in Ireland. I don't want to miss out on anything, even for a minute. There is so much to see and do. Today, I stumble upon a wool shop on my way to the park. It is brimming with options, cluttered with yarn as well as seemingly filled with stories. I ask the woman behind the counter about the store and its history, knowing that the stories of this shop will be the stories of women and the families of the town.

Sure enough, she does not disappoint. She tells of rich and poor customers, of the waning interest in knitting and then its upsurge as people look to hold on to old customs and traditions. She helps me pick the right weight and amount of wool to go with patterns for socks. My dear friend Carol has pledged to knit us both a pair of socks if I bring home the materials. At another store, I also pick up a couple of kitchen gadgets different from those at home. Before I realize it, I am running late for lunch and will have no time for journaling.

Mark is waiting for me at this quaint yet upscale upstairs restaurant recommended by the hotel clerk for its seafood. Mark is brimming with information. Last night, a wonderful old stone Methodist church that has now been made into a doctor's office caught our eye. He tells me he not only visited the medical clinic that is now housed there and got a tour, but that he then went to the library to do some research. As I already knew, the role of religion and politics here in Ireland is very complex. He talks now especially about Methodism, saying that English soldiers stationed here helped fill the pews when the English Methodists were planting churches. This church built in the 1840s served about 20 percent of the area.

I interrupt, "But that's about the time of the Great Famine. And money went to build that beautiful church?"

"Exactly why I wanted to learn more; and to learn what role the local Methodist church played in helping the victims of the famine. We know that the Church of Ireland and Church of England supported the Crown and we know the Crown's role. Since Methodists were a more populist Protestant group, I was curious to know about their role here in the South of Ireland. Have you ever heard of souperism?"

"No, do explain."

"Well, it seems that during the Great Famine some churches offered soup to famine victims. At some, the soup was nourishing. At others, there was so little nutrition in what they called soup that people expended more energy getting to the site than they received from the soup itself. Some churches were also known to require participants to denounce the Catholic Church in order to even get that little bit of sustenance. The whole situation was an abomination."

"So, did you find out the role of the Methodists here in this area?"

"Not really. It is a lot like asking the role of my white Southern ancestors during slavery. But the role of religion and religious diversity in Irish history is even more complicated. I do know that Methodists are less than five percent of the population of this area of Cork now. I can't stop myself from looking into all this, but I am happier visiting lighthouses. I am ready to head out to Sheep's Head now, are you?"

"As soon as I head up to the hotel to use the head," I say thinking I am making a great joke.

"Ow," is all he says as we make our way.

• • •

Sheep's Head is both the name of the long, narrow peninsula that forms the southeastern shore of Bantry Bay and of the lighthouse. We had planned to do some hiking as we motored around the Sheep's Head Loop but we get a late start and decide we can hike another day. As usual, we are surprised at the number of stops that appeal to us. As we begin our drive, Whiddy Island is our first temptation. We skipped over the ferry ride yesterday and find ourselves drawn to it still. But Mark is anxious to see at least one lighthouse today, so we resist the ferry ride and just stop for some pictures.

It is fun to see "our" Bere Island come into view as we drive along the bay further out the narrow peninsula. Again, we stop for pictures and to reconsider which stops to make. One hiking map offers over a dozen loops off the big loop.

We chuckle at how overwhelmed we feel in the midst of the simple, bucolic scene in front of us. Maybe we were better off on the Beara where we had fewer maps.

We stop at Lady's Well, realizing that wells played an important role in Celtic spirituality both to pagans and Christians. The site does not disappoint as it gives us that feeling of connection to Source, to the wellspring of life. Mark offers a short prayer. As he does, I am reminded of our experience yesterday at Bonane and wonder more about his connection to these sites that served both pagans and Christians. I can see him being a Druid protector of these sacred sites.

Mass Rock, our next stop, represents a period when Celtic Christians were meeting in secret to avoid destruction by English forces. So while it is not pagan, I sense that same issue of a group trying to protect its sense of meaning. Again, Mark offers a prayer for balance, for tolerance, for Oneness. I so resonate with that feeling. Next, we are drawn to the ruins of a very early church.

"It is like we are being guided through a timeline of Celtic spirituality. Every time we experience these illustrations of the transition from pagan to Christian cultures and the struggle within Christianity for what form of Christianity would be allowed here on the Emerald Isle, I feel such a tug on my heart," I say as we begin to move on again.

"Yep, and you know, I feel we both have worked hard to balance male/female energies within our own person and to find a theology/spirituality that honors the Divine Feminine as well as the traditional male form of God. This, to me, reinforces the importance of keeping up that work. I would really like to start a daily practice of reading from that Celtic book of prayers you have with you. Want to do it together?"

"Absolutely," I say without even a slight pause. "That feels really right."

As we drive along, a flood of confusion comes over me. I say to Mark, "I am trying to figure out my reaction to this timeline that has been presented to us and understand how the time periods of my *déjà vu* experience fit together. First, of course, is the question of is this about a past life I had? If so, when? Sometimes, it feels like I was a pagan in the center of the old goddess times, like when the stones would have been used as they were meant to be used. Other times I feel like I was part of that bridge to early Celtic Christianity, you know, like about 5th century; other times I feel the pain and struggle of the people being overrun by the Normans, 11th or 12th century. None of it makes sense."

"We stopped making sense as we know it quite a few days ago." Mark laughs. "As I said before, all of this is beyond incredible to me. Yet, here we are. I guess if you can believe in one past life, you can believe in more than one. Right? Maybe you were here all of those times."

"Duh, of course! And, if I were here over different centuries and if I can access those memories, I will have both a personal story to tell and a universal one."

"Yep. Wisdom suggests we find ourselves in our own story but also in the stories of those who have come before us. Maybe when you get the messages about listening to the story or stories, it is a 'both/and' kind of thing. I mean each of those times is a key one for the struggle to uphold the Divine Feminine historically. And the same can be said for upholding the sovereignty of this land of Eire and of its women. Layer on layer on layer: a theme woven through time."

"Can we stop for a few minutes? I have got to write this all down." When he pulls over and stops, I give him a big kiss on the cheek. "You are brilliant, these ideas bring it all together. Wow." Mark takes a walk while I write. The words flow as I make connections and feel a clarity I have not experienced all week. Mark returns with buttercups. I burst into tears.

"Julian of Norwich was an English, not Irish, mystic, but her words come to me now: 'All is well and all manner of things shall be well.' Let me know when you are ready for us to move on," he offers.

Moving on, there is more to see including a place named the Holed Stone, a large standing stone with a carved hole that carries a story of a bride and groom connecting their hands through the rock. It is a beautiful place, but neither of us has much to say. Certainly, nothing to say about marriage. I am reminded of CynDee's observation that I avoid that M-word.

CHAPTER EIGHT

"Finally, you get a turn," I say to Mark after thanking him for all his patience with me and my stones. "I just saw the sign. The café and trail head to Sheep's Head Lighthouse are just ahead. And, my, this view is stunning."

"Did you know that this is a fairly new lighthouse, built to guide oil tankers like the ones we have been seeing all week? Because of the cliffs and its placement on the tip of the peninsula, materials were brought in by helicopter."

"We don't intend to go by helicopter, do we?" I ask with a bit of alarm.

"No, no, but I read it is a steep trail with ups and downs. The lighthouse itself is quite a ways above sea level but the road is even higher. So we will actually be looking down and walking down to it. You can see the terrain is getting craggy. Keep an eye out; we should be close. It probably won't come into view until we are right on top of it."

"What a charming name for a café: *An Cupán Tae*," I read. "Let's go in, look around and use the facilities before we walk out to the lighthouse."

"Look," Mark points to the east. "You can see across to Mizen Head. It is so beautiful."

"What am I looking for? A place or a lighthouse?" I ask.

"It is both. It is the tip of the next peninsula east of here. Remember how I did that silly hand illustration to help us keep Beara straight in our minds? Well, that isn't a great illustration now because in truth the southern coast, which I called the thumb, isn't a smooth line but a series of smaller peninsulas and lots of inlets and bays. That is why there are so many miles of coastline."

"I hate to run off, but I need the toilet. I'll be right back," I say as I jump out of the car.

I come back with bad news. "Mark, the guy inside says it's too late in the day to take the trail. It is steep and slow going, especially with the wet stone steps due to the high tide and mist. Here's the site map."

"You...have...got...to be kidding! I can't believe it. How could I not have realized that from the pictures and research I did? I assumed it was 20 minutes, or so. How long did he say it would take?" he says as if counting to ten between each word.

"Two to two and a half hours, assuming we are accustomed to steep trails according to the clerk."

"Darn it," Mark exclaims and walks away for a moment or two. He returns with resolve to let go of his anger. "Well, that's it then. Let's ask if there is a place around here for dinner. We can take in some of the sights we skipped like the signal tower, the standing stone and I think there is even a stone circle. Though, darn it, I should have realized."

An older man is just coming up the trail. "Aye, the hike is rather long, much too late in the day to begin I would say. If you are looking for makings of a picnic supper, I suggest The Old Creamery at Kilcrohane. Only a light supper fare but all local: salmon, cheeses, brown bread and a gift shop for the lady."

I thank him and we wish him well. I then turn to Mark and ask, "So how does that sound? And we can come back first thing in the morning. If we drive straight down without any stops, we will be here in no time and then can go over to Mizen Head from here."

"You don't mind coming back?" Mark asks.

"Hardly. This is all so beautiful. Plus the light will be totally different in the morning. Let's get some shots now, go over for a bite and then choose a place to watch the sunset. One of my favorite things in the world is to watch the sun slowly sink into the ocean and disappear. We haven't done that yet. And we can see them start up the light or whatever the technical term is. Unless, you mind driving back to Bantry after dark."

"No the road wasn't that bad, narrow and winding in a few places, but OK. Sounds like a plan. A new plan, thanks to an unforced error on my part. I should have realized the trail would be steep and slow-going. Thanks for your flexibility."

"Better a path than a cable car. I'm not so afraid of falling when I am on firm ground—a control thing, I guess. Hate to think of myself as controlling, but..."

"I think being in control is a long way from being controlling. You are not controlling. But on this trip for some reason, fears are popping up for you to confront. Maybe that's part of *Finding yourself amidst the stones*. Are you aware of anything in your past that has made you fearful?"

"No, Not really. The one thing that has come up is my grandmother shaming me as a child for what she called fantasizing: you know when I thought my mom was talking and singing to me at night. There may have been fear there that blocked my connecting to the stones. I feel like that has been resolved now. You know, since the morning I spent at the Castletownbere stone circle."

"Yes, that sounded amazing," Mark acknowledges.

"As for these fears of storms and drowning and dangling in the air, I can't think of anything that happened to cause them. But I do know it would be a heck of a lot easier to soul-search at home where I feel grounded rather than half-way around the world; well, not half-way but far away. Plus, we are here on the trip of a lifetime. I feel so unsettled and torn when these messages and experiences come up. I want to delve in to get them resolved and I don't want to miss seeing these stones. Yet, I want to forget it all and just have fun," I vent.

"I always find ice cream helps," Mark offers as he heads us toward the creamery.

We drop the subject, enjoy our picnic and stop to see one of the signal towers. We had seen Martello Towers on Bere Island. These are much older. The system of signal towers represents an even earlier time than the historic lighthouses. In those days, heather was burned atop these square towers that dotted the shoreline.

Because sunset is late this time of year, we have time to go to the stone circle. It is Mark's suggestion that we make the stop at this small, unimposing circle before I take on the bigger one at Drombeg. When he steps into the circle, he offers a short prayer modeled after an Irish blessing:

> *May we find ease and joy and grace in our travels.*
>
> *May that which needs to be revealed to us, come gently.*
>
> *May we embody these revelations in ways that bring joy, peace and love in all we do and to all we serve.*

We stand amid the stones (or amidst as the Irish would say) in silence.

"Thank you," is all I can say; all I need to say.

We return to the coast road; the lighting stunning. What a gift this "accident of bad timing" has become. We find a comfortable spot to watch the orange ball of sun drop slowly into the sea. The afterglow is exquisite. Mark gets beautiful pictures looking down at the lighthouse in silhouette before we had back to town. Almost wordlessly, we climb the steps to our room, prepare for bed and fall asleep in each other's arms.

• • •

An early start with coffee and scones for the road gets us to Sheep's Head in time for a beautiful morning walk. It is treacherous in places but both of us are wide awake and ready for the challenge. The lighthouse is such a brilliant white against a sea of bright blue that it reminds me of a Greek Islands poster. I am grateful we have the sun, not only for its beauty, but because it keeps the stone steps dry.

Mark takes pictures from every imaginable angle and pokes around for what seems like hours. I use the time to soak in the sun and meditate. I ask for clarity—as well as ease and joy—on my quest as defined by the nun that first day: *May ye find yourself amidst the stones.* That phrase just keeps circling through my mind. Yet, I am just realizing she didn't actually say stone circle. Not sure the observation even matters, but it does make me curious thinking now not only about what she meant but where she thought I should go to make it happen. Maybe I don't need to be at the sacred sites themselves to do my self-exploration. And that is a good thing because I want to be with Mark as we do this lighthouse thing. Today is a day to appreciate the Cork coast—more of the amazing Wild Atlantic Way, the new marketing phrase for Ireland's coastline.

After a long cup of *tae* (I like the sound of *tae*), we continue the loop to and beyond where we drove yesterday and to Durrus at the innermost part of Dunmanus Bay. That puts us at the beginning of the Mizen Head Loop. Today, we don't make the mistake of making stops along the route.

"We need to take all these maps home because there is no way I can remember all these names or the order that we are visiting them," I say as if put upon.

"No worries, Abs. Just enjoy. The cameras on our phones record the date and mine even makes albums by date and place. As you might gather, I am also keeping tabs on everything for the lighthouse calendar I am creating. No need for you to focus on the geography when you don't enjoy it."

"Glad to hear it. Oh, I meant to ask you yesterday, about the signal towers. I was surprised that they don't excite you the way the lighthouses do. Are they going in your calendar?" I ask.

"Hmm. Interesting thought. You're right though, they don't excite me. They remind me more of smoke signals going from hilltop to hilltop, like those of Native Americans out West. Lighthouses sit on the edge of the land, where they meet the sea. They stand tall and solid and, usually, with the raging sea beating on them: unchanging beacons of light in a changing sea."

"That's downright poetic," I quip, but with admiration.

"Well, I have written a sermon or two on the subject, you know," he chuckles.

"Of course." After a pause I add, "This is not poetic, but I think our mantra should be "Go directly to the lighthouse. Do not pass go. Do not collect 500 dollars"."

"These signs to ancient ruins are hard for you to pass up, aren't they, Abs? You know we can stop if you really want to."

"I think I could spend a week on any one of these peninsulas. But we have so much else we want to see and do. I'm serious about wanting to keep moving."

"Possibilities abound, that's for sure."

"The scenery just gets more and more breathtaking. I would think we would tire of it but I don't, do you?"

"Not at all, and particularly not when there is a lighthouse in sight," he responds.

• • •

"Here's Mizen Head now," he says with mounting excitement.

"Gorgeous site again, Breathtaking. Don't remember knowing about this bridge though. Did you tell me or show me pictures of it?"

"Not sure if I did. But it is a walking bridge, Abs. No cable car."

"And it is high over the water and almost as scary looking as the cable car. Look at the water raging below," I say tensely.

"Uh, yep." That is all he says and then there is this pregnant pause. Clearly the ball is in my court, the decision to go or not go lies with me. Damn, but he is so non-reactive about everything. I am glad he doesn't push me, but still. It is aggravating when he is so neutral. I know that is irrational on my part because back at the cable car I bit his head off when he tried to sooth my fears. So he is right to leave the ball in my court. Clearly, it is my decision; part of freedom and sovereignty, isn't it? Sometimes being a grown up can be so hard, I chuckle to myself.

"It would have been less challenging to go rock climbing in Montana," I say with a weak laugh.

"We could do that some time, too, if you want," he says with a slight smile.

"You can take my arm, if that would help. And you even could keep your eyes closed, if you wanted to."

"OK, let's do it before I change my mind. But please go kind of slow."

"OK."

We make our way across. I have been so caught up in the bridge that I only now see that there is no tall tower at all. "You mean, after all this, it isn't even a lighthouse?" I asked incredulously.

"It's considered a fog station. It is the site itself and the displays in the visitors center that make it so popular and, of course, most people love the bridge."

While Mark gets lost in the visitors center displays, I duck out to a sunny spot overlooking the bridge to wait for him. I love the play of light on the water; in fact, it is mesmerizing. I realize that without Mark's encouragement and steady hand, there is no way I would have crossed that bridge. Whoa, I am learning to accept help without experiencing it as dependency. Bravo me.

I suck it up and actually look down at the water a couple of times as we cross back. It really looks treacherous down there. I cannot imagine being in a boat in seas like this. Just the thought terrifies me.

• • •

Crookhaven is next and I decide it is my favorite. First, because it is on level ground with easy access, which has become all important to me after Dursey and Mizen Head. But mostly because it is a charming little harbor village with a vintage hotel, shops and cozy looking B&Bs. The harbor has an intimacy that I like.

"Wish we had checked out of the hotel this morning. This would be a great place to stay tonight. It's just lovely," I say.

"This is the place that has the lighthouse lodgings. Remember they were already totally full when we tried to book. Now we see why. Too bad we never thought about the fact that there were alternative lodgings here. You are right, it is lovely. And we would not have had to back track. Oh, well, live and learn," Mark says philosophically.

"We aren't doing so badly for our first trip to Europe. A lot of people opt for one of those tour buses, like the one parked over there, instead of doing all the planning and research we did," I offer in our own defense.

"Yep. And I love how it all is unfolding. You?" he asks.

"Absolutely. I love it all. And look, another sign: I am getting a kick out of how many places we have seen the claim that a place is the last place before the Atlantic and America," I add.

"That is amusing, isn't it? It gets me every time. Looking out to sea I start thinking about the courageous folks who emigrated over the years. Oh wow, look carefully. Now that we are on the south side of the peninsula we can get a glimpse of the world famous Fastnet Lighthouse. Did I mention before that Fastnet is Ireland's tallest? It's the center of the great international sailing race that carries its name. And it claims to be the major lighthouse on the Atlantic-America route. She is a beauty from all the pictures, although you can't tell much from here."

He continues with enthusiasm, "I would so like to get out there. Sail around Fastnet, then see the others—Cape Clear, Long Island Point, Sherkin Island from the water. I know I can't get to Fastnet, but there are ferries from Baltimore harbor to Cape Clear and Sherkin. What would you think of staying in Baltimore for a couple of nights and taking the ferry out with me one of these days?"

"If it's not too rough. I would go on a ferry like the one to Bere Island, sure. And Baltimore is the town with the famous beacon, right?"

I have to think fast to figure out how to keep him from making a plan that will mess up the surprise reservation I have made for us at Galley Head. Mark doesn't know that I was able to get us a booking in one of the lighthouse keeper units there. It has two bedrooms, so, when Mark talked about how much he enjoyed Jack's company, I called and asked them to join us. The tricky part now is how to convince him to stay only one night in Baltimore without having to give away the secret.

"Or we could take the ferry from Shull tomorrow morning and then drive to Baltimore late in the day. That way we can easily keep our reservations at the Celtic Ross Hotel the night after. I think I got it on a non-refundable coupon deal." I hope he agrees.

"Sure, that works for me."

"Great. It's a plan then," I say, thinking how much I hated lying to him, even a little white lie to keep the surprise a surprise.

After we have enjoyed the harbor and taken a bunch of great pictures, we drive through Goleen and Durrus back to Bantry for a last night in town. I ask a question that I have been meaning to ask all through the trip. "You know, you have never really talked about where your interest in lighthouses comes from. All the sites are clearly beautiful, but what else draws you to them?"

"Never directly thought about it, Abs. But when I was a kid we visited Maine and I saw my first lighthouse. It stood so proud and stalwart and yet serene while the waves just pounded against its base. I loved the idea that it was a protector. I was never really into guns and lasers and such. Here was a non-violent protector, strength without violence, just steady and solid. I couldn't have articulated a reason at the time, but I think that was it. I had this romantic idea that being a lighthouse keeper would be the greatest job."

"I get what you said about the value of the lighthouses and what they symbolized, but didn't you think the lighthouse keeper had the loneliest job in the world?" I ask.

"I never thought about that part. Anyway, on that same trip, we went to Boston, to Beacon Hill and to King's Chapel. I loved reading about Winthrop founding Boston as 'the City on the Hill', 'the beacon to the world'. You know, words from the Sermon on the Mount. That notion of being a light reaching out was part of what drew me to ministry. Then as a Navy chaplain, when I actually was at sea, I literally experienced that feeling of coming home or coming to safety when we would come into harbor. In fact, I often use the symbol and imagery of a lighthouse in worship. You know, finding grounding in a sea change. It's classic archetypal stuff, but I never tire of it."

"Do you ever think you had a past life as a lighthouse keeper?"

"Interesting question, one that I never even considered. I still am not sure I buy into the concept of past lives, but thanks to your adventures with the stones… maybe. I know I like the idea as metaphor. And, in that spirit, yep, maybe I was a lighthouse keeper. It's kind of like you being a shepherdess, isn't it? Maybe I watched over those at sea, lighting fires on one of those old signal mounds while you watched over the sheep. I know I was captivated by the stories Sean told during our sailing adventure back in Berehaven. But past lives, really? I'm still a skeptic."

On the map, it looks like a long way back to Bantry, but it isn't bad. I just so love driving along coastal roads that this inland national road is boring. We opt for Chinese food as a break from pub food and fish dinners on our last night in Bantry. The quiet one-on-one feels great and I am relieved to find that even after days on the road, I never tire of talking with this man. The door to the hotel bar next to us is open and the sounds of *trad* music pull us in for a session and a nightcap of Irish Coffee.

. . .

Morning comes with a threat of rain, but there is no wind. The ferry ride is smooth and offers a great opportunity to see the islands in the bay and Cape Clear Lighthouse up close. It is really delightful to get a full view from the water. It reminds me of taking the Staten Island Ferry past the Statue of Liberty.

The Baltimore Beacon is next on our list. This big, white missile-shaped structure sits high on a hill overlooking Baltimore Harbour. Quite different from anything else we have seen. The harbor is lively and we are pleasantly surprised to find lodging and a great restaurant along the waterside. The village is delightful and another day flies by.

The next morning I am worried Mark will want to stay on to take a boat ride, but the rain helps keep me to my schedule. In fact, it is pouring by the time we get into Skibbereen. Our first stop is the Famine Museum. The unimaginable is memorialized here. It is sobering and unnerving. I knew the basic story, but seeing all the images is really upsetting. Mark spends some time looking for more information on souperism while I look though the archaeology books. After some quiet time in prayer, we take our leave.

Someone on the ferry recommended Field's, right in the center of town, as the place to go for lunch. It claims to be the oldest bakery in Ireland. It is also a grocery store with a busy, local cafeteria style café that helps us forget we are tourists. And the food is delicious. Then, in an effort to keep on schedule for our rendezvous time with the Sullivans without Mark catching on, I convince him to look for a bookstore. Not a hard sell since he loves them as much as I do. Even though this is a market town, we discover three great bookstores—ideal on a rainy day.

Mark thinks we are headed for the Celtic Ross Hotel along the highway. Thanks to our bookstore stops we are in perfect time for our arrival at Galley

Head. The next challenge is to keep him from wanting to go directly to the hotel. I am working that one out in my mind as we drive through intermittent showers all along N 71. Before long, the sign to Drombeg Stone Circle pops up. I get a chill.

Mark asks, "Do you want to stop?"

I shake my head. "Thanks, but I feel like I need a full day there, not just a quick peak. When the weather breaks and you come back to Baltimore, maybe I will have you drop me off here for the day."

"The whole day?" he asks.

"Yes, I feel like I want to go deeper into this thing about listening to the stones and to try to figure out what stories I am to tell. I get pieces of information in my dreams, but nothing really registers. I think a day there would help. And my intuition says this particular circle will be especially meaningful to me."

I get caught up in thoughts of the stone circle and what it might mean to me. Before I realize it, we are at the Celtic Ross Hotel and Mark is pulling in. He, of course, thinks we have a reservation. I come back to reality just in time to say "Let's go on to see Galley Head in case the heavy rains come back. It isn't far and we can get back here before dark."

"You don't want to check in first?"

"No, let's not bother," I say as nonchalantly as I can.

"OK, you know I never tire of seeing another lighthouse and actually they are fun to see in a storm. After all, that's their reason for being, but I don't want to be on these twisty, narrow lands off the national road here in a storm after dark. Going now is a good idea. Remind me not to stay too late."

That's a relief. To Mark, I say, "These views along the water are wonderful; watching the sea rage from land suits me fine."

We take lanes that follow the shoreline as best we are able. The strip of beach ahead is a blue flag beach, meaning best of best. According to the map, there is one on the other side of the lighthouse too. "We are going to the southern end of the headland known as Dundeady Island, again a fairly high rocky point, over-looking St. George's Channel. I also made a note that we are to look for ruins and an ancient wall."

"Leave it to you to find a stone circle everywhere you go," Mark teases.

"No, actually this is an old Norman fortress, not even close to what attracts me," I laugh.

"And here we are. Wow, the wind is strong. Watch the door as you get out. You are getting out, aren't you?"

"Oh, yes, this promontory is too beautiful to miss. It's just when I am on or over the water that I am squeamish." After a few minutes, I interrupt our silence, "I am cold and damp though, let's head up to the lighthouse station now."

"Let me turn the car heater on. That will help...hey, I don't believe it. That looks like Jack!"

"Surprise! We are staying here for two nights and Jack and CynDee are joining us."

"Get out. You have to be kidding me. When? How?" He is dumbfounded.

Jack and CynDee are just unloading the groceries as we pull up. I almost cry at Mark's excitement as we settle in. I have never pulled off such a surprise before. From his reaction, I would guess he has never been surprised like this before either. I am so pleased with myself and so excited that we have two uncomplicated days ahead to play with our new friends.

"What a treat, to be right on grounds, to live as the lighthouse keepers lived. And in stormy weather. No hotel reservations, I gather?" Mark exclaims.

"Nope. As I said, we have this place for the next two nights. And you stay on grounds 24/7 if you want," I add.

"And we will get to see the lighthouse in action. Do you realize, we have not really seen any in the dark of night, night coming so late at this latitude? Now we can see it all. WOW. Thanks for doing this, Abs. You are amazing" he says giving me a big hug and kiss.

"And thanks for including us. It sure is a treat. Until we actually got over to Castletownbere, I hadn't realized how into the lighthouse thing I would get. And there is no way we could have gotten a reservation here last minute. By the way, we brought all the groceries we should need, including Jameson's and Powers so we can compare whiskeys; and CynDee has offered to cook as a thank you for you hospitality," Jack beams.

"Honey, if truth be told, I am dying to get into a kitchen. None of the relatives would let me do anything. I'm not used to being catered to. Need to roll up my sleeves. That is unless you are feeling that you want to cook," CynDee directs the last part to me.

"No competition from me. I am delighted," I respond, beaming as well.

Mark leads us on a quick exploration. "Until Fastnet was built, this was the tallest and most important lighthouse in Ireland. In fact when it was first built, it was the most powerful in the world. It really is a beauty. I can't wait for us to get the full tour tomorrow, but just walking around now is amazing."

He keeps going "I read that even the original light could be seen for a distance of 30km, of course that was in clear weather. Can't imagine how close a sailor could come to this rocky shoreline in heavy fog."

"The Lusitania went down right near here, didn't it?" I ask.

"Yes ma'am, and many, many war vessels in both World War I and II," Jack adds.

"Isn't there something about the Titanic and Cork, also?" asks CynDee.

"Yep, but, of course, it wasn't where it went down. Cobh was its last port before leaving for America," Mark offers.

"CynDee has me going to Cork City next as her reward for the amount of time we spent in Sullivan country with all my family. So I was thinking we would go down to Cobh. That harbor is supposed to be something else."

"Jack Sullivan, you make me sound like a shrew," CynDee laughs. "Yes, I may drag you to some shops, but mainly we are going clubbing and you know you love it as much as I do."

"Just checking that you were paying attention," Jack laughs. Then turning to me, he asks, "You guys want to join us?"

"I'm not much for clubs, are you, Mark?"

"Not at all, but thanks for the offer. But I would like to see Cobh and, Abs, I think you would, too, right?"

"Yeah, we could meet up for lunch maybe."

"It seems like all we do is plan one thing after another. I'm just saying. There just is so much. And I don't want us to miss a thing," CynDee pipes in.

"You are so right, and I feel really caught up by it," I agree.

"I was going to suggest that we go over to the Lusitania Memorial and Old Head, the other major lighthouse near Kinsale tomorrow. We are so close and we could stop along the strand for a picnic if the weather improves. The folks in the other lighthouse keeper unit said they did that yesterday and it was fantastic," Jack offers.

"That really is appealing, Jack. It gives us time to relax in the morning, get the full lighthouse tour with the guide and then have a leisurely afternoon. I am in. What about the rest of you?" asks Mark.

Nods all around.

We enjoy a cozy evening of great food followed by great conversation over a crackling fire and a few games of Gin. They also chose some great wines which they insist we sample. As the wind picks up even more and starts howling, we can almost feel ourselves watching over the light, like we are back in the day when humans were responsible for keeping the light burning. Yet, we have the luxury of going off to bed with no duties. Mark and I sleep in the warmth and comfort of each other's arms as the wind howls and the waves crash to shore.

• • •

Morning comes, and the storm continues. Rain and high winds conspire to keep us relaxing inside our little haven of safety. I certainly am glad that we are not out at sea. But it is rather exciting from our cozy little inside niche.

By late afternoon, the rain disappears and we do take a drive to Old Head, refreshed and ready for adventure again. Not a day for the beach but still a nice coastal drive. I like Old Head a lot. It is much like Galley Head in size, shape and setting.

"Dare I ask what the plan is for tomorrow?" Mark asks. "Abs and I have been talking about using the Celtic Ross Hotel in Rosscarbery as our base for her stone circles and a return to Baltimore, to get back out to see the islands and lighthouses again. Would you guys like to hang out with us one more day?"

"We were planning to head into Cork City..." Jack's cell phone rings mid-sentence. "Excuse me, it's Sean," he says as he walks away from the table. We hear bits and pieces with tones of excitement and questioning and are dying to know what's going on. He returns to update us: "Sean's American colleague is chartering a 40-footer to sail around Cork and has asked Sean to crew for him. They want to know if we want to come with them. I said I would call him back in ten."

CynDee is the first to respond, "I assume the 'we' is you and Mark, right baby? A guys' thing and that is fine with me. Except when? And for how long? Remember, you promised me Cork City."

"Mark?"

"Appealing for sure, but Abs and I will want to talk about it. Like CynDee, I would want to know when and how long."

"He is getting the boat for five days, could leave us off at a marina along the coast if we want to only be out at sea three or four days. We would meet him first thing the day after tomorrow."

"It's fine with me. Mark, it sounds like a once in a lifetime opportunity. I can explore on my own while you are gone. Better yet, CynDee, I would love to pal around with you, if you want and if one of the places we go is Drombeg."

"Abs, are you sure?" Mark questions me.

"Of course," I answer.

"Well, Jack, so that leaves me to chime in next. If you go, that would leave us about five days together before we go home. You would become my slave for those five days and most would be spent in Cork City or up in Dublin," CynDee says in a tone that somehow combines threat and humor.

"I could manage to deal with that. So, everybody is OK with it then?" asks Jack after giving a nod and a smile to his wife. "I will call Sean back to say yes."

"We might as well backtrack to Baltimore for the ferry ride and stay over at the Celtic Ross with you tomorrow night," CynDee states.

"You know, I would love a day on my own at Drombeg. How would you all feel about dropping me off there on your way to Baltimore? You can pick me up at the stone circle or at Glandore, a sweet little town overlooking the bay that is just a couple of miles from the circle and near the hotel."

"Sounds like a plan."

CHAPTER NINE

"Here you are, Abs. Drombeg Stone Circle. On your own for the whole day. Remember now, experience it in ease and joy," Mark says as he goes to the trunk with me to get my backpack. He gives me a hug and a kiss.

"You're going to have a fantastic day, Honey. Just stay easy. Put yourself out there and let the messages come," CynDee offers out the back-seat window.

I wave goodbye and start up the short trail from the parking area to the circle.

My knees buckle at the first sight of the stones. I have been impressed and impacted by the others, but this one is really outstanding. Magnificent in its simplicity, the circle lays in a flat meadow, nestled between rolling hills of green pastures. I can see all the way to where the sea meets the horizon, with the spectacular green to blue on blue that is quintessentially Ireland. The setting surpasses even my ideal of a perfect site, and the circle itself is even more appealing than the circle in my watercolor. I find it unbelievably beautiful and just stunning.

There are seventeen pillar stones of various heights. The recumbent stone across from the entrance is said to be aligned for winter solstice, a fact I cannot experience this sunny May day. How cool it would be to see these places on the actual day of their alignment. Yet, so few people who live here in Ireland even bother. I guess it's like people who live on the west coast of Florida not bothering to see the sun drop into the ocean at sunset. We have become so disconnected from the natural cycles of sun and moon and sky.

I try to imagine the solstice celebrations that took place to welcome the return of the sun. To the Ancient Ones, who lived in the open and whose lives depended on the bounty of the earth, it must have been a joyful day. "Here Comes the Sun"

I sing. I feel like a diva of song, despite barely being able to carry a tune. My heart is light and I feel pure joy.

I am freer here than at the other stone circles. Is it the energy of the stones or the work that I have been doing to remove my blocks and resistance? I can feel that I am going deeper each time I enter a new stone circle. It gives me the chills. To reinforce this openness, I speak out loud, with the stones as my witness:

> *I consciously release myself from any lingering thoughts of acting foolish or silly and from the negative experience of my grandmother' stern face and scolding voice.*
>
> *I ask that I be able to hear my mom's voice again, perhaps even see her as I did as a little girl.*
>
> *I ask to be able to hear, or experience, or see the guides that have been trying to reach me as I visit the stones.*
>
> *I ask that in doing so I find any aspects of myself that have been obscured from my awareness.*

I then enter the circle prayerfully and stand in the center, just soaking in the energy. I lose any sense of time as I move around the circle stopping to touch, really to caress each stone; then a second time to build momentum, and a third time with intention. Next, I go to the center space and twirl myself three times: clockwise again like a dervish. Whew.

Light-headed, I go over to the flattest stone, the one across from the circle entrance and sit. I rest for a moment and just soak in the vibrational energy around me. I feel fully free and fully present. I am hopeful that I now will be able to connect to those who have been trying to reach me. The Hag? My mother? The shepherdess?

Breathe in love, breathe out peace, as the chant goes. Then, I begin singing "You Lift Me Up" or as much of it as I can remember. I get the feeling that the stones hold more mystery and power and had an even greater purpose than I comprehend. I am feeling hopeful that I am beginning to connect to their energy in a meaningful way.

I offer up this simple prayer:

> *May I be of open-heart;*
>
> *May I know I am One with the Universe.*

A lamb comes galloping over as if being chased by a bee and I laugh. Lightness of heart is such an important thing for me to learn. Very Zen, these stone circles, very Zen.

Another song enters my consciousness: "Lady of the Season's Laughter", a favorite of mine. I always associate it with my mother. Did she sing it to me as a lullaby when I was a baby? Did I just imagine her singing it to sooth me as a child? Why did I let it fade from memory until now? I sing what I remember of it, humming the parts where the words are long forgotten.

After a good length of time sitting silently with the stones, I decide to try to capture the beauty around me on my phone. I take a picture from each direction, looking inward and then outward. I also try to get a picture of all 17 stones. However, like the stones in a Zen garden, I cannot see or capture the image of all at one time. Intentional on the part of my Neolithic Ancestors? Or accidental? Another part of the mystery.

My attention is drawn to the stream, a spring-fed pool of water and the fire pit. A sign explains that this was a *fulacht fiadh*, a specific kind of cooking pit. Stones were heated and then placed in the water and then the food could be heated. Mark and I saw one at Bonane, but this one has a stronger pull. I have cooked here, lived in the nearby huts and worshipped at the circle. What is that expression of CynDee's: *holy moly!*

I wish she were here to call in the shepherdess. I want to know more.

I hear someone coming. At first, I wonder if I am getting my wish. However, it is a group of four women tourists much like myself. Fortunately, they are quiet and respectful as they experience the circle. When they reach the pool where I sit, one asks if they are disturbing me. That opens a discussion. I learn they are Canadians, from Ottawa, actually not that far from my birth home in Watertown, New York. They share an openness to learning about the metaphysical and spiritual meanings of stone circles. What a gift to meet up with seemingly like-minded people.

Soon, an Irish tour guide with a group of Americans in tow enters the site and moves everyone to the inside of the circle. He talks academically about the archaeology of the site and we all eavesdrop.

We move closer and hear him say, "The builders were hunter-gatherers. This was a simplistic calendar monument, nothing more. Neopagans try to make more of it, but in reality it was simply a giant sundial. Well, I stand corrected: in some cases the alignment was to the moon not the sun, but you get the idea. Call it a moon dial. Ha-ha." Many of his group politely laugh at his lame joke and begin asking questions based on his version of history.

I look to the other women to see if they are feeling the same rage I feel.

"What arrogance!" one of them says.

"I don't know what it was all about, where they came from, and how they did it but these ancient monuments were celestial instruments not mere sundials! We just came from Newgrange and that whole Boyne Valley complex. What power and energy even now," exclaims the redhead.

"Somehow they worked with energy, didn't they? Crystals, vibration. I have read that both were used," says the third.

"The Bible says 'with eyes to see and ears to hear'. This gentleman just does not get it," offers the woman who called him arrogant.

"The English always underestimated the Irish and so never looked deeper into places like Newgrange," says the fourth.

"Right, but even in England, the rulers disrespected the ancient stones, dismantling some entirely, messing with some like at Avebury, or building churches over the sacred sites to claim the power for the Church," says the redhead.

"I am beginning to understand now why I am getting messages to tell the story, the stories of the stones." I surprise myself that I actually say this aloud.

"Do tell us more," one of the women pleads.

So I tell an abbreviated story of what I have been experiencing. This is the first I have talked to strangers about any of it. In fact, I haven't even written anyone at home. Their interest and acceptance of the possibility of it all being true is more than affirming. It empowers me. So I tell them even more.

"We must dash off, but will you keep in touch? And when your book comes out, we want to buy it," says the informal group leader.

"Oh, I am not sure there will be a book, but I would love to stay in touch. Let's exchange contact info," I reply.

"There will be a book, dear. There will be a book," she smiles and nods emphatically as she says it.

• • •

After they leave, I suddenly realize that I am already beginning to tell the story. As I tell the story of my trip to the stones and my opening to their messages, I am starting to fulfill the charge. What a joyful feeling. I enjoy the picnic lunch CynDee prepared for me from last night's left overs. This is the first time all day I have thought about Mark or wondered how they are doing. I would have enjoyed the boat ride on a calm day like today and would have had fun. But there was no other way to get here alone and I wanted to do this more. I am so glad I did; and on this day, when these women came also. There are no accidents.

The sun makes me drowsy and I find a way of laying my backpack against the bank of the knoll so I can lie back onto it. Watching the shapes and movement of the white puffy clouds, whose scientific name I once knew, relaxes me even more. There is a gentle voice whispering to me. Is it the shepherdess I wonder? Then I realize it is my mom. Her voice is soothing just as I remember hearing it as a kid:

Listen, my lamb, my dear sweet daughter who has grown into a lovely woman. There is no harm in listening. It is safe for you to connect with me, to connect with our ancestors, and to connect with the shepherdess. Her name is Jane. You can trust her. She loved you as she would have loved a daughter of her own. No harm will come to you by listening to the story of your past life and all the other stories of the Mother. I love you, she loves you, love is all around you.

I am jolted back to reality by an invasion of tourists, loud and boisterous and irreverent. Five young Scandinavians jumping on the altar stone, taking stupid pictures of one another. Really, can they be any ruder? Really? At least they aren't American. We have a enough bad reputation as boisterous travelers. I fiddle with my phone, checking out the pictures in my gallery just to avoid interacting with them, which is unnecessary given how self-absorbed they are. Thankfully, they are quickly bored and tromp off.

All that disruption aside, I wonder if I really did connect with the spirit of my mother? "Mom, did you have more to say?" I ask plaintively. But the connection is gone.

I think about walking over to Glandore. Mark said that if I wasn't here, they would meet me at the inn there. I am restless and can't imagine anything more will come to me here. Yet, I don't want to leave. I still have not connected with the shepherdess, the key to what I sense is an important story for me to hear.

I walk to the adjacent pasture and mindlessly watch the lambs frolicking in the far field. I pick buttercups and do my ritual. Then, I return to my backpack to get my journal out in hopes of capturing some of this amazing day. But I keep nodding off until I give up writing and put my head on the backpack for another little nap.

My dear daughter, you are being called to an earlier time and place. You are safe, you can move back and forth between these places and times through the power of the stones. Not physically as your man fears, but through voice and thought and heart-centered feeling. For now, just let yourself listen, to me, to Jane, to the Hag and to all who bring you messages that can help you find yourself and tell the stories. Simply ask if they are here for your Higher Good. If they say yes, you can trust them. All others, those not of the Light, will be rejected by your Higher Self.

Call it memory, call it time travel if you like, but come with me to the time and place where you will know yourself in differing ways, know yourself to be a healer, a protector of women and of the Mother. You were a priestess, too, a keeper of the Temple Fires. Come learn your own Power and help the world remember the Divine Feminine, help the world find Balance, help it heal.

It is no surprise you are drawn to your man here who also was a priest and a Druid. He was both healer and councilor. He just does not yet remember.

His steady manner in this lifetime will give you the support you did not have with your grandmother. But let us also acknowledge that my passing and your grandmother's stern ways taught you strength. You will not fall; you will not fail. Be comforted by my words of reassurance. Let them allow you to remember more and more and to bring forth more of your gifts.

Your man is not yet ready to hear and see for himself. But tell the stories to him, answer his questions and that will help you find your voice as it opens him to further exploration.

It is time, my dear girl. Open. Open to your wisdom. You are more powerful than you know. You have many gifts, among them is the gift of storytelling.

Open your heart. Open to all you have been and all you can be.

"Abs, wake up. Are you, OK?" It's Mark and he sounds alarmed.

"Wow, I was in a very deep sleep, almost like I had to come back into my body to answer you. But yes, I am OK. It must be later than I realized."

"You know this stuff is so out of my comfort zone. I saw you lying there and panicked. I mean, do you think it safe to let yourself be so vulnerable?"

"You mean to tourists or to spirits?" I say lightly, teasing a bit but also warmed by his concern.

"It does sound a little foolish, I admit. Just so glad you are OK. And did you have a good day?" he asks.

"It was amazing and I will tell you all about it tonight. But right now I need a few minutes to get my bearings," I say as I give him a deep kiss, which promises more, and I whisper, "And thank you for caring." Of course, as soon as I do that, I lose some of the dream. I come around quickly and signal I am ready to talk, asking, "And what about you? And where are CynDee and Jack?"

"The harbor ride was great and the weather perfect. I just dropped CynDee and Jack off at the Glandore Inn. I think they wanted to have a heated discussion and I was a third wheel. Besides, I wanted to see this place and also wanted some time to talk to you on our own."

"That all sounds curious. Anything wrong?" I ask with concern.

"Not wrong, it is just that Sean called to say his friend Doug can't charter the boat tomorrow, rather it will be postponed two days. CynDee is upset that it is interfering with their time in Cork City. Well, and I wanted to check in with where you were on the whole thing. Tell me honestly what your reaction is to the idea of my going, especially now that there is a delay."

"Wow, that's a lot to take in, from the dreamland to trip planning and logistics. Hmm. Let me take a breath to switch gears. First, as for your yachting adventure, I say go for it. We still will get some quality alone time, right? I mean I have loved hanging out with the two of them, but I want some time just with you," I respond.

"Glad to hear that. It is exactly what I have been thinking. It has been great to share things with these guys and I can't wait to sail, but I want us to have some time like those first few days, just us. In fact, I was thinking that tomorrow we could go to Kinsale. It's supposed to be upscale but with historic forts, a castle with wine tasting, a great marina and top notch restaurants. We can get a sweet little B&B overlooking the bay, where we can walk to stores and pubs."

"Sounds like you have it figured out and the plan sounds wonderful. All that is left is for me to check to see if CynDee still wants to hang out with me at least part of the time you guys are gone. We could even leave one of the cars right at the hotel or in Kinsale. I can't imagine she is going to veto the trip for Jack, is she?"

"I don't think so. Fingers crossed. Let's go see."

As we prepare to leave, I ask Mark to take a moment to stand at the altar stone with me. We hold hands and pray silently together. He is here with me now and I also feel our connection over lifetimes, even if he doesn't.

"Wow, Abs, now that I take time to really look around and soak in this place, I see you have found your watercolor essence, haven't you? Not a stone-by-stone depiction of the circle, but certainly the spirit of this place is in your nursery room picture. God works in mysterious ways…"

"It really is very like my watercolor, isn't it? Wow!"

We leave for Glandore filled with spirit and love. I can barely make out the village in the distance as we drive away from my precious Drombeg. As we near and I see the harbor, I have a powerful sense of having walked this route before. I am not even surprised by the feeling.

The meal, the conversation, the rest of the evening are kind of a blur. I know I half-heartedly participated, I also know I am still caught up in my day at Drombeg. I don't even remember getting into bed.

I wake with a start and this feeling of having been in an elevator that suddenly dropped ten floors.

"Sorry, Abs. Didn't mean to wake you. Thought I would go for a run. Why don't you just take your time? We said goodbye to the Sullivans last night so there is no rush. The shower is nice and big, perhaps we can share it when I get back," Mark whispers as he kisses me on the forehead.

"Ah hah, sure," I murmur and turn over, returning to sleep or to some semblance of sleep. I feel I was visiting my mom and feeling a deeper bond with her than I have ever felt before. It feels so good. I thought I had outgrown my need for her love and support. Now, I realize I may have ignored it, but I did not outgrow it.

"Ew, Mark, you are wet and cold," I exclaim, awaking abruptly after what seems like only minutes later.

"Back from my run. The mist is so thick I am soaked. I'm going to hop in the shower. Join me. It will wake you up."

"I bet it will," I retort as I sit up and look out at the soupy day.

We gather the laundry as we dress, planning to put it in the machines while we are at breakfast. And a wonderful breakfast it is. All the full Irish plus an amazing breakfast buffet.

"I can see why this place is so popular with the business trade," he says with exuberance. "Are you OK?" he adds.

"Yeah, but I had a powerful dream, and I still haven't processed all of the experiences of Drombeg from yesterday. I feel as foggy inside as the view we have of this inlet. Hope they both lift soon. Once we are on the road, I will tell you all about it. You are such a good listener and I know you will help me sort it all out. But here are our eggs; let's leave it till later."

"Sounds like a plan. I heard the waitress tell that couple over there that this area of Rosscarbery is known for its black pudding, so I got one sausage link from the buffet. Want to try?"

"No way, even if Rosscarbery makes the best, it still is made with blood. The idea of something made with blood disgusts me. I don't even like liver." My face reinforces that distaste.

He just laughs and moves on. "You know, I think that couple over there seem to be the only Americans in the place. I love that we don't keep running into folks from the States."

"Actually, except for Jack and CynDee, we really haven't run into any Americans. I stand corrected, one guy that first night in Kenmare. Do you think Jack and CynDee are OK? They really were snapping at each other last night."

"I think that's just their way of rebalancing things when one or the other is feeling put upon. After 25 years of marriage I would guess it's how they give each other space but also not end up feeling taken for granted," he says nonchalantly. "Done? How about we move the laundry to the dryer and take our coffee to the lounge where we can look into the harbor mist while the laundry dries. We also can figure out where we want to go these next couple of days. I picked up a couple of brochures in the lobby that look intriguing and we have wi-fi here."

Sitting by the window he continues, "Listen to this place. It hits all the notes: standing stones, a sacred well, a 6th century monastic settlement begun by the Celtic St. Mologna, known for beekeeping, then a 13th century abbey with a 15th century tower. In the churches of today, we can also see Henry Clarke stained glass windows, East Indian-inspired mosaics, a chalice and a labyrinth. In quotations 'All where the river meets the bay in the little village of Timoleague'."

"Sounds idyllic," I respond.

"Maybe you had numerous lives there too. Let's go find out," Mark teases. Then continues "It's on the way to Kinsale, the place I suggested yesterday. This brochure further describes Kinsale as a heritage town with forts, castle, marina, yacht club, upscale restaurants, cafés, traditional pubs and shops. It's also near where I need to meet the guys. How's that for a choice?"

"Perfect, but no lighthouse?" I joke.

"Oh, did I forget to mention: the Old Head Light House is actually Old Head of Kinsale Lighthouse?" he gives me an exaggerated smirk.

"Is that the one we visited from Galley Head after the rainstorm?"

"Yep. If you are game, I thought it would be nice to go on a brighter day to get better pictures."

"Sure, if the weather cooperates, I'm game. Let's reserve a B&B right in the town so we can walk, as we did back in Castletownbere. Oh, now I remember, you actually already suggested that yesterday."

I think I talked all the way from Rosscarbery to Timoleague. Mark primarily listened as I told him all about my day's experience at Drombeg.

"What a breakthrough. I remember you telling me about being able to connect with your mom's spirit as a child. I am so glad you have that back. As for Jane, the shepherdess, I guess hers is like a visit from an angel. It will come when you relax and least expect it. This is probably a silly question, but are you planning on exploring all this further with CynDee while Jack and I are at sea?"

"Yes, I definitely want to go back to Drombeg with CynDee. Last night, she agreed to come with me for a day or two and then we would head back Cobh. She is going to get permission to leave their car at the marina and I will take care of making a reservation here."

"Just be careful. I don't want to lose you to any of those past lives you keep alluding to."

"Mark Andrews, I do believe the power of the stones is reaching you."

"Saved by the bell. Here we are in Timoleague with its Christian abbey. I am on home turf here."

As we drive around this absolutely charming village looking for parking, the ruins of the 13th century abbey stand silently above the harbor along a fast flowing river that spills into the bay. The place is pure magic and the lingering mist adds to the mystical experience of walking the grounds, standing under arches and next to old Celtic crosses looking out to the water. I so love these crosses.

"This place is extraordinary. I loved Kilcatherine, but this is so much more extensive, and it holds a gentle, but powerful positive energy. Even though it was built in Norman times, it feels very Celtic," I say out loud.

"Well, it was built on holy Celtic ground and by the Franciscans so it would be gentler and more Celtic than Roman. You know your ideas must be growing on me. I can see myself having lived and worshipped here in another time. It is that powerful."

"Hmm," I respond, giving him a squeeze.

We visit the churches in the village that are stately and beautiful in keeping with this place that for so long has been deeply faith-centered. I take time to walk the modern labyrinth in front of one of the Catholic churches while Mark climbs the long set of stone steps going up to the church. It is the first labyrinth I have seen here in Ireland. I am struck by how similar the experience of walking it is to the ritual of rounding the stones. I guess both put us symbolically and experientially in touch with the circles of life, and the ebb and flow of energy at every level that make up our existence

We cap off the tour of Timoleague with a visit to the sacred well up the hill at the edge of town. What a jewel. We sit for a long while just admiring the view. A large white statue of the Virgin Mary reminds us of the statuary on Healy Pass overlooking the town and out to sea. It is the simplicity of the well that holds our attention.

"Remember the ditty we said as kids: 'water, water everywhere and not a drop to drink'?" Mark breaks the silence to ask. "It keeps running through my head. As I sit here I am thinking of the Ancients who protected and revered these natural springs and wells: pure water, water as Source, water as Life. Now the world is so polluted. I think you are on to something. We both need to tell the stories of the time when the elements were honored, and the human race did not declare dominion over Nature."

"Yeah, and, you know, I am getting more and more comfortable with whatever comes to me. I get the Hag story and how to speak about aging, sovereignty and male/female balance now. I get the story about how We Are One and that these wars of one religious faction suppressing another are wrong. Not sure how to tell them yet, but I trust that the way will be revealed. Now, it is only this story of Jane and my past lives that confuses me. I don't get what I am supposed to learn, what I am supposed to do with what I learn, or how to go about it."

"I think it is always easier to tell other people's story or the big cultural stories. But the stories we have lived and their meaning, that can allude us. But we learn from telling our stories, and it sounds like you are meant to reach deep and find the blocks that keep you from telling yours. Perhaps, both today and in past lives."

"I think you are right. Walking the labyrinth, I felt an awareness of the archetypal pattern, of going round and round until I reach center and of opening to a new insight; then being released from the pattern and walking out from the center, lighter and wiser. I do hope that's what will come from all this," I share.

"It is interesting that you started this trip feeling so free and open. In different ways I came needing to relax and find renewal. Now, we're both finding ourselves between stories. Ireland is helping us both sort things out and be refreshed, like the holy well here is continually refreshed."

"Hmm. You are right. Outwardly, it appears you have more change occurring, but I certainly am being guided to make changes too."

The drive around the bay tops off the experience of Timoleague beautifully. The mist lifts and the sea opens to us as we head east to Kinsale.

Kinsale proves to be the perfect place for us. Our B&B is right in the town so we can walk everywhere. And do we walk; up the steep hill and around to Charles Fort high about the cove. We are rewarded by great views of rusty-orange sails slicing through the wind with the quays and historic village in the background. We sit, talk, and, later, sit quietly again just enjoying the sun, the wind and the colorful vistas. We pass two great pubs on the hillside coming down but neither is open for lunch. On impulse we go for Chinese, our second time here in Ireland, and then explore the town.

This is a town that caters to tourists more than any we have visited so far. So we get *trad* music starting early and going late. Good thing we are in town, I think, as we do a pub crawl through the streets. Neither of us drinks that much and, in fact, we switch to soft drinks before the night is over. Nonetheless, it is nice not to need the car. *Ól, Ceol agus Craic*, (drink, music and fun) has become our new favorite Irish expression.

• • •

The next day, a long walk to James Fort, in the direction of the sea, takes us past a pristine scene of yachts to a bustling shipyard and beyond. After Charles Fort, the remains of this fort are disappointing, but the walk is exhilarating. We quicken our pace as we see the rain coming off the sea but get caught along a stretch where there are no shops. Then we come to a wonderful little bakery with a counter overlooking the harbor and the best, biggest and yummiest meringues ever made. We talk with the college student serving us who supplies coffee generously as we dry out and watch the pouring rain outside the window. Politics, culture, generational hopes, and personal aspirations…all delightful.

Finally, the rain let's up and becomes just a drizzle. We walk back to explore bookstores and galleries. Mark checks out the navigation section in the first bookstore we come to while I ask about local authors who write about the area. The delightful woman at the counter suggests Alice Taylor, from the neighboring town, who writes about rural Ireland in the fifties. She has written a zillion books it seems. I choose *The Parish*, thinking Mark might enjoy it. I also ask if she has anything like *McCarthy's Bar* to recommend. She has never heard of the book, even though it was on the top of the Irish bestseller list a few years ago. We agree she should order it for tourists like us. Then I find Virginia Woolf's *To a Lighthouse*.

"Hey, Mark, did you ever read *To a Lighthouse*?"

"Kind of outdated, don't you think? Lizzie was reading it for her women's book club a long time ago. She wanted me to read it too. But I kept falling asleep trying to slog through it, waiting for them to get to the darn lighthouse—very wordy. As I remember, it was hailed for depicting the constraints of patriarchy—for women, but also men—in the early 20th century."

"The part about what the lighthouse represented to each of them might be kind of fun to revisit now that we have been visiting different ones and also because we have been talking about sovereignty. I might see if it's on Kindle."

"That's an idea; and I have another idea: lunch. Pub or café?"

We choose a lovely café down the street where for a couple of hours just talking and people watching. A thirty-something couple's argument prompts me to bring up an issue that sometimes worries me. "What about us, Mark? Do you think it is odd that we haven't had one spat, one conflict?"

"Well, nothing has come up that has bothered me. What about you?"

"No, I feel good about everything. You pay attention to things important to me but give me space. I like joining you in your passions but not feeling pressured to be at your elbow every minute. That is super important to me. I love that we talk and learn from each other and I am having more fun than I have had in a very long time," I allow.

"Good. I like to think we can trust each other to bring things up and confront them before they become problems. I've done enough premarital and marriage counseling over the years to know how critical communication is in any relationship and as you know I am a no-drama person," Mark states.

"True enough, but sometimes I wonder," I admit.

"Wonder what? Do you want drama? Like the young couple over there? Or like fighting and making up Who's-Afraid-of-Virginia-Woolf-style? Or just more tension? Are you worried that there isn't enough spark between us? Maybe, you find the absence of these things boring?" he asks with a tone which borders on defensiveness.

"No, not at all. There is spark. In fact, I have no complaints with anything," I say blushing a little. "I guess it's just I have never been with a guy like you. Sometimes it doesn't feel real. I guess that's what makes me uneasy, concerned we won't last. I kind of equate intensity with investment and you are just so easy going," I scramble to explain.

"Well, I have never been seen as lacking in intensity, even though I am laid back. I guess I see where you make the connection to investment. But I think of investment as a word that implies ownership or rights to something. It is not the same as love. Remember, men are evolving, too, you know. Not every guy wants to play King of the Castle. I certainly don't. In fact, I was never a fiery guy nor a demanding guy. I have mellowed even more as a minister. I long ago learned to cultivate a non-anxious presence, nip conflict in the bud and all that. And, of course, Lizzie and our daughter taught me a lot about women."

"I see the wisdom in all that, and I think you're right. I guess I just need to learn to trust that easy is OK. Ease and joy are new to me. While I am at it, one more question that I have been mulling over." I take a deep breath before I ask, "Do you think we will do as well when we get home?"

"I can't promise I won't get testy if you interrupt me six times while I am writing a guest sermon, or that the congregational ladies with casseroles won't infringe on our privacy or that my daughter will include you in family get-togethers without a fuss. But I would like to think that if you can handle it, so can I."

He continues, "You know, I was very happy for thirty years of marriage to Lizzie. We married young, took on traditional roles, never thinking much about it. Wouldn't change a moment of it. But, as I was saying yesterday at the well, that is the old story. As I let go of Lizzie and the grief of her loss, I also am realizing that the story of my life is changing too. The old story of who I am doesn't serve my future. The new story is barely unfolding. I am still in the process of letting go. So being in the moment is all I want right now. All I can offer."

He takes a breath, then adds, "I like where we are. I like you in my life, but I am just taking one day at a time, trying to live in the present. Not ready to speculate or worry about the future. Is that something that feels right to you too?"

"Actually, it is," I add quietly, my wheels and heart turning.

"Good, because I like us together. You challenge me and I like that. Let's go explore the town some more," he says in a way that indicates he wants to be done talking about it.

We walk silently, drawn down to the quay and to the boats.

I break the silence with a question, "Did you want to drive out to Old Head? If so, we should go before dinner while it's light out."

We drive out and find this approach as beautiful as the approach from the west. It is fun to be revisiting this classic lighthouse with so much history. In fact, all these lighthouses are growing on me. I am beginning to see the similarities and differences. I am beginning to imagine who lived there and operated them and what they witnessed. We stay quite a while just listening to the waves hammering the shore as the tide comes in.

"Let's stop at the Lusitania Monument on the way back. You know the Lusitania was lost right out there," Mark says pointing out to sea.

"I'm not sure I want to think about that or the fierceness of storms coming up on these waters. You are going to be out there."

"And we will stay safe. We'll come back in one piece. I promise."

CHAPTER TEN

S o, they are off, sailing away on their little adventure at sea. Shall we head on to Drombeg to meet your Jane?" CynDee asks crisply.

"Are you upset with them for going?" I ask.

"Yeah, but I do get it. It is pretty much a once-in-a-lifetime opportunity. It's just that Jack and I both work a lot of hours and we had to rearrange Heaven and Earth to get this much time off; and, well, I wanted to spend more of it partying and letting off steam. We had a great time with the family, at the pubs and with you guys, but I want more times at the clubs. I really like a blast of big city life now and again. I may be a small-town girl from Tennessee but I ain't into backwoods livin'. City life keeps me loving life in a small town."

"Did you go clubbing last night and was it as much fun as you expected?" I ask.

"Yes, it was awesome. Hearing all those Irish accents took it over the top. That's also why I am kinda pissed off to see them leave. But I'll get over it. There is a different vibe here than when we visit a U.S. city. I hate missing out on it. But we will return to Cork City when they are finished playing sailor. Let's get to your stone circle."

"Are you sure? It is so totally different than what you came to Ireland for," I seek confirmation.

"Yeah. It is not what I imagined doing or being interested in doing, but it is one hell of an adventure. I do love new things. Now, fill me in on what happened the day you went to the circle on your own," CynDee says directing me to move on.

I tell her the whole story and we catch up with each other on the way, talking continually except for a pit stop. Of course, we buy chocolate too.

"So, this is the place of magic, huh?" CynDee asks as we park.

"For me and I hope for you too. Did I tell you that I almost fell to my knees as I came up the path? And did I tell you about my watercolor?"

"Honey, yes, I think you told me everything. You told me about your early morning trip back to 'our' Castletownbere circle where you felt released from your grandmother's criticism; you told me about that Bonane place where you got messages about the Holy Grail; and you told me all about your experience here. And I swear I was listenin' to it all. But to tell the truth, some of it just went over my head. But I sure can feel the energy here. It is more powerful than before. I can't imagine what we are going to hear next."

We walk to the entrance of the stone circle, standing quietly and just breathing in the energy of the circle and of the site itself. Slowly we proceed between the stones so that we are inside the ring. I begin walking the circle clockwise, pausing and touching each stone as I go. CynDee walks directly to the center and begins turning and turning, arms open to the sky, like Julie Andrews in *Sound of Music*. I expect her to start singing "The Hills Are Alive" any second. And, by gosh, she does.

When she finishes, I clap. She blushes and we both start to laugh, the joyful laugh of a fulfilling moment shared between friends. I doubt we would have gotten to know each other back home. But here, we have become sister travelers, each supporting the other on life's journey of self-discovery—different world views, experiences and interests, opening to Spirit and the Divine Feminine in our own way.

"CynDee, you know I am bursting to get your help connecting to Jane, my shepherdess, but I want you to have your own time with the stones first. Oh, did I tell you that her name is Jane? Believe it or not, I actually got that piece of information on my own."

"See, Honey, I told you to just be patient. Good for you. But no need for you to leave me here on my own."

"I insist. There may be an important message here for you and it is not fair for you to get caught up in being the conduit between Jane and me at the expense of your own experience. I am going to let you have some time alone here in the big circle, while I go back over to the well. Join me when you want."

She starts to protest, but then gives a smile and a nod and stays at the circle while I move on.

I find a place on the rock around the well where I can see my reflection and I slowly drop buttercups into the pool; one petal at a time, each in gratitude for an aspect of the life I have been given. As always, I name my friend Judy, my mom and my dad, but this time I give special thanks for the renewed connection to my mom. What a gift. Tears come to my eyes.

Then I am overcome by a flash of anger toward my grandmother whose intim-idation robbed me of the connection I might have had with my mom's spirit. How dare she have done so? Release, breathe, release, I tell myself. It begins to work. How many times did I stuff down this anger as a child just to cope? How great it is that I am finally learning the power of naming a negative thought and then trusting that I can release it. Another amazing gift and part of finding myself as in the nun's blessing. Wow.

I ask to see what lies before me; how I am to tell the stories. I specifically ask for Jane and information about what she wants me to know. I don't get Jane di-rectly, but I do get a strong sense of the past, of having sat in this very spot before, of having been cold and scared and of having been rescued and brought to this place. Brought to the fire pit I am now facing, to a place of warmth and safety and then to the healing waters of this well. Chills go up and down my spine as this knowing feeling grows stronger.

"Are you all right?" I hear CynDee say as I realize she has come up behind me.

"Yeah, I am. I'm having this overpowering sense that I was here in another lifetime and that it was a place of sanctuary. No direct message from Jane, but I think this is what she wants me to know."

"Well, Honey, if it is, you can confirm it with her right now. 'Cuz she is here now. In fact, she is cheering you on."

"Really?" I ask.

"Yes! She is pacing back and forth. Even though she is pleased, she is still very impatient."

"Doesn't she see I am trying," I say in exasperation.

"Steady now, Honey, just take deep breaths. Jane is saying you think too much. She says to get out of your head and open your heart. Feel it. Be there with her. Release your criticism of yourself. OMG. I feel like I am channeling her or some-thing...holy moly."

She wants to speak to you through me...she is starting:

Yes, my dear, my cara, you lived here. This place was your refuge. Here you became a woman and developed your gifts as a healer. You lived in many lifetimes serving the Mother and you taught the Mysteries. I will now tell you more about the lifetime that brought you here to this community.

You. You—the one who sees me. Get out your little box that captures voices, so you will not miss the words I am to tell you. For it is a strain for me to communicate in the energies that match your frequency. I will only tell you this story once. SO LISTEN. Then it will be your responsibility to tell the story to others.

We dutifully set up our phones to record her words, in CynDee's voice:

We set out across the Celtic Sea from Glastonbury. We were sad to leave behind our sisters and brothers, but we were needed here. A group of us banded together to answer the call. The Norman brutes were invading Ireland and destroying native communities; both the Old Religion of our peoples and the Celtic Christianity of the Irish were being trampled. Standing stones were being toppled, abbeys burned, and many people slain who were in the path of these self-righteous crusaders.

Our community has had lots of experience standing up to outsiders. Many times, over the ages, we were attacked. Many were threatened by the power of the Mother. Glastonbury and Avalon were targeted because of its importance to the Mother. She has always been revered there. The Atlanteans hid their crystals in the Tor, the Great Goddesses developed Avalon. The Greeks were among those who came to study the mysteries. Arthur brought the power of his throne to Glastonbury. Mother Mary and Anna came for sanctuary. It was here that the Divine Feminine was strongest. It was here that the threat was most pronounced.

We learned how to hold our ground. We learned to summon the forces of Nature to protect our sacred ways.

We learned to survive, to thrive despite the cruelty and hatred of the Normans and other invaders. In the lifetime I now present to you, you were but a seed within your mother's womb when we set out for Ireland from the shores of England. In fact, had she known she was carrying you, she might not have set forth with us on the arduous journey to Ireland.

Listen to the story. Put this story together with all you are learning about yourself and about Ireland. Then, tell these stories so others will know all we did to keep the Divine Feminine alive. Inspire them to reconnect with the Mother energy so needed for this beautiful blue-green planet to survive.

You were there; you were part of that time long ago when the flame burned bright despite the hardships. We kept the Spirit of the Mother alive. You were brave, you were true. I could not have been prouder of you if you had been my own daughter.

You were a daughter of the Moon. You embodied the spirit of the Mother. Born at fireside, you had the Blessing of Brigid, the Fire of her Protection, the Light and Love of the Goddess.

Brigid was known to us in Beckery Chapel. Her time in Glastonbury had kept the spirit of Avalon alive through the trials and tribulations of early

Christianity. At first, the Christian monks had lived compatibly with those who venerated the Goddess. All were living and experiencing the Mother/ Father energy, Merlin and Arthur, especially. But then kings succumbed to the Roman idea of empire, of male domination...of a God who had no place for women. But I digress.

In the lifetime I am now describing, the assault on the Mother, on Mary Magdalene, and even on the true energies of Mother Mary came from the Norman raiders. These brutes came in to Ireland to change the landscape; to create square towers where stone circles had prevailed, to change the energy and wrench people from the connection to the land, to tear down that which honored the Mother and to assert a militaristic energy and a religion that worshipped power, patriarchy and ascendancy. You were part of resisting their influence. You were part of keeping the Mother Spirit alive and well in the south of Ireland.

Our Destination was what you modern people call the Beara Peninsula, where you first heard my voice calling to you. We were called by the Hag of Beara, the Goddess in her most aged form. She fiercely held ground there. She and Manannan mac Lir kept the Normans from the shore. He, as God of the Sea, blew storms in and away in patterns that disrupted Norman ships from landing. She saw that the wind and rocks discouraged those who made land from staying long.

The presence of those who held the old ways was fierce, but it was under constant attack. Those who knew the secrets of the standing stones, the rituals of the stone circles, and the words to open the portals of the dolmens were few and far between. So, we were called, and we came willingly. All who could safely fit in the boat came to create a new settlement.

But, as a group, we never made it to Beara. You got here to Drombeg and later visited Beara. My spirit and, of course, your mother's spirit traveled with you. We were so proud to see you thrive, build community and share the Mysteries here. But back to our journey. We were run aground as we neared Cobh at a place now called Ballycotton. We first made land near Youghal, a Viking fishing village. But the Normans were all around us. We had to move on even though the seas were rough; there was more danger in resting and waiting, than in sailing on. We stayed as close to shore as possible without running aground or being bashed to pieces on the rocks.

All the while your mother retched, and her stomach struggled to hold on to the life within. At times, I looked at her and thought we would lose you both, but she persevered. We all appealed to the Goddess to support us as *we tried to get to the place where she had asked us to come. I admit that at times I gave up hope. I looked at your mother, I looked at the sea, and I questioned why we had given up our home and our safety to be about in the turbulence, the unfriendly seas of Ireland.*

But your mother was certain that the Goddess would protect us. She had faith that The Mother had a purpose for us and that we would fulfill that purpose. All good things have a price she said, rubbing her belly and smiling with love at the life within her. I figured if she could have faith, that I too could find the strength to carry on. And you, dear little one, you provided the symbol of hope. You were the future, you were our hearts, and you would be blessed with the Spirit of the Goddess. Your father had been the Merlin of his time, your mother was a sister of Avalon and of Beckery. You were meant to carry on the tradition. If we survived this awful journey at sea, I vowed to see to it that you would receive training to pick up the mantle of your lineage.

We were shepherds and shepherdesses and this sea trial was a test of all our metal. To live in the elements in a different way, to be battered and bounced around by the wind and water, to have no stone nor fire circle to keep our grounding, to watch the stars while floating with our movement greater than the movement of the heavens was disconcerting, unsettling even during calm seas. And then the storms came.

What you now would call networks of those who honored the Mother lived in communities on the knolls where stone circles marked the land along the shores of Eire. They knew we were coming and communities set out fires to help us navigate the stormy sea.

But the winds were blowing fiercely, the seas rough and our ability to ground the energies grew faint—fear of Normans added to obscuring our path. We could no longer connect with the people and the energies that would support our journey. Instead, everything became a scramble to find landing places where water and food could be had, where there was safe harbor, where we could rest our arms, ground our feet.

Then came the big blow. Our boat was destroyed on the rocks. We made it to the shore of an island close to the mainland. Thank the Mother. The first night we made camp on the sea side, windy and cold but we knew not where the Normans were and could not chance our fires being seen. In the morning, we woke to see a lovely, small fishermen's cove and a beautiful sandy beach that stretched for miles, creating a lovely crescent strand as far as the eye could see. We were on an island with a high hill which we could hide behind if we spied troops coming toward it. Most exciting of all was a smaller island, closer to shore, by the cove which connected to the mainland at low tide. It is there we hoped to settle ourselves. If only long enough to rest, but hopefully it would be safe to stay until after you were born, and your mother was ready to travel again. That was my continual prayer to Brigid.

Our scouts went out to find out just where the Normans were and to get a sense of who else was about. We had no knowledge of this place you now call Ballycotton. We knew only that we had not yet reached Cobh where our contacts were to be made. We took to shore clamming, fishing and searching the grasses and sea cliffs for eggs whilst we waited. Fresh water was found. All in all we celebrated the moment, hoping and praying we would not have to set out to sea again right away.

The scouts returned with word that the people they encountered were wary of strangers but not unfriendly. A Norman keep, or tower-like castle, had been established in Shanagarry, the "old garden" settlement down the road and in the middle of the crescent shore. The farmers and sheep herders sent out a silent alarm when troops came through, but generally the action was elsewhere. We could be fairly certain of safety if we kept a low profile on the wee island and in the cliffs to the west of the cove. The good news also was that we had made it to Munster, the place you now call Cork. Sadly, though, we were still very far away from Beara Peninsula that had been our destination.

We later learned there was an underground of Celtic church peoples avoiding the Normans too. A Celtic priest who kept to the old ways helped us. His community was not Roman, nor Norman. They survived, and they helped us survive.

An Old Road along the shore led from Ballycotton up to Shanagarry—the Old Garden. Indeed beautiful. And all along the road we could see the big island looming over our shoulder, protecting the bay and reminding us of the marriage of the sea earth and sky—the original trinity of the Celtic peoples. We were safe, we were content, we settled in and trusted that if we were to move on we would receive a message from the Goddess to do so.

Your mother was not well. We feared for her pregnancy. I desperately wanted to get her to Kildare, where the Sisters of Brigid, skilled in midwifery could look after her. But we were too far away. We would have to make do with our own fire, call in the spirit of Brigid, and use our own best midwifery skills.

So little one, you were our first born on Irish soil. A sister of Avalon and of Beckery, born to the land of Brigid, Herself. As I was to represent the aged Hag, your mother and you were the mother and maiden. We were the trinity of sisters that would form Goddess circles here in Erin as our ancestors had done in Avalon and the Ancient Ones of Danu had done here in Ireland. All would be well. As another sister would one day say: 'All will be well. If not well, then not yet done'.

You were our heart. Keeping you alive and seeing you thrive kept us all going, contented us to build a small island community.

Sadly, your mother did not live to see you grow into the beautiful young girl you became. It was I who taught you the old ways and prepared you for your role as priestess. But much happened that I could not prevent, and you ended up here in Drombeg. So here we meet today.

The rest of the story you must discover yourself. Find the Old Road, find yourself in the story of the time we lived together. Only when this is done will you be whole and strong again. Only then will you be able to tell the stories with deep and true heart.

An eternity passes. "OMG, where did she go? CynDee, why did you stop?" I say with my heart in my mouth.

"I am so sorry, Honey, but the energy was just too strong, her vibration too intense. I could not hold it. That's all I could get."

"I am overwhelmed. I don't know what to say or where to begin. I do hope the recording is clear because I have a feeling I am going to want to play it again and again," I say breathlessly.

"Holy moly! That was something else. I sure hope it's recorded. I couldn't possibly repeat what all she said. What a story."

"It sure is. And now I must find this Old Road."

"Sorry, Honey. I sure wish I could have gone on longer but that's all I could get…and I am exhausted. Got any candy bars left?"

"Of course. Here you are. How insensitive of me. Let's say our goodbyes and get you some lunch." We say our goodbyes, express our gratitude and take our leave. If I were not so stunned I would probably feel sadness in departing, but I am too caught up in the story.

I can't stop thanking CynDee as we drive on to Leap where I treat her to a late pub lunch followed by a walk to the famous waterfall nearby. We frolic along the stream at the bottom of the waterfall where someone has placed little fairy houses to attract tourists. It releases some of the pent-up energy I have been holding since we listened to Jane.

"Fancy an ice cream?" CynDee asks, playfully referring to the sandwich sign like so many we have seen.

"Yes, and then I 'fancy' going back to the hotel. Hope you don't mind, but I am beat. I noticed there are great walking paths along the water around the hotel if you aren't into napping."

"Honey, your Jane exhausted me. This channeling thing is something else. A nap sounds good to me, and I never nap."

For dinner we walk up the hill to the village of Rosscarbery. I am first to notice a display map of the area and see that it illustrates where the local stone circles and standing stones are located. "Dare I suggest we visit these tomorrow?" I ask.

"Honey, leave it to you to find even more of these things—and just when I thought we were done and ready to party," she chuckles. "But sure: In for a penny, in for a pound, as my mawmaw—you know, my grandmama—used to say. Never did I think I would come to Ireland and do this, but OK. Besides, I don't think Jane is going to let either of us rest until you get the whole story. Enough for tonight. I want to talk about something else over dinner, go back to the pool for a swim and then straight to bed," she states without equivocation.

"And I want to email all this to Mark. Not sure when he will have Internet connectivity to read it, but this is too big and moving too fast for me to wait to catch him up when he gets back. Then, I'll try to read up on this Shanagarry place."

"Yeah and look up the Old Road so we can find it tomorrow," CynDee adds.

"You are OK with doing that?"

"Honey, as I said, I don't think Jane will let me forget about it, even if I tried."

• • •

A new day dawns and still all I can think about is yesterday's experience at Drombeg. I try to hold back talking about it with CynDee as we dress and go down to breakfast. I wrote in my journal while she went for a morning swim. Yet, the whole thing still has a hold on me. I know I am not very good company over breakfast.

"Earth to Abagail. Hey, Honey, snap out of it. You have found a way to connect with your mama and that tickles my heart. Try to enjoy it. Lighten up. I still have my mama but I'd like to think when she passes, I can speak with her too. Now, my daddy is gone, but if he did by chance make it to Heaven, I still have nothin' to say to him. But back to you and your situation. You gotta come out of your fog. Let's go find a way for you to speak directly with your shepherdess— your Auntie Jane—and then we can go on to other things."

"Thanks, CynDee. What would I do without you?" I say as we start our new day of exploration. The plan is to find the stone circles pictured on the town square map we saw last night. Then, we will head east to find the Old Road. It proves a bit more complicated than we had imagined.

We must be circling around the place without seeing it. This is so frustrating. We have asked two people who said opposite things and tried to follow the map in the town square as well as Google Maps. Finally, we find it. Then we must duck under an electrified fence to get to it.

The stone circle is small, very different than Drombeg and it doesn't seem to speak to either of us.

"You know, Honey, I think we are trying too hard, traipsing hither and yon. I remember a customer telling me once that Spirit came to her when she least expected it. And then there is the thing about fairies and how they say that you must lighten up to attract them. Just like Jane tells you to get out of your head, maybe she is also telling us to stop trying so hard."

"You may very well be right." I pause to truly consider her words. "But I would like to try just one more: the one just above Clonakilty, Templebryan. Maybe it is just the fact it translates as Druid's Temple, but my gut says it's worth it," I say with mild conviction.

"Damn if I know, Honey. I gave up trying to figure it out back a ways. I am just along for the ride…you know, Ethel to your Lucy. Let's go and find out. If it proves easy to find and not all muddy and yucky, then we are meant to be there. If it's a hassle, I say we drop it. Deal?"

"Deal," I agree.

It is easy, it is not muddy, and it reminds me of Ardgroom in a way. We approach it with interest and respect, but I am not tense as I was back at the last one. I open with:

> *Ancient Ones, we are here to listen.*
>
> *We are here to hear the stories.*
>
> *We seek guidance to the Old Road.*
>
> *Help us to do your bidding.*

CynDee joins me in my little buttercup ritual and we sit patiently on the crystal block in the center, enjoying the view. I can feel the crystal energy move up into my body.

"Jane is here," CynDee says calmly. "Turn the recorder on."

> *Now you must go to the Old Garden, a place you call Shanagarry, you must find the ancient Old Road and tell the story of the circle that reared you…of the man who took away your youth, who dishonored your sovereignty, and*

of the men and women who rescued you…who brought you hence. It was not a time of safety for women.

What time has been safe for women? How did the world let honoring our Mother go? You can no longer deny the pain of that time. You can no longer avoid the darkness and shadow. Face these things and you will be strong again. You will be a healer and a storyteller.

"Jane, I have a question. Is there a way you can teach Abby to hear you directly so that she may reach you when I am not able to be with her?" CynDee asks aloud. She then repeats the reply she gets:

In good time. Be patient. You are to here to help her, as you help many in your own way. You are already a woman of a big heart. These experiences will open your sacred heart. Your gifts will be amplified. You will continue to reach out to others. You will be blessed. Now, remind my cara to stop thinking, to lighten up, to be Love not Fear.

"Well, I guess we go into Clonakilty for some lunch and then plan our route to this Shanagarry. You can buy me a glass of wine and some chocolate to go with it, Honey, because I feel my battery is dead as a door nail. Then, when I am recharged we can get back into it."

"You are the best, thank you!" I hug her to me as tears of gratitude stream down my face.

CHAPTER ELEVEN

H oney, good news. The chocolate and the wine and the food worked their magic. I am ready and so is Google Maps. It shows there is no problem in getting to Shanagarry. Straight across on the main road here to Middleton and turn south. Jack and I were actually at that very round-about when we went to the Jameson Distillery. Cell service works just fine there but we won't need GPS. Easy peasy. It's only about an hour and a half away. I suggest we go get the lay of the land and then get ourselves a room. It stays light out until late and its midweek. Maybe we can find out about the Old Road today even. It's odd that there wasn't but that one line about the Old Road on Google, but we will find it."

"I can't wait," I respond.

"OK, but first I would like to stop in the salon we passed on the way here. We can get our nails done and I can get a chance to see how they do things here. It's nearer the city than Castletownbere and probably has the latest ideas for me to take home. An hour tops. My treat."

"What can I say, if you really want to. Cross your fingers that they can take us."

With full tummies and pretty nails, we head out, me with trepidation, CynDee with unbounding enthusiasm. She keeps us on route and talks non-stop about her observations at the salon and about her own business back in the states. I like the patter. It keeps me from surfacing this fear I have of facing the story of the Old Road. I said I can't wait, but on another level I am scared. Everything has been going so well. I have heard it said that we find ourselves through the recognition and retelling of our own story. I am beginning to realize that I can't tell this story Jane wants me to tell until I face something dark and painful first. Hope it doesn't upset the apple cart, as the saying goes.

"Oh, Honey, look. Katie just texted an update on the guys. Let's see. They are loving the sailboat. No surprise there. They have logged in a plan that takes them west to Fastnet and then goes back east to Hook Lighthouse near Waterford. We pick them up on their way back to Cobh. That's it. Short but sweet."

"I just hope they have good weather. The more I have seen of the sea the more concerned I have become. Mark and I stopped at the Lusitania Memorial. It was sobering. And we also now have Jane's story of the big blow as she called it."

"Best not to draw that kind of energy to us. Positive thinking is my motto."

"You are so right, I know better than to worry, especially raising two adventurous sons. But I have been thinking about how I must be denying whatever dark and horrible thing happened to me in Shanagarry. So how do I let dark things surface but still be a positive and upbeat person?"

"Not sure they are on the same plane, Honey, and I am no expert. Probably Mark, with his experience as a pastor is a better one for you to kick stuff like that around with. I only know that I believe that old saw 'the truth will set you free' and I believe in a loving God who watches over us. That's what keeps me light and positive. Oh, look, see how far out the tide is. Here we are at least ten miles from the sea and the water that was here when Jack and I drove by is almost totally gone out. I do love the sea and all its mysteries. Don't care all that much about the lighthouses but the ocean itself fascinates me," she says.

"And what about you and the stones? Jane and I have used you to get me going on this new path, but what about you? Does it freak you out to realize how psychic you are? Does it embolden you to do something with your gifts of connecting to the Otherworld?" I ask.

There is silence in the car for a long time, at least a relatively long time, given how we usually gab continually.

"Really, Honey, I don't think much about myself like you do. I don't mean any offense, not to say you are wrong, just saying I get up, spend my day doin' what I do, takin' things as they come and then doin' the same the next day. No day is the same, but there is no grand design or angst over any of it. I live in the moment 'til the moment gets to be too much and then I go dancin' and partyin' and let go."

"You have such gifts and common sense wisdom, and you so seem to live in the moment. And I kind of make a big deal of everything. It is hard for me to imagine," I say truthfully.

"I am just me. I know I help people sort things out by listening to their stories and sharing bits and pieces with others when I think folks will benefit from hearing about other experiences, but I am just a simple hairdresser who helps people look and feel better, inside and out. Now, I have new experiences to share and that's a great thing. Plus, we have had fun, right? An adventure I couldn't have dreamed up and somehow I imagine it ain't over yet."

Just then we come to a T in the road. There is more I want to say and ask but I need to focus on the road. I see the sign to Shanagarry and Ballycotton to the right and a public beach sign for Garryvoe Beach almost straight ahead. I go for its parking lot.

"Holy moly. Abby, look! That must be THE island. It is shaped so perfectly, it looks artificial and it has a lighthouse smack dab in the center. Mark will get a kick out of that."

It is both gentle and imposing. And it commands attention from every inch of the bay, a bay we later learn is named Ardnahinch.

We sit soaking it in until finally we are ready to go walk the pebbled beach. The beach stretches on in both directions for as far as we can see; forming a gentle crescent of sand and stones, rimming the blue waters. A grouping of travel trailers, holiday caravans to the Irish, suggests the place will be busy come summer. Today, we see only one guy walking his dog, an elderly couple sitting on a bench and a guy digging for clams or oysters. Even the vintage seaside hotel on the inward side of the road is quiet.

We walk toward the guy who is digging to ask if he knows anything about the Old Road. He doesn't speak English, at least he doesn't understand us, and seems frightened by our questions. CynDee allows that it is probably because of fishing rights; seems there are a lot of restrictions, going back to the lords of the castle kind of thinking.

"Let's get some ice cream over at that little store and ask if they know," CynDee offers with still unbridled enthusiasm.

I agree, but realize I am still in a bit of a fog as I let the fact that we are here sink in. The young girl behind the counter has no idea about the Old Road and asks if we have Googled it. I nod. We continue on into Shanagarry with the island staring at us most of the way. I want to stare back but need to keep my eyes to the road.

"Here we are at another T. Turn right. We are now in Shanagarry. Oh, look an old stone manor house there and a pottery studio...and now a Kilkenny Design Center. We went in one of those in downtown Cork. I am going to love this place. Slow down a bit more. On the right is a sign to the Ballymaloe Cooking School. I saw in a magazine that it is one of the top ones in Ireland. I think I will call to see if they have any day classes open."

"Did you want me to turn and follow the sign?" I ask.

"No, Honey, I will check them out online later. Let's stick to the main road and see where it takes us."

"OK, then. I'm going to pull over, so we can walk a bit in this park and have a look at the castle ruins hidden in the trees. Something about it draws me to it."

"Whatever. Remember, I am here as the Ethel to your Lucy," she laughs. "Seriously, this is exciting. Maybe I should be the Nora to your Nick, you know, since we have a big mystery to solve."

I ignore her banter as I try to hone my intuition and focus myself. "There is definitely something here I am supposed to experience, but we don't want to take the time now to climb through that fence. See that guy trimming bushes? Let's ask him about the Old Road."

"So is it the castle ruins ye want to see? I can point out a place in the fence for ye to slip through. Your man William Penn owned it 'til he took up and went to America and started your Pennsylvania. It would be the earlier Normans, who built it though. Penn Himself was a Quaker man. 'Twas the Normans that built square towers, you know, not like the ancient round tower over in Coyne, early Celtic tower that one. Surprising, the Normans didn't destroy it. They were raiders and invaders, you know. Mind now, in today's world many are big names—like your man Kennedy. The Fitzgeralds would have been Normans 'til they stayed and took over the land up Limerick way and became respectable Irishmen. I fear bad things went on in this tower in early days."

"We are definitely interested in coming back to look at the tower and the castle ruins. Will you be here?"

"Aye, sometimes. I work for the village so I have other duties. But I will be here if you need me."

That sounds a bit odd. He seems like an interesting guy, yet I am so eager to find the Old Road that I don't engage with him more. "Right now, we're wondering if you knew about an Old Road and where it might be?"

"Well, missus, now it may be that there was such a road long ago. A road up from Ballycotton that followed closer to the water. If you were to walk as the crow flies right on through there and over the creek," he says pointing to thick brush and trees. "But it would be all gone now…and ye canna go back in there. All bog land it is. Thickets and then bog. You would sink in, you see. Like quicksand it would be in places. No, there would be nothing now fer you to see."

We thank him profusely and take our leave.

We ask again at the gas station on the corner, but that fellow doesn't have a clue. So we turn down toward Ballycotton, looking out to the bay, mesmerized by the island and trying to imagine where the road would be.

We pass an old stone church to our right as we enter Ballycotton. A breakfront stone wall and steps leading down to the water are on our left. The road becomes the main street and we drive through the row of shops as the road rises. Then we notice a stately white building below the road and on the hillside overlooking the water.

"That's the place we should stay. The Bay View Hotel," CynDee reads the entrance sign as I concentrate on driving up the narrowing street. "It is lovely and the view is of the island. It is too perfect. What do you say, Abby?"

"Agreed, it looks fantastic. And it is getting late. But let's just go to the end of the street first. I think it ends right at the sea. Then we can find a place to turn around, come back to get a room, and ditch the car. I can't look and drive too."

The street climbs uphill before dipping down to the sea. Suddenly, we see a jetty, I think it is called, and a beautiful little harbor. It's a postcard-perfect picture of the RNLI lifeboat station, a bright orange lifeboat like the one we saw in Castletownbere and an array of fishing boats and small crafts bobbing up and down in a playful display. It's like a child's armada of toy plastic boats. This is the most unique harbor we have seen. I love it already.

The road veers to the right up to a high point with a cliff walk and public parking. I stop so we can get a full view of both the smaller, closer island and of the big island with the lighthouse. The cliff walk looks as though it extends all the way to Cobh. Although I realize that is impossible. We see beautiful, expansive views of the ocean. Of course, my eyes keep returning to the big island. It has got to be the one Jane says they shipwrecked on; the little one has to be where I was born. Chills run up and down my spine.

We check in, securing a room with a view, and then walk through the garden and find some steps that give us access to the beach. A wide breakwater forms the outer wall of the man-made basin. We walk on over to the orange lifeboat. The whole place is just so picturesque, even more so than the sweet harbor in *Ondine*.

We are as close to the big island as you can get and have a full view of the little island that in some ways is even more alluring. We are looking east now and I can't help but think of Mark off there somewhere looking at lighthouses when here I am in front of one of the best.

"The brochure in the hotel said they give lighthouse tours. Let's sign up for one. It is a short ride and I am dying to get to that magical island. What do you think, Honey?"

"I would love to as long as it isn't too windy," my standard reply to boating questions.

"Hey, I just noticed the lighthouse is black. That's pretty unusual and isn't it weird I have been looking at it all the way from Garryvoe and just realized it," CynDee observes.

"Perceptions can be weird. We will have to remember to ask about it on the tour. I think it is rare for them not to be white. If Mark were here, he would know. I wonder if the guys stopped here? I wonder if Mark got my message that we were coming over here? Tonight I will email him our location. Maybe Doug and Sean can even drop them off here. It would be fun to watch them sail into this beautiful little harbor. To think this is where Jane sent us. Too much!"

At this time of day, it is pretty quiet. We can't find the boat tour guy, so we call his mobile number. He will take us tomorrow. We are to be down here at 10 am.

"Shall we try that great pub we passed and then just go back and crash? I find that I am just exhausted from all this," I suggest.

"OK, with me. I might actually catch up on emails and a couple of my shows on Netflix if it won't keep you up."

"And I want to see if there is anything from Mark. Plus, we have to text Katie and the guys to tell them where we are. But not to worry about the television. Nothing will disturb me once I hit the pillow."

• • •

My sleep is again deep and as if I travel someplace else and return to my body in a jolt. I always find that sleep helps me process things. Maybe I communicate with my guides, maybe I just go deep into my unconscious. Either way, I always feel guided and restored come morning, especially if I can wake naturally. This morning when I wake I go through my morning ritual of gratitude silently so as not to trigger conversation from CynDee. She is great, but quite a talker. I need some quiet with all that is churning within me.

When I do admit to being awake, we dress and head down for breakfast. It is cool, but we take coffee out on the terrace after polishing off huge plates of food from their scrumptious breakfast buffet. The view is so beautiful and calming. I am especially relieved that the day is calm with only a few high fluffy clouds in the sky.

The hotel itself is lovely, with a warm wood main staircase and a formal lobby. There is an art gallery featuring a local artist whom I really like, especially her renditions of the island. I was too tired last night to absorb any of it. We made a good choice.

Before we know it, it is time for our boat ride. Our boatman is friendly. CynDee engages him as I quietly take in the sea, the islands and the rocky coast line. It all holds meaning and memory, but I cannot yet articulate what I am feeling and sensing. I do get the sense I was born here in another lifetime. To think I have access to that lifetime. To think I am to learn enough about it to write about it is mind blowing. Why me? Why now? The only thing clear is that I have been guided all the way here—nudged even—and I must see it through.

I realize that CynDee is asking our boat guy, George, about the Old Road. I tune in only to hear him say he doesn't know. But he does reinforce the idea that this harbor was a busy one in olden times and has no doubt there would have been a way up to Shanagarry. As he points toward the breakfront and bank, I can see just how far the present road and shops are from the water. Interesting angle.

"Aye, now, here you are now. Mind your step. We'll be tying up here and going up to the lighthouse now."

What I had thought was a winding path is actually angular and more modern. Nonetheless, my mind flashes to pictures of the High Tor in Glastonbury. I wonder if Jane and my mother felt the connection to their home when they arrived here. Jane told us they arrived in the dark. I can imagine when they looked around the next morning they were stirred by the similarity. Of course, there was no lighthouse here then, but I bet there was some kind of ancient signal tower. I get chills the more I imagine us all being here: my family and community in another lifetime.

George is telling us all about the history of the lighthouse. CynDee's question about why it is black attracts my attention: seems it is to avoid confusion with the one at the east side of the bay. I am so glad CynDee keeps engaging with him. I will want to hear it all from her later so I can pass it on to Mark, but for now my mind is on the past.

We stop to take a zillion pictures as George unlocks the lighthouse door and waits for us to enter. I so am missing Mark at this moment. He would love this. He would also be intrigued by the Jane story. We go up to the balcony which has absolutely wondrous views. Looking out to sea, I so badly want to see him. I wave as if they can see us. Reluctant to leave our perch overlooking this bay we have already, in this lifetime, come to love, we follow George down to the boat and head back to the cove.

"Ye did well to choose today, lasses, for a big blow is coming tomorrow the telly says."

"Our men are sailing somewhere here off the coast for a couple more days. Will they be affected?" I question George.

"Good sailors take warning. Not to worry, missus. Mind your step now and 'twas my pleasure to have ye come to Ballycotton Island with me."

"I sure worked up an appetite. The pub up the hill for lunch?" asks CynDee.

"Works for me. Then maybe a leisurely glass of wine from the hotel terrace?"

"Ladies, would ye be wanting lunch now? There is a women's club meeting today in the dining room. Would you mind eating at the bar?" the waitress asks as she steers us to the right.

The bar proves great fun as we chat with a couple of local men who are retired from the RNLI—lifeboat people. The more talkative one is a former captain.

"We spent some time in Castletownbere where I first saw one of your orange lifeboats and learned of the RNLI, but would you remind me what the letters stand for?" I ask.

"Aye, 'tis The Royal National Lifeboat Institution," he replies proudly.

"That's why I couldn't remember. I am confused by the fact it sounds so British but serves both Ireland and the UK, right?"

"Aye, right enough, 'tis one of the best examples of our all working together. Ye know the expression about necessity being the mother of invention, well it drives cooperation as well. I was stationed in Castletownbere for a time. More of the big international fishing boats and oil tankers are there. Here we have more calls on the recreational side of things."

The two gentlemen regale us with stories through our lunch. We reluctantly say goodbye and agree we might be back to see them again.

As much fun as the pub lunch was, we are both glad to be back outside. There is nothing like this beautiful weather, the terrace view and a glass of Chardonnay. I notice the tide has gone out a great deal. "You know, the tide is so low now that I can see a stretch of beach along the stone wall and cliff. It looks like this time of day we might even be able to walk to Shanagarry. What do you say we do it?" I suggest.

"Well if we do, we couldn't get back up on land way until beyond the pottery shop. That is too far a walk for me, but I am game to go for a mile or so."

"You are on then, let's do a mile."

We get water bottles and stow our phones and a few euros in our pockets and start out around the sandy crescent. We are not too far beyond the stone steps we noticed coming into Ballycotton yesterday when I think I see something.

"Oh my! Look at this! These stones have been intentionally placed—like cobblestones. They are tall and thin but laid out like up-ended bricks. They are really embedded and old. We have found it! These are pieces of the Old Road, I am sure of it!"

We dance, we stomp, we take pictures. Finally, we plunk ourselves down in the sand and just stare at the stones. We are very pleased with ourselves.

"Honey, you did it. Great work. This has to be a remnant of the Old Road. Look how straight those stones are laid and how deep they go. And it makes sense. Not that far from the old stone steps leading up to the oldest part of town. Yet, I guess I can understand that people walking the beach never consider that these stones were part of an old road built at sea level."

"I bet the beach kept eroding until it came up to and finally destroyed the Old Road. This breakwall was built to keep the cliff from further erosion. Amazing."

"This calls for celebration. Too bad we only have bottled water with us. Ooo. Jane's here with us. She says: *Ye found The Old Road.* Can you hear or see her? I will do my best to keep up with her, but get out the phone to record it."

> *Aye, dearie, ye found the Old Road…and the picture is beginning to fill in, is it not?*

"Tell her, I get the sense that I walked this road, with her and with our people… mostly women, but some men too. And that we went to a gathering of some sort, over that way," I say pointing beyond the shore of the most inward part of the bay, about where I thought the Shanagarry Design Center roof could be seen.

> *Talk to me directly, my cara. I can hear and see you and it will help you build our connection. This one who helps us has her own life to lead, after all. Do you know the nature and importance of the gathering?*

"Wow! I am actually hearing her myself! CynDee, are you hearing her too?" I ask in surprise.

"Go, girl, I am with you," adds CynDee.

I answer Jane, "The gathering was a kind of worship. We met to honor the goddess but yet it feels it was also Christian…"

> *Aye, we met together: followers of Patrick and Brigit and those of us who honored the Goddess.*

"I thought the Church rejected all those pagan ideas?" I ask.

> *That, dear one, is one of the stories you are to tell. The story of how we— Celtic Christians and followers of the Mother—together kept the Divine Feminine from eradication in spite of those who tried to destroy Her.*

"But I know so little. I just sense the love and power of Mother Earth and that today that earlier understanding of the Divine Feminine is reemerging."

> *Aye, lass. And you are to tell others, help them resonate with the Word, the Story. In the first of days, here in Ireland and over in the mists of Avalon where you were born, people worshipped the Mother.*

"I was born in Avalon? I thought you said I was born here?" Now I am really confused.

> *Aye. In a long, long ago lifetime, you were born in the mists of Avalon, under the Great Tor of Glastonbury. I do not mean to confuse you, but I want*

*you to learn about what you might think of as your lineage. We were sisters
in that lifetime. Our people heeded the ancient ways. When the Christian
monks first came, our communities co-existed and came to accept one
another, to learn from one another. St Brigit was a big part of that, coming
over…her face is carved into their great tower, you know, and her Spirit
was incorporated into early Christianity in Britain as here is Ireland. Mary,
Mother of Christ, and Brigit were sisters in the understanding of the Great
Goddess. Mary Magdalene carried forth the tradition as did we.*

Are you saying they were pagan?

*There was not the kind of separation you modern day people think. Christ
Himself brought a message of Oneness and pagan actually means earth-
based and the Mother is Mother Earth. We were priestesses, dear. Keeping
alive the ancient mysteries of Atlantis and Egypt and Sumer. The Kings of
your Old Testament married queens from our line that go back to Atlantis.
Are you remembering Atlantis in your dreams?*

"No, but I won't be surprised if I do from here on out. I am coming to believe
that any of this is possible. But are you saying Christ knew and was part of this?
He was the Son of the Divine Mother and the Divine Father…like in days before, like Isis and Osiris? I have been reading about the ancient mysteries on the
Internet. More and more is being revealed and made available to our time, isn't it?"

*Aye, dear. For those with eyes to see and ears to hear, all will be revealed.
We are all One. Early Christianity held with the ancient beliefs as well as
loved and honored the Christ who came as Jesus…You know of the Grail?
Of Arthur? Of Percival? Of the merging of the Old Religion with the
followers of the Christ? They kept alive the memory of the struggle. Here in
Celtic lands we kept alive the energies of the Mother. But when the Romans
came, they tried to wipe it out. Avalon and Camelot were about keeping the
balance and about holding on to the mysteries.*

*But it was the Normans whose fierce attempts to destroy us led to our
journey here in the lifetime that you are now exploring. That English Pope
Adrian was behind it all, sending the Normans in to destroy the Irish
Church, bringing their own form of Christianity that put down women
and rejected the ways of the Old Religion. They started their destruction in
Waterford and moved up to Dublin and then came back down here along
the coast. Then they rampaged throughout Ireland, even to Brigid's beloved
Kildare.*

"When was this?"

In what you would call the 12th century, dear. That is the lifetime you are now coming to remember. It happened again in a later time period with a man called Cromwell who tried to eradicate the Irish way.

In this lifetime we speak of, as I have said, your mother and I were sisters of Avalon. We were asked by the Hag of Beara and the women of Kildare to come to Ireland to help sustain the seeds of the Divine Feminine which were being destroyed by the Norman conquerors whose ideas of Christianity included plunder and grabs for power and land. They cared not for the people or the land itself. They only wanted domain over the land. Men and women who objected were slain, places of worship like the beloved stone circles you have been visiting were forbidden. In many cases they were destroyed.

Because the same had happened in Britain, we knew well about such destruction. Places like Avebury had been disrupted. The ley lines weaving the Mary and Michael paths from Mount St. Michael through Glastonbury, Avebury and on to the far coast of England were disturbed. Either the powers that be tore them apart or built churches over them. This went on for centuries. Yes, this assault continued, dear, led by different powers at different times. But I have told you all this before.

What you now would call Celtic Christians even had to meet in secret. Did you not come across mass stones as you traveled? There is one up ahead. People took the Old Road and met there to worship the Christ. It is evidence of how secretive those who followed the early Celtic Christianity had to be.

"And what did our group do once we were here?"

Our mission was to reactivate centers of Feminine energy at sacred sites through rituals we knew and could teach others. The Light of the Ancients was fading. Much of the knowledge of working with the Light that your Jesus brought back to the consciousness of the people was distorted or lost as early Christians struggled to survive persecution. Old Atlantean mysteries involving crystal activation of the stones themselves were not passed on as before. Much also was lost when the libraries of Alexandria burned.

Thankfully, the Celtic tradition had been an oral one. All was not entirely lost. The Druids still carried forth the mysteries. Bards and storytellers and those you call Gypsies using Tarot cards passed on the mysteries to those with eyes to see and ears to hear.

"And how was I part of this?"

You were my apprentice, learning the old ways of the crystals and the plants.
Our group met on the small, flat island west of the big island. At low tide
we could walk over and if need be stay through the changing of the tides.
We walked this road of service to the Mother together many, many circles
of time. You learned the cycles of the sun, the stars and especially the moon.
You were to carry on the ancient mysteries.

"What happened?"

What do you feel and know inside yourself, dear?

"I can sense that I walked this road, many times, and in joy…but I also sense
fear—being scared and cold and shaking. What am I not remembering? Did
something bad happen?"

Aye, dear. Now that you have walked the Old Road as far as it can take you
in modern times, return to Shanagarry. You will find your answer there.
You will face the darkness. You cannot tell the stories until you come to the
experience from inside yourself. Fear not, your mother of many lifetimes,
The Mother of All Lifetimes, and I will be with you.

"That's it. She is gone," CynDee says as she flops back into the sand and lays
there speechless.

We soak in the sun until suddenly I realize the tide is coming in and we soon
will be without beach. "Hey, look! We better start back."

"No worries, we can always run up the steps and walk along the top of the cliff,
if it looks like the tide is going to overcome us."

"We can make it." We laugh as we begin a skipping like motion to avoid the
incoming waves. Soon we are back below the hotel.

"A beer?"

"I think I will stay with wine, but yes, let's have a drink." We sit companion-
ably on the terrace watching the tide come in. We chat on, but my mind wanders
to our beach conversation with Jane, and her piercing words *tell the story*. How can
I? Even if I come to know it in more detail, how will I tell it and to whom? I was
a teacher all my life, not a storyteller, not a writer. But first things first. The life
I lived here is coming back to me. Do the remains of the Norman castle next to
the church in the parking lot hold more answers? Shall I ask CynDee to explore
it with me?

So I ask, "Feel like a ride up to Shanagarry to check out the park and the
old castle? We can try out the pub near the bus stop on the way back. I am very
itchy to see what the tower is all about. Since you are going to be at the cooking

school in the morning, I would appreciate your coming up tonight. You might hear something or notice something that I miss. Maybe Jane will appear again. I promise not to stay long. I plan on going back in the morning after I drop you off at the cooking school."

• • •

The park is quiet. The old growth trees are inviting and we spend a bit of time soaking in the peaceful feeling of the earth under our feet. From here, we cannot see the water or the island, but we know it to be beyond the thickets and trees that bar our view and deny us access. We also now know that the Old Road is there, just beyond our view.

I try to communicate my thinking. "So the Old Road must have come up here, at least to the creek. And this path must have led over to the castle. Let's first walk to the other side of the church and see if we can get in there, maybe even find more signs of the Old Road. It may have continued parallel to the present road."

"OK, Honey, follow your intuition and I will follow you."

We get a good view from behind the church but there is no way to get over to the ruins. No doubt, for safety's sake everything is blocked off.

"OK, back to the park and in through the bushes," I say taking the lead.

We find the hole in the fencing that our groundskeeper friend had pointed to yesterday. With each of us holding branches back for the other, we come to a clearing very near the ruins. I begin to tremble.

"Breathe deep, Honey. Relax and just keep breathing deep, deep breaths. There you are, all is OK. You are safe. Just keep listening to my voice until you feel better," CynDee guides me.

"See that door? Something bad happened to me here and I was down there. Beyond that door. Dark and scary." Suddenly, I feel cold and clammy. "CynDee, I was in there—in the dungeon, a prisoner…and, oh my God, this pain, stabbing pain, under my right breast like I was stabbed. Ugh! No I was kicked. Thank God you are here with me." I grab her arm and squeeze, hoping, I guess, that it will help.

"Holy moly. Abby? What can I do?"

"Just steady me, feels like broken ribs. Can't walk. Let's just stand here a bit."

"Keep breathing. Deeper. Steady. That's the girl. Now, come sit on this stump. Slowly now, keep breathing."

She helps me get over to the stump. It hurts to sit; but once I sit, the pain eases a bit. "That bastard beat me," I say.

"Who? What are you talking about?"

141

"The lord of the castle, when I told him I was pledged to the Mother…he went ballistic. Beat me, threw me in the dungeon…Dark. Cold. Rats."

"How do you know this? When? How long? What the hell?"

"Don't know how I know. I just know."

"Relax and breathe into the pain. Let your mind be still. Just until you get the pain under control. Remind yourself that you are here, with me, in this lifetime. He can't hurt you here. This is just a memory. It is a flashback to another time and place. Keep breathing." She keeps repeating that last part over and over until I finally feel relief from the pain, and can put some distance between me and the memory.

Finally, I feel myself again. "Thanks, CynDee, you are a lifesaver."

"Well, Honey, I really didn't know how to help. I just guess I was guided. Not really anything I ever did before. I just knew to keep you breathing deep. Wait, now I am seeing something…something about what happened here. I see a man coming, a guard maybe."

"Yes, I am getting that he let me out! It was dark. A gate over there was left open and someone took me stumbling down the Old Road to Jane. Jane met me."

"So, the man I just saw is my signal to tell you to look beyond the beatings and the imprisonment. I am being told that now that you have experienced the attack, relived the beatings and the darkness of the dungeon, you can let go of the pain. Remind yourself that your ribs are fine. The pain did its job; it got your attention. But it can go away now. You are in this present lifetime and you are whole and free of pain and you are safe."

I do as she tells me. I consciously let go. I give it up. After quite a few minutes, I feel much better. "CynDee, it worked. I feel OK. The pain is gone. How did you know what to do? Thank God you were here." I embrace her as my tears flow.

"I have no idea where those words came from. This is new territory for me. I haven't a clue. I'm just glad they helped. So now, do you think it best to just drop this whole thing for now?"

"And go shopping?" I laugh. Then add, "You are sounding like Mark when he wants me to move on. But I need to keep going. I am clearly guided to do this exploration, whatever it is. I am confident it is safe, even though I don't know what else to expect. And somehow, I think that was the worst of it."

"Guess I am destined to play a role in all this too. Honey, I am done for today. Can we go get a drink now or do you need more time here?" she asks.

"You are right, we have done plenty for today. Let's get something to drink, have dinner and then maybe I can journal and sleep on it before coming back tomorrow morning."

"Are you sure you are OK? You just had one hell of a mind-blowing experience. And are you sure you want to come alone tomorrow? You could always wait until afternoon. The cooking class is only half day."

"It's hard to believe, but once the pain went away, I started feeling this huge sense of relief. Right now, I feel good. I think I want to come back on my own. Thanks for your offer. It is good to be reminded that I can always wait until later in the day if I get cold feet. Let's clear our path through the bushes as we go back so I can get over here more easily tomorrow."

We chose a pub on the main street. It is friendly, but seems newer and seems to appeal to a younger crowd. Of course, it may just be the time of day. The food is good and we enjoy the quiet. No music scheduled for the evening so we head back to the hotel. I am relieved because I just want to curl up and read for a bit. I no longer feel any pain or anxiety, but I do feel very tired. I so wish Mark was here. And I do want to email him before I go to bed. Not sure when he will see it but there is so much going on. I want to keep him updated.

When I turn on my computer, I find a message from him that must have come in while we were eating. He tells me they came into port (although he doesn't say what port) for groceries and a meal but there was no mooring available for the night. They are anchored off shore and going to bed early. He is sorry to have missed me. He ends with: "I love you." Wow. We have casually used the words "love you" before, and maybe I am reading something into it that isn't there, but this "I love you" seems deeper and more serious. Perhaps the adage "absence makes the heart grow fonder" is at work. We shall see.

CHAPTER TWELVE

Morning comes and I find myself clearer and more energetic than I imagined I would be. After leaving CynDee off for her class and avoiding the free range chickens and rooster in the lane leading from the cooking school to the road, I go straight to the park. My friendly groundskeeper is trimming again so I say hello. I refrain from telling him what I am up to or how glad I am to know he is within shouting distance. Not that I plan to be attacked, but it is unnerving to be going back to that tower door.

I get over there more easily thanks to the path we opened up yesterday. I find a stump and sit on it looking straight at the door that held such a charge for me yesterday. I am so grateful CynDee walked me through a process of releasing the pain of that memory. I know I want to explore it further. I only hope I can do so without the pain returning.

So I call the guides that I have called in at the stone circles. I call in my mother and I call in Jane. I ask that they help call in memories of the time I lived here in Shanagarry without the experience of pain. Perhaps that is too much to ask, but I figure it is worth a try. "Ask and ye shall receive", right?

Soon, I feel that cold, dark feeling of yesterday; the only difference is that today I am not thrown by it. I name it and sit with the knowing that I am about to find out more about my past; and that I am OK. There is no present threat.

Someone or something is here. "Whose there? Who are you?" I ask aloud.

> *I am you in the lifetime that you seek to understand. We are one. Yet, it seems you are struggling to remember. Jane tells me we must speak. She wants me to tell you all so you can tell our story to others.*

She wants us to be remembered for keeping the spirit of the stones alive. She wants people in your time to know the importance of honoring the Mother. She wants you to know in your heart and in your bones the sacrifices we made; the hardships we endured; how those who followed the Old Way were persecuted.

"Were you—was I—locked in this tower?"

Aye, in a dank, dark stone hole down in the bowels of the tower. At first, I dreaded the coming of those who would take me again to the lord who put me in here. Just the sight of him repulsed me. But then, he went away; I feared even more that I would be left to rot.

I coundna barely look at the man without wanting to vomit. He and his kind ruined our world. Them and their square towers. He said he wanted me, that I was to be his.

Fourteen and a virgin made me ripe for conquest. When I refused his advances, he slapped me silly. So hard that I fell to the ground. It was then that he kicked me. I shouted out in pain. Jane came to my defense. Then he threatened her. When she stood up to him and said I could not marry him; that I was already pledged to the work of the Mother, he went wild. He spat at her and slapped her until she fell to the ground and then he kicked her too. It was just awful.

I had come to my feet by then. I begged him to stop. I asked him did he not see his own mother in Jane's eyes. I asked him how we could venerate Mother Mary and yet harm Jane, or me or any of us. His eyes burned into me, at me, he exploded in rage and he dragged me away by my hair.

When we got to his chambers, I continued to plead with him. I tried to explain that I was already promised. That angered him more. He threw me into a chair and slapped me some more before pulling me upright and glaring into my face. He had such a look of hate in his eyes. Again, I tried to explain that I had taken vows as a healer, vows to the Mother to remain a virgin and that I was bound to my community.

Sadly, this enraged him more. "How dare you compare yourself to Mother Mary! Who are you to refuse me as your sovereign? He kept shouting as he ripped my shift and denuded me. Taking me right there on the floor. Ripping into me and violating me while all the while shouting ugly, awful words until I finally fainted. When I woke, I was imprisoned. Here. Your world tells stories about princesses in towers, but this was a stinking, rat-infested hole that no woman, no person should have to endure.

"How long were you here?"

At least two moons. For the first few weeks, I was not aware of much, in and out of knowing, barely surviving and praying for the healing of my wounds and sobbing about the violence that had been done me. A kind guard brought me water and a wee drop of ale now and again to ease the pain and to allow me to clean my cuts. Slowly, I began to take in my surroundings, to eat the little that was given me and to befriend my guard.

"Did the Norman lord return?"

Nay, thank the Mother. He did not. I feared his return, then I feared he, and everyone, would just leave me, moving on to their next raiding campaign. I began to think I would die in that hole.

"How did you survive?"

I prayed, I conducted healing rituals for myself where I called in Brigid, goddess and saint, and I watched the sun and moon and stars through the tiny slit that brought a wee bit of light and air to the hold. After the second full moon, my guard brought a message to hold fast, a rescue was being planned.

I am losing our connection. I can say no more at this time. Goodbye for now.

"Must you go?" I ask in alarm.
I hear a different voice next:

You did well, my cara. I will tell the story from here.

"Is that you, Jane?"

Aye, I shall take over the story from the lass. She still holds the pain. I hope that when you tell the story she will be released from all of it. That both of you will let go of all the pain and trauma. It is my fervent hope that you will then be completely free.

We sequestered you aboard a fishing boat in the harbor waiting for a time to set sail to Glandore where I knew you would be safe. Do you remember being hidden in the bow of the boat? Do you remember my tears as we said goodbye? I could not go with you. My absence would have been noticed and

147

they would have punished those who remained in our community. Everyone would have been flogged to an inch of their lives.

You had lived in Glandore and protected the stone circle of Drombeg in a previous lifetime so I knew you would be safe there. Do you remember now? Did you remember when you sat there by the fire pit? Could you feel the energy of community and of welcome?

By that time, the stones energies were fading. I could no longer teleport you there, but the Irish fishermen knew our suffering and were as disturbed by the Norman lords and their rape of the land as we were. Your rape enraged them further for you were young and beautiful and had always been kind to them when you passed them on the Old Road. So they took pity and they helped you escape.

The Normans were especially hard on us. They were not sure who we were. Word of our healing abilities intimidated them but they could not find us doing anything against their laws or their God. We worked the land and our crops surpassed all others, our berries were the plumpest, our sheep the wooliest and our lambs the most succulent. When their lordship stayed at the Shanagarry Tower House, they came to us for his food. He wanted the best and his servants knew that. We grew the best food so they came to us.

We ministered to the oppressed. We suffered with them but we also taught them things that they had forgotten, like how to commune with the devas of form and get help from the elementals, not just for planting but to hide from and to resist the invaders.

Celtic Christianity was closer to our ways than to this new form of Christianity the Normans brought over in their boats. Like the Vikings before them, the Normans ravaged the countryside; but these ones also took pains to destroy the Irish way of viewing the world. Nature and The Mother had no place in their patriarchy. The Mother directed us to help keep her name alive. Even as they elevated Mary in the Roman way, they destroyed the true spirit of the Divine Feminine wherever they could. No Mother wishes to be on a pedestal. She wishes to be among her children, to be love and to create anew. Just as Jesus wished to be seen as a shepherd to His flock, not a sign of crucifixion, sin and suffering.

Her energies, the energies of the Earth were being suppressed. People began thinking smaller and smaller. Bowing to raw power, succumbing to the abuse, believing themselves unworthy. Conformity and subjugation replaced sovereignty, not just women but men too. Both lost their sense of self, souls got weary…

We had promised the Ancient Ones we would protect the portals. I was so proud of you, dear one. You suffered through, you remembered your lessons and you put your gifts to good use in service of the Mother.

Whoa. That sure is a lot to take in. It all came up so fast I didn't think to record it. I get out my journal and write away madly. This serves two purposes: I capture the story before it overwhelms me and fades away; and it calms and grounds me to go through the physical motion of writing and seeing words on the page.

A notification of a text interrupts as I am finishing up. CynDee has a ride to the Design Center so I do not have to pick her up. Good, because I feel a little too wobbly to drive.

I take time to shake off all the feelings attached to the dungeon experience. The release comes much easier today than yesterday. I thank Jane for having my past-self connect with me. That allowed me to hear it firsthand but not experience the raw pain I felt yesterday. I thank my past self as well.

As I leave the ruins and walk back into the park, my friendly groundskeeper comes over to say good morning. I have this vague sense that he is my protector. Was he the guard who helped me in that other lifetime? Or is it simply that his presence in the park gave me a feeling that I had back up if I needed it? It all is too much for me to bring up. I can't even speak yet. Fortunately, he doesn't ask anything of me, but just talks about the storm brewing to the west. I explain that I am meeting someone, say goodbye and thank him in the weakest of voices.

I then begin walking to the Design Center, which is right next to the church. I feel better walking. I feel with each step I am coming to terms with what I have heard. It was so unbelievable that it hasn't completely registered.

I so wish Mark was here. He isn't, but the church is. There are no cars in the parking lot but the church door is unlocked. I go in and take a pew in the back and just start sobbing. Sobbing and shaking, I just allow the release to continue.

On some level none of it is real. On another level it is all too real. Images came to mind that could be from a movie. They can't be from a life of mine. But Jane says they are and what she says and what the other version of myself says ring true. Maybe I never saw or experienced my guides because I have blocked the ability to see or experience my past. Maybe, now that I realize and have named the fact that I was raped and imprisoned, I am free. Knowing I survived such degradation and pain in a past life may be the key to my fully living this life. Finding myself in the stones, listening to my story, listening to the dark as well as the light. It is all right here before me.

I pray once more with a grateful heart. I specifically ask for the complete release of this past life experience. I place it all in a bubble of white light and ask the angels to lift it up and away. I ask to be free of it. I offer gratitude for the strength the experience is giving me. I ask for release from any fear, pain, or anger that remains. Only when a beam of light crosses the altar do I feel heard. I have been released. I know in my heart that all will be well. I add a deep thank you to Jane for her insistence that I explore the life I lived along the Old Road. I pray for guidance that a new road, a new story will emerge.

At first, I assume I will have left CynDee waiting. After all, it feels like I have experienced and released an entire lifetime since her text message. But, actually, I arrive first. The tea room is to the back and the wide expanse of windows offers an amazing view of the bay, the island and the lighthouse. I sit where I can look out to the sandy beach—where I now know the old road used to be, where I can see the island that now has even more significance to me. I go over the escape images in my mind. This time they are less vivid and the feeling I get is being grateful to be free rather than the feeling of running in desperation and fear. I find myself feeling more grateful than upset.

I have been given a window into the past. I feel stronger and more powerful and more capable than ever before. It was jarring, but already I am feeling better for having experienced it. And I am really excited that now I can once again connect with my mom, and now also to Jane and to my past self—awesome.

And here's CynDee.

"That was totally fabulous. I loved the chef. He is dreamy with a great accent and the kindest eyes. He said he never works in someone else's kitchen, but made an exception for Ballymaloe. He was so smooth," she gushes.

"Did you learn anything?" I ask, teasingly.

"A little, but mainly I just watched everybody and listened to the chatter. I was the only American so it was really fun to meet all these Irish women. I feel like I have been totally immersed in the Sullivan family for two weeks—a fortnight, you know, and these women were from all over Ireland, and like our age mostly and very interesting."

"The whole thing was fantastic," she reports. "I signed up for a full day tomorrow. The place is beautiful and the chef's really nice—and knowledgeable. It is the best day I have had. I loved it!"

"That was gonna be my next question," I chuckle, enjoying her exuberance.

"You can tell I liked it, huh?" she grins. "Tomorrow we do a whole dinner, then stay to eat what we made and after lunch work on fancy desserts. I got talking to two women from Cork—Cork City, I should say—who are taking a couple of days off for 'holiday'. Once I got used to the fast pace of their talk and their accent, we had a ball. I love hearing about different families and how people do stuff. And they had great suggestions of places to really party in Cork City when Jack and I go back."

"So, they are coming back tomorrow too?" I ask.

"Yeah. Oh! I asked if you could join us for lunch but they only serve those who are taking a class."

"Thanks for trying, but it's OK. Ready to hear what I did this morning? Brace yourself. First, I went back to that door we found yesterday. Then, a voice came to me…"

"Jane? You finally spoke to Jane on your own?"

"Not at first. The voice was actually me—me in the lifetime I spent here."

"You're kiddin'. What the…"

"I got more of a sense of her and the words just came inside my head. She basically told me I had been torn away from Jane and my community by this lord who went into a rage when I wouldn't marry him. He raped me and kept me in that dungeon. After she told me that, she faded away and Jane came. She described my escape—along the Old Road and out to the island. Then I was sneaked by boat to Glandore and lived at Drombeg. It all makes sense now."

"Holy moly, this is like one of my romance paperbacks. Are you OK? You seem so calm. And here I was blathering on about cooking school. I am so sorry."

"I am surprisingly OK. I mean it is not as if it happened here in this lifetime. While it shook me and felt really weird as she spoke to me, I didn't feel the pain like I did yesterday. I sat stunned for a good long bit. I wrote in my journal until your text came in. Then, as I was leaving that sweet groundskeeper came and chatted. You know, it just dawned on me. I think in the other lifetime, he could well have been the guard who helped me escape! That gives me chills."

After a quick breath, I continue, "Anyway, then I stopped at the church for a good cry and prayer. I had a catharsis of sorts and am feeling OK now. I was glad you called to say you had a ride over here. The time in the church and then the time here looking out at the island have calmed me."

"Honey, this is all amazing. I can't believe you are taking it so well."

"Ever had a feeling there was a deep, dark secret about you and then finding out what it is and realizing the feeling before was worse than how you felt after? I kind of feel freer. I named it and released it and now it has no hold over me," I say proudly.

"Let's just hope that remains true, Honey. I do hope you are done with it. Here comes our server. Think you can eat?"

"Yeah, actually I am starved."

So I have a cup of soup and some wonderful brown bread while CynDee just gets dessert, her yummy looking sticky toffee pudding. She says she had lots of rich samples during class but no desserts. I envy her metabolism. I gain weight just looking at dessert. But I have a bite just to see what I am missing.

"I learned today that the Irish, and I guess the Brits, too, call lots of things 'pudding'. There are the black and white breakfast sausages called puddings, there are Yorkshire pudding variations, there are these dense steamed puddings. I think having any dessert is called 'having pudding'. I am fixin' to try them all." CynDee's infectious laugh brings attention to our table from those around us.

"So how about some shopping therapy? I walked right back here to the café and skipped over all that gorgeous stuff. Did you look yet? I bought a couple of things with Jack when we were in the downtown store so I'm good here, but I can't wait to get to the pottery gallery."

"So let's walk down there and have a look. Pottery is so heavy, I can't imagine schlepping any home, but I would love to look and to help you spend your money."

"Ha," she says with a grin.

The lane back to the pottery gallery comes to a fork, with a private mansion to the left. We take a peek. Then we return to the right fork. There is a parking lot to the side and then just beyond the gallery we see the entrance to an old cemetery.

"Can we have a look down there first? It is in line with the Old Road if we assume it extended behind the castle and along the bay."

"I love all the honeysuckle and these old Celtic crosses," she comments as we walk.

"Hey, guess what? I am getting a message, loud and clear," I say with excitement.

"Go, girl. So is it Jane?"

"Something about Celtic crosses, not sure, yeah, I think it is Jane."

Remember. Past, present and future are represented by your Celtic Cross. The spirit of Stonehenge, of Orkney, of Drombeg, of all the stone circles is kept alive in the circle at the center of the cross.

The magic of the Newgrange spiral, the labyrinth, the circle and the cross are all part of the sacred geometry. They are keys to keeping the portals open to the Otherworld. Keep opening to the Ancient Mysteries. There is so much to be told.

"OK, don't know what I am supposed to do with that, but OK I will try."

"This is getting weirder. The past life stuff is hard enough to get my arms around, but portals and time being simultaneous? Holy moly, here we go again. Aren't you getting a little freaked out by all this?" CynDee asks. "Let's go have a look in the shop."

There actually is a potter at work whom I watch while CynDee shops. CynDee buys a few items and has them shipped while I browse. I find a beautiful display of pottery with the Newgrange triple spiral. I choose a small flat piece that can be a serving plate for cheese and bring it to the counter.

"Know anything about the old castle ruins?" I ask the young clerk.

"Sure, the owner here owns those old ruins too. At least, I think he still owns it. He was going to make it into some kind of shopping centre but the plans fell through. That's all I know."

"I will check it out online, then, thanks."

We decide to go back to Ballycotton for a cliff walk. Each of us walks with our own thoughts and at our own pace. CynDee singing a tune and I wrapped up in the events of the morning and their meaning. The walk is breathtaking.

Jane comes to me.

> *Aye, my cara, this was your escape route. You were safe with us the night of the escape, but we knew they would come looking for you at first light. The watchman on the big island was a friend; He agreed to hide you until the following night when you could leave in the darkness. You were whisked off to our people in Glandore. You were safe; there you protected the ancient portal and there you kept the mysteries alive through your stories and your leadership.*

> *Others also endured pain, violation and degradation—our sisters, all our people suffered much throughout the centuries of serving and protecting the Mother. You cannot truly tell the story without acknowledging the suffering. More importantly, remember the support, the love, the courage of those who got you to safety.*

> *I am so proud of you, my cara. You are owning and releasing all of it. You are safe now. You are complete now. You are ready to tell the stories.*

After walking in silence with all that, I finally shout out to CynDee that I think I will head back to the hotel for a nap. She comes closer so we can talk, saying she is thinking of walking in to the shops and checking out a salon, if there is one.

We walk together to the place where I split off to go to the hotel. I am glad for the time alone. It has been a long and stressful day.

Abruptly, she turns back toward me. "Honey, what are we doing? We should be celebrating not getting all somber. If you are to totally release all that you have been through we have to move, dance, shake it all out. Let go, really let go. I say we go down to the beach, put our toes in, skip some rocks, dance and run until we are out of breath, then collapse on the sand—with chocolate…and wine. You go down now. I will run up to the room and get us a bottle of wine and the chocolate and be right behind you."

She is quite something and, once again, her instincts are spot on.

CHAPTER THIRTEEN

CynDee is so right. The beach is cleansing and wondrously refreshing. My nap is all the better after the physical movement and the wine.

CynDee still goes to the shops. When she gets back, we turn on the TV to check the weather while getting ready for dinner. The news remains the same, "storm warning."

"I can't believe we still haven't heard from them. Nothing, not even from Katie." I shake my head in frustration.

"My guess is that they were waiting to see what the storm was going to do and then got caught up in getting to a safe berth and don't have a new plan for tomorrow yet. Jack would just assume that I wasn't worrying, because I know what a good sailor Sean is. After all, Sean knows these waters and these weather patterns. I think he has even sailed in the Fastnet Race."

"That makes sense—and Mark is so damn non-anxious that he probably isn't concerned, not even realizing that I will be concerned."

"Does his calm, mild manner irritate you?" she asks.

"Sometimes I feel as confused as Lois Lane, dating both Clark Kent and Superman."

"Honey, no offense but that makes absolutely no sense."

"Well, I love his easy going, supportive, thoughtful self. Sometimes though, like with Lois and Clark, I want him to just react, get mad, get passionate.

"Honey cut to the chase. Are you saying he is not good in bed?"

"No, he is fine in that department," I laugh. "I guess it is that I am always waiting for the other shoe to drop; you know, to hear he is harboring resentments, particularly about my independence—back to this whole sovereignty thing. Flashbacks to life with my ex who would just blow up now and again, like a volcano if he felt his power had been threatened."

"Well, lose that image. You may have chosen fire and bluster the first time around. Now you have chosen water and flow. Anyway, did it ever dawn on you that he might like your independence? Maybe that is what he really likes about you. The man is not nineteen, you know. I would guess he knows what he wants and what he doesn't want. As the Sullivan women here in Ireland would say: 'Get yourself sorted, dear'."

"Hmm." I say no more.

"Now, do tell about the Superman part."

I laugh again, "You sure have a way of getting me out of my mumble jumble of words, don't you? I guess I mean that the part of him that is always protecting people, championing people and causes. I really like that. But he doesn't do it in some super macho way. It is with a quiet strength I adore. Maybe Superman isn't the right image. It isn't about super powers. But it is this non-violent strength and constant readiness to come-to-the-rescue vibe I really like."

"So, tell me again, what's the problem?" She pauses for effect and then adds, "Just sayin'."

I toss my pillow at her in jest.

After playfully picking up another pillow and holding it up against her chest, she says "Truce. Let's go to dinner. How about back at the pub on the hill, the one in the Inn? Maybe our RNLI guys will be there. We can have a drink at the bar and then eat in the dining room. The food is delicious. We can see what their take is on the impending storm."

We are greeted right away upon arrival. "Now, Arty, would you look at who's back now. Our favorite American ladies. Will ye not have a drink with us?" Ian asks.

We tell them about finding the Old Road and about our visit to the lighthouse and CynDee's cooking class. Not sure they understand her accent, but they laugh at the right places. We do not mention my past life story and thankfully they don't ask why we were looking for the Old Road.

Their take on the storm is that it will come in the night, that it is not a "raging disaster" and that "our lads" will hear the weather report and take heed.

After a second drink, we say goodnight and go into the dining room for dinner at a window seat overlooking the water and within sight of the island. It holds even more magic on this gloomy night. I shudder to think of my past life experience. The notion of being hidden and protected by the watchman brings tears.

"Are you OK?" asks CynDee. "You aren't letting yourself get upset about the storm, are you? Everyone is saying there really is no need to worry."

"Well, I am trying to heed the advice but, truthfully, I am worried. But just now I was thinking about my escape from the dungeon and the watchman who protected me in that lifetime."

"Honey, I don't have any experience with this past life stuff, but it stands to reason that it is going to take some time to get beyond it. Even if you did do this big release, some stuff will remain and need sorting. If we can have flashbacks to traumas in this lifetime, I suppose we can have them to a past lifetime. Be gentle with yourself."

"You're right and seeing the lighthouse and knowing its beam shines brightly out into the sea is reassuring. There was no lighthouse in the days of the other story and still Jane, my mother and the others survived and made it to land. The guys will be OK." Silently, I add a prayer: *Great Mother/Father God, let that be true. Please keep them safe.*

Dinner is delicious but rich and filling. Despite the drizzle, we walk a bit before returning to the hotel. CynDee finishes telling me about her afternoon uptown after we played on the beach. Each of her stories, of course, is funnier than the last. Jane should be putting the storytelling on CynDee, not me.

Once more, before going to bed, we text the guys and Katie. No word back.

"I still can't believe we haven't heard from the guys about when they are coming in and where. What do they think? That we are just sitting around waiting? That they came to Ireland for a long guys' only weekend? That we don't have things we want to do too?" CynDee complains.

"The Hag of Beara," I murmur.

"What?"

"You know, the story of the Hag of Beara that I am to tell? It is the first one that I feel I now can tell with any depth of understanding. And I get its importance to today's world. I don't know how I tell the story, but hopefully that will be revealed to me. And I trust that Mark will have some insight to share.

"Still don't get what you are driving at, Honey. How does she fit in with our guys being jerks about contacting us?" she asks.

"You know that Mark and I visited the rock on the north shore of Beara near Eyeries. Legend has it that it represents the Hag waiting for her husband/lover Manannan, God of the Sea, to return. I got these intense feelings of anger from the stone about how the story gets depicted. Later legends, written I say by men, have her sitting waiting for her man, Manannan, to return from sea. Somehow the fact that she was a goddess with immense powers is ignored. Instead she is memorialized in one story at least as passively sitting, waiting. So, I spout off at Mark, about how she was the goddess, not Tammy Wynette 'waiting for her man'. You should have seen the look on his face! But he was cool, only a bit defensive. It started our whole amazing conversation about sovereignty. So now I am saying I don't want to be that woman just sitting waiting for her man to come home from sea. At the same time, I want to go down to the jetty and sit there waiting and praying for him to come in."

"Honey, you two are way too academic for me. All I know is that Jack is going to hear from me about it—and he is going to take me to a fancy romantic place for dinner."

"To tell you the truth, while I have been missing Mark and while I have had the storm warnings playing non-stop in the back of my head, I have totally lost track of the days."

"Humph. I forgot too. Earlier today, I signed up for cooking school class for tomorrow not even thinking about it being day five of their trip. And I'm the one who insisted Jack go no longer than five days."

"Well, I say go ahead with it. Either I can pick them up somewhere on my own or they can just hang out until you are done with class and we can go together. Ha, they can wait for us, huh? When I think about it, there is no reason they can't hang out until we are ready to come after them. And I don't know about Jack, but Mark would say, 'of course we can, who said I was demanding you be there waiting'?'"

"True. Jack would probably just shrug and go get a beer and text me the name of the bar."

"Why do we let ourselves get so caught up in roles and expectations and even worse, in imagining and anticipating others' expectations?" I ask with exasperation at myself.

"That's just how we were reared. And because we love them and because it is damn hard to balance independence and partnership," my wise friend opines.

"Yeah." I pause to let that ripple across my mind. "You know, Mark is always saying that in pastoral counseling all he really did was urge communication, communication and more communication. Not having cell service sure points out how important communication is, doesn't it?"

"Uh-huh. So, if I go ahead with cooking class, what are you doing tomorrow?"

"I actually would love a day, sitting out on the terrace, writing. The mandate to find myself and tell the stories has been with me since day one of the trip. I want to reflect on how finding out the story of this past life is helping me find myself. I feel it has, but I need to go deeper into it."

"Well, it certainly explains your fear of the sea for one thing," CynDee observes.

"Hadn't thought about that, but you are right. And it would explain my trust issues with men. I would like to reflect on that before Mark gets here. I know I hold back and he has given me absolutely no reason not to trust him."

"Well, that's a day's work," CynDee laughs.

"So, you mean I won't actually have time to also write a draft of my first novel? You certainly keep me real, girl. Have I thanked you for being here and helping me? You have been more than Ethel to my Lucy. I can't thank you enough," I say with tears in my eyes.

Then she gets a more serious tone. "You know, Honey, that these fears and all your emotions are connected, right? You have amped up the worry thing since you found out about the Old Road. Don't let fear get to you. Choose love not fear. Always chose LOVE." She pauses for a brief second and then starts in again, "It's been an amazing ride. Who would have thought my visit to Ireland would be all woo-woo stuff about channeling and past lives and myths and legends and ancient mysteries? If I didn't like the cooking class so much, I might stay back to be part of this 'getting sorted,' too. It is so fascinating. But what are you going to do if the wind and rain get bad? I hope you won't freak."

"I am going to sit by the window in our lovely lobby and drink tea, try not to worry and try to concentrate on Jane stuff. Or maybe, instead of tea, I will drink wine or even Jameson's if it is really stormy. Now that I think about it, I first want to go to the Design Center café for breakfast. Want to come too, before your cooking class? I so love that view. And if I want to keep an eye on the storm, that is the place. Then I will come back here to work."

"Sure. And really, are we agreed that we are going to tell the guys to hold tight that we will pick them up after cooking class?" CynDee asks.

"Yeah, works for me. Then they can come back here, wash up and take us out for a fabulous dinner as you suggested," I add.

"Well, we have that sorted. I know the perfect place. The people who started the cooking school have a restaurant and guesthouse just down the road, Ballymaloe House. It is rated as one of the top hundred in the world, not Ireland, Honey, but The World."

"Well then, we have to go. Sounds fantastic."

Just before turning in for the night I write Mark a long email and a short text. There still is no word from them. I urge CynDee to check in with Katie. She does, and reports Katie's reply is "No word, but no worries." We check the weather a final time on the television and online. No 24/7 weather station TV channel but we get weather.com. Same report: "Storm coming sometime around midnight or after. Small Craft warning in effect for entire southern coast of Ireland."

"Remember, Honey. No worries. Pleasant dreams. Dream of fine dining tomorrow night in Ballymaloe." CynDee turns out the lights and I hear her turn over and fall to sleep almost instantly.

I lie awake awhile reviewing all the voices that said not to worry about the storm and then nod off.

Pounding rain wakens me and the wind and waves raging outside. It is pitch-black and at first, I can't get my bearings. Then the phone rings. It is Ian from the pub. "Lass, I thought ye would want to know that the lifeboat call came in and a rescue is in progress as we speak. Your man, now, is still at sea, is he now? What is the name of his vessel?"

"I don't remember. My God! I don't remember. I know there was a name on the side of the boat, but I wasn't paying any attention... what happened? Has the boat capsized? Are the men in this freezing water? How far out? Oh my. What a disaster!" I see Mark in the water, flailing. He has his life jacket on, but the waves, the swell, like those pictures of the Lusitania. Oh, My. God. I need to wake CynDee. I need her to call Katie; I don't care if it is the middle of the night. No worries, she said. I promise I will come back in one piece, he said. And now, there he is out in this raging storm. Damn it. But maybe it isn't them. We need to know the name of the boat. Why didn't it register with me? Why didn't I write it down?

Things have been going so smoothly. So easy to think we are immune, invulnerable when things are going smoothly. Mark is always saying "all will be well." But what if it isn't? What if he drowns? Oh. My. God. I can't breathe. I can see the big orange lifeboat bobbing up and down, slowly heading out to sea to find them. "Hurry, hurry," I yell. "Hurry, damn it, hurry!"

"Abby! Abby, what the hell? Are you OK? Wake up, wake up. You are having a nightmare. Wake up, Honey. It's OK. Whatever you think, it is OK. You are here with me in Ballycotton. You are OK," she says as she shakes me. "Is it about your past life? Are you in the dungeon? Out at sea? What's wrong?"

She finally gets through to me and I just burst into tears in her arms.

"What was all that about? That dungeon and past life stuff? Jane should have left you alone."

"No, it was about Mark and Jack. I dreamed that Ian called, you know the guy from the pub, saying that the guys were going down at sea. God, it was so vivid. I never dream like that."

"Let's give you a shot of Jack's whiskey and get you calmed down. You are shaking like a leaf."

"I heard this pounding rain, but, actually, it isn't even storming that much outside, is it?"

"No. It is not a gale-force storm by my reckoning. What got into you?"

"I don't know." I shake my head.

After encouraging me to sip the whiskey and to breathe slowly and deeply between sips, CynDee asks "Do you think you can go back to sleep now?"

"I think I exhausted myself and that whiskey is doing the trick. Yes, and I am so sorry I woke you. Thank you, again. Thank you."

"Well, if my soufflé falls tomorrow in cooking class it will be all your fault."

"You are going to make soufflés?" I ask drowsily.

"Go to sleep, Lucy,"

"Good night, Ethel."

The sunshine streaming in the window wakes me from a deep sleep. I don't hear any noise and look over to find CynDee's bed is empty. I drag myself to the shower, then get back under the covers to dry off and mull over what happened last night. I cringe as I remember my nightmare. I am embarrassed about waking CynDee and still a bit rattled by how vivid my dream was. I have never been clairvoyant and pray that the dream was not a premonition.

In the light of day, I have more clarity and I very much doubt there was anything to it other than having suppressed my worries. Everyone told me not to worry, but in truth I was scared. And if I am truly honest, maybe I also was surprised how much this guy means to me, how devastated I would be if he was no longer part of my life.

CynDee pops back into the room. "Hey, Honey, rise and shine. We best get going. I just went down for coffee, texted Katie and checked the weather. She hasn't gotten back to me, but it seems that storm wasn't as bad as predicted and for sure the lifeboat guys were not called out. I was told practically everybody in town gets an alert when the boat is going out and it hasn't happened since last October according to the gal at the desk."

"That's a relief. Thanks for checking and for last night. Sorry I woke you," I say sheepishly.

"No problem. Now let's hustle. I am starved. I can't work with food all day on an empty stomach."

We both have quiche and salmon for breakfast as we look out at the island we have come to love so much. "Not only does it command this whole bay, but it is so different: a black lighthouse sitting on a mound of perfectly manicured grass, rather than a white lighthouse placed on a rocky point. Still has an iconic look about it."

"Aren't you becoming the lighthouse expert?" she teases.

"Seriously, it is so different. It feels so much more gentle than the others. All it needs is a flock of sheep grazing on the hill. It is kind of pastoral. Remember the *Little Prince* finding his sheep? That's the feeling I get," I muse.

"Never heard of your little prince, but it does have a gentle sense of power, doesn't it? We better get going. I don't want to be late to class. Ha, don't think I ever said those words before," she chuckles.

• • •

After leaving CynDee off, I am drawn back to the tower and the castle ruins. One last time, I tell myself. I want to see if I have truly released the experience; and if not, sort out why. The path is getting well worn by now. I calmly approach the old door and sit on my stump. Perhaps Jane will come. And she does:

Aye, my cara, Knowledge of this story sets you free. You will remember the story and you will tell the story, but you also will be released from the fear, the pain, the victimization you once felt.

Aye, this is where you were imprisoned. This is where you were violated. This is where a single, small worm of a man, one of wealth and power aggrieved you for not surrendering yourself to him. He would not accept that you were bequeathed to follow the goddess, to be a priestess and storyteller among your community, to carry the flame to others. He was attracted to your light, but he wanted to possess it.

The dark dungeon, like the darkness over the land had to be overcome by light. Failure to honor the firmament and the earth created great danger. You were a light worker. Your example was important for all to see. The story of your escape was the story of love and light overcoming darkness and abuse of power. It had to happen. It had to happen so the story could be told. For many years, it helped people find the courage to stand up to abuse. Your story, like the stories of so many women of the light, was lost. Now, you have it back. You must tell it.

I was with you the night of your escape. I met you and the guardsman who helped you escape along the causeway and took you to our island. I so wanted you to stay with us. You had become like a daughter to me after your mother's death. We had traveled in sisterhood from settlement to settlement bringing the message of Avalon to renew the Irish spirit. The locals were drowning under the accursed Normans. We were more than sisters in community, we were light workers.... I helped bring you into the world. I cared for you when your mother no longer could. You were the child I never was able to bear. You were beloved among us. Men and women alike teared at the thought of having to send you away, but we knew we must.

When you escaped under moonlight, the Goddess was with you, my cara, and she is with you now. You were to tell the story of The Divine Feminine then, and you are to do so now. Healing is in the story. Balance comes from honoring the Feminine as well as the Masculine. Tell them, tell those who have eyes to see. Call them to Divine Purpose.

Our sister community beyond the big bay agreed to take you in, to continue your training and give you a home. A small group went with you, sailing off the next night before the protection of the tides was lifted and before the soldiers came searching. I watched from the cliff as you sailed off to the west. It was too dark to see you leave, but I looked out to sea for a long time anyway and prayed to the Mother that you would be well.

I never saw you after you left us—at first it was too dangerous, I might have been followed. The lord of the tower was mighty angry and revengeful. We all stayed clear. We were all watched. I would hear of you. Of your service to the Mother…by then my body was forsaking me and travel could I not, but I kept track of your doings. I sent my prayers and my love. Did you feel it? Do you feel it now, dear one? Will you tell the story—the love, the sacrifice, the sense of Oneness with the Universe—Mother Earth, Father Sky and the Sea together bringing the deep waters of the sacred wells to meet the roaring waters of the ocean vast?

And now you see the fierce ocean forces must be balanced by the soft gentle breezes. The sun, the moon, and the stars all align to bring us light and balance. And when we are love and light, all is well. And all will be well. So it has been said through eternity.

Take up the charge in your new lifetime. Be Fiercely Feminine. Let love and light and will be known. Tell the stories, my cara. Tell the stories.

CHAPTER FOURTEEN

My head is so full. I head straight toward the hotel to write without delay. Strange how much like home it is beginning to feel after only a few days. I feel as though the corner of the terrace facing the island belongs to me. My first stop is at the Ballycotton Stores and Post Office to buy a new writing pad. I like working with yellow pads and am hoping to find one there. Also, I want a new pen, a souvenir pen, but a good pen I can dedicate to this tell-the-story crusade, for which I have been recruited. No. Drafted. Bless you, Jane, it has been quite a ride and I am overwhelmed by all the stories you want me to tell, all the expectations you have of me, and the emotions you have stirred up with this past life stuff.

The shop doesn't have yellow pads, but it has spiral notebooks. I buy three. Their scrumptious looking tea biscuits call to me. I take some for my lunch. And I get two big pieces of chocolate loaf. That I learn is the Irish term for big squares of chocolate cake with chocolate icing, Mark's favorite. I have been so caught up in the revisit to the tower this morning that I feel kind of guilty. I forgot to check to see if they called. They have not. Strangely, I am no longer worried or anxious about their safety. They will be home soon.

Meanwhile, I intend to write. Not sure if I am writing because I am to write an article or book or if I only need to make notes to tell oral stories. I do know that I must capture what I can as soon as possible, before it disappears from memory. Also, I have so much swirling around in my head that I am looking to unload some of it to paper.

I have always been active and involved but never a torchbearer. I stood in front of a classroom for years, but never did much public speaking. I wrote curricula but never stories. Not only am I feeling emotionally overwhelmed by these experiences at the stones, but I am overwhelmed by the daunting task Jane has given me.

But I am not one to shirk a duty, so I roll up my sleeves to see what I can do. I get set up in the lobby by the window looking out toward the lighthouse, making myself right at home. It is too cold to sit out on the terrace. In fact, I position myself as far away from the door as possible to avoid a draft. I also want my back to the reception desk, so I can nibble on my tea biscuits later. With great formality and ritual, I unwrap my new pen and notebooks and get myself organized. First glitch is how to label the notebooks. There is the Hag story. There is the story of the lineage from the Ancient Ones to Avalon and beyond. Then there are the Celtic mysteries, stories held by the stone circles, the story of my past life and the story of how learning about past lives impacts my present life. What do I do with it all?

Tell the story of the Mother. Tell the stories of the triple goddesses. Tell how the early Celtic Church embraced the Divine Feminine through Brigit and the three Marys.

Yes, and tell our story of time here in Ballycotton. Tell of how we struggled to keep the Spirit of the Mother alive as the Normans were systematically wiping out the Old Religion and early Celtic Christianity.

Tell of the forces that shunned those of us who followed Her way, besmirched Her character, destroyed many of our ritual sites that celebrated and kept balance in the hearts and minds of the people. More and more folks listened to those Masculine forces that sought to remove the Divine Feminine. To replace Her Love and Light with Power and Will; To make the Christ-energy into a warrior energy. And tell of the forces for good, for balance, for community from Camelot to Kildare.

You heard these stories as a child. We were grooming you to be a priestess like myself. Tell them to help reclaim the Divine Feminine. Help the world find balance once again.

"Jane! Stop!" I scream. Then I lower my voice. "This is too much, too much. I am only one person, I cannot right the wrongs of centuries of abuse and neglect and wrong thinking. Give me a break."

"Ma'am, are you alright now?" asks the clerk as she comes around to the center of the lobby.

"I am fine. Just lost it over something I was reading. So sorry to disturb you. At least there were no guests out here. I do apologize." I feel so stupid.

"Perfectly fine. 'Tis fine. No worries. You make yourself at home now."

She must think I am a total idiot. When I shake off my embarrassment, I turn my attention back to Jane.

Using my inside voice, literally, I try to talk with Jane:

Forgive me for the outburst, Jane. Please know that I am so appreciative and humbled that you reached out to me. Your persistence motivated me to open up, to listen not only to you but to my mom and to dimensions beyond what I knew to be possible. You guided me to face unacknowledged blocks within me—my shadow and my fears. Already, I feel more trusting, more expansive, more secure. I do appreciate the love and the confidence in me that you have expressed. I deeply thank you and hope you will remain as my guide.

I will not give up on your request to tell the stories. But I can't deal with the intensity I am experiencing. I'm new to this, I am not even sure what "this" is. Maybe it is about vibration or frequency, like when you said back at Drombeg that you could not continue channeling through CynDee. That it exhausted you. I am exhausted too. Exhilarated in many ways, but over-whelmed and exhausted by what you are asking of me.

Right now, it makes my head swim. It is overtaking my present life, and making me question whether I can do any of it. You keep repeating your command and piling it on. I cannot deal with it all. You have had this bottled up waiting for me to open to it for what—centuries? But it is all new to me and overwhelming. Please ease up. I am trying.

There's a magic question I used to teach my students that applies here, I think: In what ways might we make this work? Please help me with that. I don't want you to go away. I just need you to ease up and offer up clues as to how to do it. Guide me.

I feel heard but there is no answer or response.

I do settle down and write though. The question of "In what ways might I make this work?" re-energizes me. I start with a timeline. After classroom teaching for 25 years, my lesson planning skills kick in and I feel at home with a process of capturing information and chunking it into manageable pieces. I visually show the interfaces and overlaps and gaps. It helps me "get sorted" as my Irish friends say. That phrase keeps making me smile.

Next, I remember that I have recordings of some of Jane's messages on my phone. I take the time to save them up to the cloud while I have good wi-fi service. I have one more to go, when suddenly, someone is grabbing my shoulders from behind. I jump and let out another scream. The receptionist will surely think I am crazy.

I turn. It is Mark.

"Hey, Abs. Didn't mean to scare you." Then both Mark and Jack yell, "Surprise!" grinning ear to ear, tanned and scruffy looking—an outdoorsy look that is rather sexy. Mark's hug is intense and there is a longing in it that sure says he missed me.

"Where's CynDee?" Jack asks looking around the lobby while Mark continues to stand with his arm around me.

"Cooking class in Shanagarry, the next village over. We didn't know when you were coming so went ahead with plans," I offer without apology.

"Yeah, glad you did. We wanted to surprise you. We were excited when Doug and Sean told us that they could drop us off right here in Ballycotton. Our plan was to come in first thing this morning and catch you still in bed. But, with the storm, we had to moor further east last night. Anyway, we can't be late since you didn't know when we were coming, right?" This is Jack at his most charming.

I just start laughing—joyful that they are home safe, that they are in such good spirits and so happy to be back with us. I am sorry CynDee is missing this homecoming. I also am amused at myself for the worry, and fretting, and nightmare, and complaining that I put myself through unnecessarily, expectations and projections and roles and all that crap. I hope I have let go. Or at least I can see it for what it is as I go forward in this relationship. Sovereignty. Hag of Beara, thank you for your wisdom, your guidance, for giving me clarity.

I actually don't say any of that. But I do ask one question, "Guys, what were you going to do if we were out?"

"We figured we would need a second room tonight anyway, so we would just get a room, shower and get ready for when you returned. Then we would take you out for a nice meal."

"CynDee has an idea on that score. The cooking school people own a topnotch restaurant just a few miles from here."

"Why am I not surprised? Good though. Can't wait to see her, even though I know she'll bust my chops."

I never understand that kind of banter between couples, but *c'est la vie*. Maybe because I was an only child. Whatever. I simply reply, "The class ends at 3:30. Do you want to take the car or shall we all go?"

"I don't like the idea of driving your car without being on your insurance. Do you mind driving?" Jack answers.

"No. I don't mind. I was planning on it anyway," I reply.

"Hey, buddy, how about heading out to lunch on your own and we meet you back here at say 3:00 to go get her?" Mark suggests.

I jump in. "There's a great pub up the hill. We have been talking to two retired RNLI guys at the bar whom you will really like. Tell them that you are CynDee's man and they'll be delighted. In fact, if they are there, please buy them a pint on us. They were so kind when I was worrying about the storm. They were also great fun, good *craic* as they would say."

"It's a plan. I will go get the second room and then check out the pub. A hearty pub meal and a pint sound perfect. See you later."

"I desperately need a shower. Can I interest you in joining me?" Mark asks.

"Just a shower?" I tease. Then add, "I am so glad you are here. So much has happened that I want to share. Though right now, I have forgotten it all. I missed you. I was concerned when the storm came up. And I want to hear all about it." By then we are up in the room and have started undressing each other. No conversation needed.

Mark stops, "Before I go any further Abs, I need to know. Are you OK? I got your emails and this past life stuff and the dungeon and…everything. You didn't say it outright, but I guess you were raped as well as abused by that thug?" His tone is so gentle despite his outrage and his eyes are so beseeching.

"Yes, yes," I whisper. I start crying as he takes me in his arms and just holds me. When I stop crying, I repeat how good it is to have him home.

"Is this OK, Abs? Is it OK to touch you?" he asks as he draws me toward the shower.

I nod yes. Then in a moment, I find myself saying "Your kindness and love brought the tears. I am touched by your caring. But I am OK. I don't know how to describe what it was like to discover this past life and even harder to explain how it felt to relive its horrors. On some level, I felt the pain and the shame and the fear. Yet, at the same time it was muted, surreal. You know, like a walkthrough of a play not the real thing. I faced the darkness of it all. I know I released a lot of the emotion and the emotional baggage connected to the abuse and fear of being left in that hole of a dungeon. Then, I wonder if there is more work to do. Will there be other painful past lives to uncover?"

"Sounds like you did lots of work on your own. I am so sorry I was not here to support you."

"You are here now and that is all that matters," I say, wiping away the last of the tears.

"How about we first just stand in the shower, let the water wash over us. Cleansing, healing, renewing as it flows down and over our bodies. Even though the abuse you suffered was long ago or in some other dimension or whatever this is all about, may you be TOTALLY released from any lingering fears or hurts. May you feel whole. *All shall be well. All manner of things shall be well.*"

From shower to bed to the gentlest of love making to a depth of passion we had not yet experienced together. Time seems suspended. Three o'clock arrives and we scramble to dress to meet Jack. I give the chocolate loaf to Mark to eat in the car as we race to the lobby. After all, he missed lunch.

Jack grins but says nothing about our rushing in late. Then he talks a blue streak about the pub, its historic wall of lighthouse pictures and the guys with whom he shared a pint, or two. "Oh, and the guys taught me an Irish expression I am supposed to share with you and CynDee: *fáilte ar ais.* It means 'welcome back'. They said they have been waiting for you to return so they could teach it to you."

CynDee is as surprised to have Jack greet her as I was when they first arrived. She and her new friends walk out the door of the cooking school and Jack picks her up and twirls her around. She obviously enjoys it and seems to enjoy showing him off to her new Irish friends.

We all chatter back and forth on the way back to the hotel, not getting into much. Neither of us points out the Old Road or the tower, but we do go on and on about the big island. The guys share their perspective of coming in by sea. We share our impressions coming along the Garryvoe road.

"I booked a second room and already settled in and showered. I didn't think you would want to go in to Cork City tonight. I figured we would all want one last night together before splitting off to go our separate ways. Hope that is OK. And I also made the reservation for four at the Ballymaloe House. A little birdy told me that is the place to go for dinner tonight," Jack reports.

"Well, then, let me move my things over. You can help me settle in to the new room," CynDee replies with a wink. They go upstairs while we go for a long walk.

I show Mark the Old Road and tell him the story of finding it. We sit at the beach and discuss what it all has meant to me. We speculate on why this became a central theme of the trip and what the learnings are for each of us. We agree we both have grown through it all even though we experienced it differently. Mark holds to a kind of Jungian interpretation—that I am picking up on the collective unconscious and that the myths I have heard over the years are coming out, probably as catalysts for change, for exploring my shadow self. I, on the other hand, have totally come to believe in past lives and our power to let go and release past life trauma. I believe the spirit of my mother has led me to connection with the Divine Mother, and that Jane is the link.

"I love this kind of conversation. It has qualities that are hard to describe and hard to find in another person. Very special qualities," I say as I lean over to give him a kiss.

"Yep, not exactly easy to express on one of those match-up service profiles," Mark replies.

"I didn't know you had used a dating service. Tell me more."

"Well, I didn't really. I considered it but didn't have the heart, or the whatever, to sign up. Then I met you at the adult ed class and never gave it another thought. Shall we walk some more? I would like to take that cliff walk looking down on the harbor and get some shots of the lighthouse from that angle, especially with the sun behind us. It should be spectacular."

It is spectacular, even more so than the other day. "I think it is the light, the changing light on the water and the shadows it makes on the rocks and mountains that makes this such a fascinating and magical country," Mark observes.

"And the winds and breezes. I heard locals talk about 'enjoying the fresh' and I get it now—this sea air is gloriously cleansing and uplifting," I add as I twirl around for full effect.

"I think their ruddy cheeks come from the outdoors, not the pub. What I see is lots of people walking. While people meet and greet at the local pub, I have seen very few actually inebriated," Mark opines.

We return to get ready for dinner. This time we wait for CynDee and Jack. We are close to the restaurant, so we have plenty of time. Mark drives which allows me to get a good look at the stone wall and beachfront as we drive out of town back toward Shanagarry. I point to the well-marked turnoff for Ballymaloe. We follow a long, open lane back to the manor house. Several buildings have been tastefully added to the manor house grounds; more accommodations it appears.

The grounds are beautiful. Tall, old growth hardwoods, flowering white and purple bushes of different varieties and shades with enough mowed grass to create two golf courses. We walk together for a while, down what could be a fairy path. Then the guys go to look at the stables while CynDee and I check out the gift shop.

"How'd we miss this wonderful café?" CynDee asks as we see the signs for tempting breakfast and lunch specials, and some remaining loaves of soda bread in the bakery case. "I could eat my way around Ireland. It will be kind of sad to leave. Though, I got to say, I am getting itchy. The girls report everything is OK at the salon, but it is time. It's like the circus act of spinning plates. You got to keep giving them a boost to keep them twirlin'"

"I will miss you. And I will be forever grateful for your companionship and support through this exploration amid the stones."

"Now, girl, the Irish would say 'amidst the stones'. It has been my pleasure. Will I have stories to tell when I get home. Ha. That will please Jane, an extra bonus. That is, I hope she trusts me to get it right. She never paid me any mind. So, what's the latest with her anyway?"

"That's right, I didn't tell you. Right before the guys came back, I had a big meltdown with Jane. After I left you off at the cooking school, I made another stop at the tower and then came back to write. She started talking again, at both places. You know, that intense, beseeching, driving voice. Going over what she has said but in a different order and with new information added. I just got so overwhelmed. I shouted for her to stop."

"Really? Holy moly. You shouted at a spirit? I never heard tell. How did she take that?" CynDee is more flustered than I have ever seen her.

"She was silent. After I collected myself, I apologized. I thanked her and asked her to work with me."

"What did she say to that?" CynDee asks more calmly.

"Nothing. Total silence. But shortly after that I really got to work. I felt inspired and I got a lot done. So, I took that as a sign she understood and was helping me get started."

"Good for you. You own it now, girl. It's that sovereignty thing again. I would like to think she respects you for it and is going to help you rather than push you," CynDee offers.

"I like that interpretation. Frankly, since Mark got back, I haven't been thinking about telling the stories. Although, of course, I am telling him the story. It all kind of spirals around, doesn't it?"

"Speaking of the guys, let's get them and head in for dinner."

• • •

The manor house itself is quintessentially Ireland. Yet, it is a country elegance aspect that we hadn't chosen until now. I could get used to it though. At least, now and again, it would be nice. The stone building, bedecked in ivy and flowering rhododendrons, has a white entry with a classic, high fan-shaped window above the door. I can imagine women in long gowns and men in tuxes milling around before a formal banquet.

The floral arrangements in the foyer are exquisite. There are more flowers on each table and in every nook. The best of Irish white linen and tasteful Irish china, crystal and place setting with more knives and forks than I know how to use adorn each table. I feel under-dressed to say the least. But CynDee and the guys are nonplussed so I try to "get over myself" as the Irish say.

For starters (what the Irish call appetizers) everyone else wants oysters and mussels while I go for a beet salad. We all have a tough time choosing entrées. Ireland is known for its beef, its lamb, its salmon and its duck and all are on the menu. We finally order one of each with a plan to share. The plates come beautifully presented with snippets of herbs and little edible flowers, all presumably from the extensive gardens we saw on our walk. It is all delicious.

We try each other's dishes. We marvel at the sauces, the freshness and flavor. It really is a meal to be savored. We note that the service is as good as the food. Local Irish youth, it would seem, are working at a high standard.

Realizing it is our last night together and hoping to see Ian and Arty, our Irish buddies, we forgo dessert and opt for a stop at the pub. It is Mark's first visit. But he gets to be part of the hearty *fáilte ar ais,* the welcome back, we receive. Ian challenges us to repeat the Irish we have learned, saying we will be tested after a few more drinks. The beer and the stories flow while we practice the only three expressions we know:

Sláinte and the more advanced *sláinte agus táinte*

Craic and then the new *ol, ceol agus craic*

Fáilte and then *fáilte ar ais*

Reluctantly, we raise our glasses one last time and head back to the hotel. *Sláinte;* goodbyes, all around.

CynDee and Jack will leave by bus for their car tomorrow morning. As we stroll back to the hotel, we begin saying our own goodbyes. We promise to stay in touch and even talk about getting together back home to share pictures and stories. I am blown away by what CynDee and I have shared in only a few days. There really are not words. We say goodbye with a tearful embrace. As to be expected, CynDee is more loquacious than I. She offers the last word or two.

"Honey, you write those stories now and if you make them into a book, you all better visit and we will have a grand ol' signin' party. Between Jack and me, there will be at least three counties of people there to hear you and buy a copy. Jack, we could have it at the fire hall, don't you think?"

I hadn't realized Jack was even listening, but he nods vigorously and shakes Mark's hand, adding "And I will introduce you to the American Sullivans."

"That would be amazing. What a picture to keep in mind as I try to write," I say as tears form.

"None of this cryin' nonsense. You write, girl. No stallin'. Just call on Jane or call me up if you need a good goosin'."

I swear she is laying the accent on thicker than ever, but perhaps it is just the wine talking. "And what about you, CynDee? What will you be doing with all we experienced and with your amazing gifts?"

"Honey, I pass it all on. I listen. I help people shape their responses to what God has given them, and I give them a boost now and again. Just like doin' hair. I work my magic while they are in the chair, gettin' beautiful. Now I have more stories and ways to help people sort themselves out. Not to worry, Honey. I have had a blast and loved every minute. The guys may have had their big adventure at sea, but we had a mighty adventure ourselves amidst those stones."

"OK, you two. Let's call it a night. You can always talk on the phone when you get home. Goodbyes are hard, but at least we will be just a day's ride away and can meet up," Mark adds with a note of finality in his voice. "Let us bless our time together, the memories we created and the connection we made. It has been really great."

"*Sláinte*," Jack offers as he raises an imaginary glass in a salute while Mark holds the door of the hotel for us all to enter.

"I am surprised at how hard that goodbye was. We only met a couple of weeks ago, but we sure shared a lot, didn't we? And you and CynDee really connected," Mark observes as we walk into our room.

"Yeah, she was so amazing through this whole adventure with the stones. Who would have thought? And it all came about because you guys connected through sailing. Speaking of sailing, you guys told about your adventures at sea, but now tell me about your own experience, Mark. Was it what you expected? Did you get amazing pictures for your lighthouse calendar? Did it feed your soul?" I ask as we slip beneath the covers.

"The pictures are great. Let's order room service for the morning and I will entertain you with my travelogue: *Mark's Adventure at Sea*." He laughs and continues in a more serious tone, "Well, you know the whole thing for me—for the entire trip—was to get away, relax and be free of duties and expectations. Just live in the moment. Keep working on letting go of what I need to let go of, without letting go of that which is meant to always be a part of me.

"Well," he continues, "there is no better way to be in the moment and to feel free of spirit than sailing. The setting was magnificent, the guys great and the chance to sail to Fastnet the dream of a lifetime. So yep, it was great. Yep. That's it. More than free from responsibilities and roles, I became a free spirit out there riding the waves. It was just what I needed. I have more to tell you, but I am too tired tonight, too sleepy after all that wine and beer. And it is wonderful to be in a real bed…"

I think he falls asleep before he finishes the sentence. I had drunk less because I was the designated driver so I am not sleepy. I pick up my phone, check emails and send a quick note to the boys. I also make a mental note to pick up the car in the morning. We left it in front of the pub. Saying my prayers of gratitude settles me down and leads me into a deep and restful sleep.

"Good morning, buttercup," Mark says, as he puts his arms around me in a full-body embrace. After leisurely love making, he suggests, "Let's make some coffee and order room service and then just laze around for a while."

"Um, fine with me. I'll just lie here a bit longer." I lie there until the bathroom calls.

When I return, there is coffee on each of our night stands, the pillows are fluffed, and Mark is back in bed waiting for me. He has his computer out ready for the slide show.

Indeed, his pictures are stunning. He has photos of lighthouses from all angles and in all different lighting, and a couple of night shots that are absolutely beautiful. "Wow, you have the makings of a great calendar, and you should do one of those Snapfish photo albums too. Tell me more about the places you went to that we didn't see together."

"Shall do. You know, Abs, there is another aspect of *Mark's Adventure at Sea* that I haven't told you about yet." He pauses for what seems like a long time. Then he continues, "Actually, I had a harrowing experience, a life-threatening and life-changing experience while out there. Shh, now, it is all fine.

"Let me start at the beginning.... It was while we were tying everything down in preparation for the upcoming storm. Interestingly enough, it would have been right around the time you said you began to worry about me. Anyway, I had my harness on because I had been up securing lines, when this huge swell came from nowhere. I literally went flying, flying and swinging out over the sea. Had I not had the harness on, I would have gone overboard. I would be gone. It was terrifying. It only lasted a minute or two. Yet, those minutes were really intense. You know how people say their whole life passes by? Well, it's true.

"The skipper righted the boat. I got my footing and it was over. But, for those few moments, I saw my entire life in review. It was terrifying and exhilarating and shocking. I just thank God I had that harness on and lived to tell the story."

"Oh, Mark. That's just awful!" I say as I hold him for dear life.

"Yep, it was. And yet, it really was freeing. You know, I took courses on death and dying in seminary. I have counseled the dying and the bereaved. I walked with Lizzie through her battle with cancer and was present with her at her passing. Somehow though, I had never truly contemplated my own death, my mortality. Looking God in the eye and asking if He was going to take me now: that was quite an experience. Just like you read about I found myself saying 'God, if it is my time, I am ready. But if it need not be my time, I vow to live this life to its fullest, no holds barred.' Talk about freeing. It was amazing."

"I'm still thinking how I might have lost you at sea..."

"But I wasn't and here I am with you...." A knock at the door interrupts him. "And, oh, good, the food is here, and more coffee. Would you like to be served in bed, Abs, or come to the little table by the window?" Mark says, seemingly delighted to move the conversation on to lighter things.

"I love the idea of breakfast in bed, but I don't find it very comfortable. The table, please."

"Yep, be my guest, then." After we are seated and begin eating, Mark continues, "Before the waiter arrived, I was about to say how much I love lying in bed with you, talking, just being together. It makes me think of the questions you raised back in Kinsale about what will happen when we return. I think of the casserole ladies, even the church board members, and of my daughter. None are ready for us, for me, to have someone move in with me. Yet, I want to spend more time with you. I want to wake up with you at my side. Maybe not every day and maybe it won't be what either of us want to commit to forever. I am not asking for that. In fact, I am not sure I am ready for that or even that I ever want to marry again. But I do want to see what unfolds."

"Me too. You have put in words my own feelings. As for other people, my teaching career is done, my boys are no longer home, and appearances don't matter much. I do get that your circumstances are different, but it makes me angry to think that other people's judgments could get in the way of what is developing between us. Maybe we should just rent a place back on Beara overlooking our favorite cove and stay in Ireland for a few months. Then go home when we know where we are as a couple."

"Are you serious?" he asks.

"I don't really know; the words just came out. Perhaps, or perhaps it's just a fantasy. I guess I would consider it."

"Oops, Abs, look at the time. We have to get going."

"Mark Andrews, are you avoiding our conversation? That is not like you."

"It is mind blowing, but no I'm not avoiding it," he laughs. "I hadn't gotten around to telling you, but I have a surprise. Not that big a surprise, but last night, I asked Ian if he knew of someone with a decent sized fishing boat that would take us out for a tour around the two islands, go along the cliffs and show us Ballycotton from the water. I checked that the winds would be light, no high waves or chop, so I figured you would be amenable," he says with questioning eyes.

"If you are sure it will be smooth out there, OK. How big did you say the boat would be?" I ask.

"Well, it's no ferry, but it sounds solid and certainly ready for sea. Plus, we will never be more than a little way from shore. I thought you might want to get up close to the places Jane says you lived in that other lifetime. The thing is when I asked Ian, he offered to do it himself. We meet him at 10 a.m. He will drop us at the big island when we are finished. He is arranging for the guy with the boat tour to allow us to join his lighthouse tour and return with him on the last boat leaving the island. While you were in the bathroom and I was ordering room service, I asked them to pack us a picnic lunch. So, get your gear together and we'll spend the day out, if that is OK."

"It's more than OK, it's wonderful. I never would have thought to do that, but it would be great to get up close and personal to the little island, especially. And, you know, I think now that I know the story of what happened to me in that past life, the fear of the sea is fading. I don't want to be out in a raging storm, but this sounds fine."

Ian waves from his boat as he sees us approach. *"Fáilte ar ais*, lass. Ye didna know ye would be seeing me again now, did ye? Ha-ha. Your man is worth his weight, is he not? Mind the step now, as ye come aboard me wee vessel," he says laying the accent on for effect.

I greet Ian with a quick kiss on the cheek. Once I am on firm footing, I tell Mark what a treat it is and give him a full kiss as his thanks.

"'Tis no bother at all. Didna realize you would want to be doing this or I would have offered before. Best though that your man come along. I gather himself is the lighthouse enthusiast. Set yourselves down now and we will be off."

"Ian, as we go around, we would love it if you tell us all you know about the history of this area," Mark says.

As Mark finishes speaking, I hear Jane's voice: *Fáilte ar ais, my cara, Fáilte ar ais.*

CHAPTER FIFTEEN

After a fabulous tour, Ian drops us off at the lighthouse dock and we allow as how we might come back to the Inn on the Harbour for dinner and one more farewell drink. I had told Mark how great the food was and, of course, we both experienced the *craic* of the pub last night. And, after all, how could we resist another night of storytelling.

"It's beautiful, isn't it?" I comment as we get our land legs back and look around.

"Yep, but it is so different than I expected. I envisioned circumnavigating the island on foot and having a quiet, intimate picnic on the ocean side, just the two of us. From afar it seems like pasture land on a hillside. But up close, these modern facilities, paths and fences take away some of the magic. When we were sailing in, I was too busy crewing to notice."

"I was surprised too. I had this perception of a grassy knoll with a winding road from the very first time I saw the island and it persisted. I thought it had something to do with the past life memories fogging up my perceptions. Yet, CynDee agreed. For instance, at first sight, neither of us noticed that the lighthouse itself is painted black. All in all, it is interesting that we saw something much more mystical than the up close reality."

"Reminds me of our discussion of Virginia Woolf's *To a Light House* where everyone envisions it differently and all have vastly different expectations," Mark recollects.

"Speaking of differing expectations, while I loved our 'picnic' on the Beara, there is no way in hell I would do it here," I say using my hands to make little quotation marks in the air over the words "do it". "I stared as if hypnotized by the island for too many hours. I don't think I can rid myself of the idea that hundreds of eyes and probably a bunch of telescopes and binoculars are on us, right now."

"It is mesmerizing, no argument there. But we can be discreet, you know."

"I feel like this island is too much in the center of everything."

"Ah, well. Another idyllic spot will reveal itself. We still have a few days before our flight home," he says in exaggerated sadness.

"Speaking of these next few days, do you have any thoughts about where to spend them?" I ask.

"Not really, I know I am ready to move on in the morning. I had figured that it would be your turn to choose since you and CynDee had accommodated Jack and me about the sailing adventure, but clearly you were meant to come here as much as I was meant to go out to sea," he observes.

"That's for sure. Maybe, that's the answer. Maybe, we need to ask for guidance. The Universe seems to be co-creating the path of our trip. Let's take time to clear our minds and meditate on it."

"Good idea. I am very attuned to the notion of co-creation these days. I like to think it describes my relationship with God and also how I want to be in relationship. Some people get annoyed when new words are insinuated into the lexicon, but I find it super helpful. Taking turns is good too," he says with a grin as he adds "You want to lead us in opening to Spirit on this one?"

"Sure," I respond. "Since we are the sole visitors to the island at the moment and no boats are coming in, we know we have some degree of privacy. Let's do something similar to what we have done at the stone circles.

> *Mother/Father God, Ancient Ones, All who guide and teach us.*
>
> *Direct us to a place that furthers our understanding of our life's purpose*
>
> *That further opens us to the Love and Joy that is ours to experience*
>
> *That helps us to move forward along the path we each are meant to follow, individually and together.*

I close with, "Blessed Be."

Mark adds, "Amen."

"Getting any guidance?" I ask a few minutes later.

"Images of a round tower and the feeling of a place like Timoleague. Perhaps an abbey, Abby."

"Ha-ha, never thought of my name being connected to an abbey. But now that I am aware of past lives, who knows?"

"Actually, Abagail, as you probably know already, is a Hebrew name, meaning Father's joy. So that doesn't help us here in Ireland. Interesting to think about visiting an abbey though. I have come to love abbeys, at least abbey ruins. I haven't visited an up-and-running one. We seem more into earlier eras."

"Kildare came to me. Maybe because Jane said we had visited there in my Ballycotton lifetime, maybe something else. Just know the name came in."

"Kildare is landlocked. Not one lighthouse. Horse racing though. I suppose we could do that every day, right?" Mark deadpans.

"Mark Andrews, you know full well that Kildare is more than that. It is the sacred site of Brigid's Well and Brigid's Flame and the abbey built by St. Brigit," I say in mock disgust.

"Yep, and actually I love how the spelling of the name changed ever so slightly through the centuries as she evolved. There is Brighid or Brigid, the goddess who bridged the Old Religion and Christianity, Bridgit who started the early co-ed monastery, St. Brigit, Brigit, or Brede who is called the Mary of Gael, the legendary mid-wife to Jesus. And Kildare with its ancient well, its round tower, and cathedral are all part of the mystique. It is a perfect place for us. Instead of God by many names, we have goddess by many spellings."

"Ha! Let's do it then. The more we say, the more I realize how right it is. And I do so love the Irish. They think nothing of honoring the goddess and the saint as one. They have no problem with venerating her as a saint who worked with St. Patrick to grow Christianity in the 5th century equally with her acting as the mid-wife to Mary at the birth of Jesus centuries before. I love that non-linear thinking," I say excitedly.

"There are so many stories related to Brigit. I can't wait to find out how we each experience her ourselves. And then there is your past life connection. I haven't been with you at sacred sites since you started directly communicating with Jane. I have to admit I am fascinated and anxious to witness it. I do hope though that my skepticism won't get in your way."

"Speaking of Jane, could you feel her presence with us on the boat ride with Ian?" I ask.

"What? No..."

"She whispered *Fáilte ar ais, my cara, Fáilte ar ais*. Fun to realize that she now speaks to me in Irish phrases. Actually, I only know three and she used one of them, but still."

"Or maybe you can imagine her using Irish now that you know the phrases," Mark offers a different interpretation. "I still can't quite get my head around the idea of a Jane who actually speaks to you," he confesses.

"It's not a head thing. It's a heart thing. I have no idea how any of this works and I have no coherent cosmology to spout. But that is the one thing I know. The connection comes from the heart not the head. I am just learning to go with my intuition and it feels so freeing. I can't wait to develop it more. But I haven't a clue where it is leading me or why. But, as we rounded the small island, I got all these stirring feelings like information was being downloaded to me, like I was gaining insights about working with crystals and energies. I can't put my finger on any of it yet, nor can I describe it to you any better than that. But, wow, something is changing inside me."

"Never a dull moment with you, my cara. Who knows what the future holds or what changes are in store for any of us. Want to walk up top?"

"Mark, do you realize that 'my cara' is Jane's pet name for me?"

"Wow, really? It came out without much thought behind it, but I have been thinking about John O'Donahue's book *Anam Cara*. You know, where he talks about the Irish idea that everyone needs a best friend/confessor. Modern day folks call it a soul mate for lack of a clearer term. I just liked the idea of calling you 'my cara'. But the Jane connection is totally coincidental."

"I like it, but I am beginning to think nothing in life is coincidental. You may discover some past life stories of your own, if not amidst the stones, then amidst the abbeys. Did I tell you, Jane and my mother approve of you, by the way? "

"Why do I feel like a school boy being checked out by a girl's mom?" he asks with an awkward laugh.

"I like the idea of *anam cara*. I want to hear more about it and his book too. I do know that we talk in a way that is special. You have my back and support me even when you don't agree with how I am interpreting something. I also feel I can tell you anything and you will accept me and respect it as my experience. I can't quite get my tongue around what I want to say. I guess it is that there is a special quality in your listening and responding to me that touches me deeply and that I am beginning to rely on."

"Hmm. I like that. I think O'Donahue would too."

We chug up the hill, with me slightly behind. I don't remember even being conscious of the incline when CynDee and I came over. Of course, today is so much warmer and Mark is going faster. I am so enthralled by the view from this fascinating island that I can't help but stop to take it all it. I love the greens and blues and shimmering iridescent bands of light all around. I wish I were a painter. And, of course, with all this stopping and thinking, I lag further behind.

Mark began humming as we started the climb. He is now humming joyful songs but only a few lines of a tune before he changes it. Some are familiar but I am not able to place them by name. Finally, I catch up with him and ask.

"Oh, that one was from Sunday school: 'I Love to Tell the Story', the one before was 'Tell Me the Story'. Did you ever play the game where you tried to see how many songs that you could sing that had a certain word in the title? For example, red. You could start with 'Rudolf, the Red nose Reindeer', then 'Red River Valley'. You get the idea. Want to play the game using the word story?"

"Sounds fun, just remember I am not a singer." So we amuse ourselves until we arrive at the lighthouse.

"Of course, the idea of story has been coming up all through the trip. I have been thinking about how important story is and how clearly that is evident here in Ireland. Besides the amazing scenery, the color and light changing it all the time, I think the thing I like best is the storytelling. Everyone has a story for the occasion and if they don't have one, they make one up. It gives vitality to the simplest things in life as well as makes sense or light of the most profound," Mark offers.

"I keep wondering when Jane keeps saying 'tell the story' if she means orally or if I am meant to write a book? Historical fiction? Anthology or short stories on the Divine Feminine? I just don't know."

"Perhaps that's the next question you ask her, or yourself, especially when we get to our next sacred site. You seem to get the best and strongest information at the stones, right? We even can make a stone circle stop on the way to Kildare. In fact, I might like to stop at the Rock of Cashel on our way. Different period, later period than your stone circles, but Doug was telling us about his visit there. He said he had a moment when he swore he saw a period bagpipe marching band round a corner, and then it vanished. So you are not alone in finding magic and mysticism at these sacred sites."

"You guys were telling campfire stories without a campfire?"

"Sailors call it spinning a yarn. Shall we find a spot to sit with our picnic lunch and spin another yarn or two? I am starved."

The Bayview Hotel provided a lovely lunch of cold poached salmon, cold asparagus, hardboiled eggs, a fruit salad and croissants, plus bottled water. Mark also pulls out two single serving bottles of white wine.

"Where did those come from?" I ask with surprise.

"The pub last night, after I made arrangements with Ian. I bought them separately and slipped them into my coat pockets while you were talking to CynDee and Jack."

"Well, aren't you something," I laugh.

"As you know, I had ulterior motives. I still think no one cares what we do here behind the lighthouse. And besides, we can be discreet. No one will see a thing." He moves closer as he speaks.

"Well, it is true we haven't seen or heard a soul," I say as I slowly acquiesce to his touch. After making love discreetly as Mark promised, we lie together in silence.

"Mm. There is something about lying here looking up at the clouds together after love-making that makes it even richer. I like our new tradition a lot, Mark Andrews," I murmur.

"Me too. I feel so free and uninhibited here with you. I like it," he says.

"I sure hope we can continue to feel like this back home. Have you thought anymore about how you are going to introduce our deepening relationship to the folks?"

"Indirectly. I have indirectly. I have been thinking a lot about story: the stories we are told, the stories we tell ourselves, the stories that shape our world, the stories from which we get our strength and the stories we allow to limit us.

"I once gave a sermon entitled *A New Story for a New Time*. It was a number of years ago, perhaps the first year of the Obama presidency. His message offered such hope. Not since Kennedy had I seen America daring to dream the dream again. Martin Luther King's Beloved Community seemed so near. People once again seemed willing to step back into the story of the country we aspired to create. You remember my passion for the idea of the City on the Hill, the Beacon of Light stuff. I truly believe we have been placed here on earth at this time to reignite the experiment of co-creating a community of love. So Obama's 'Yes We Can' theme fired me up. I wanted to get the congregation fired up, not in a political but in a spiritual way, about possibilities for our future.

"I think the congregation expected the sermon to be about the Gospel, telling the good news of the coming of the Christ. But instead of the New Testament, I used a quotation from Thomas Berry, the modern Catholic priest and eco-theologian, as the central theme. I still remember most of it:

> *It is all a question of story. We are in trouble now because we do not have a good story. We are in between stories. The old story, the account of how we fit into it, is no longer effective. Yet, we have not learned the new story.*

"At the time, I was preaching about how as a community and as a country we needed a new story that brings us together again as a people: a story that gets us out of the entrenched positional approach to problems and away from identity politics; that embodies the Christ-based life of Love, which I believe we are meant to live and model to others."

"That's beautiful and very inspirational, Mark, and certainly timely. At first, I didn't see how it relates to being here in Ireland. Although when I think about it more, I see it: after centuries of division, the story of Ireland's Peace Accord is inspirational. Who would have believed that there would be peace in Ireland in our lifetime?"

"Yep, that is huge and a wonderful example of changing the narrative. Speaking of changing the narrative, here comes the tour boat. Where did the time go? I can't believe the boat is here already. There was a lot more I wanted to say about story."

"I think we know where the time went," I laugh. "But let's remember to pick this up later. And I still want you to answer my question about what you see happening when we go home. It looks like George has a family of five this trip. We should go meet them at the lighthouse door. You probably want to get some more photos before they get in the way of your shots. I will take the garbage over to the bin while you take your pictures."

"OK, good idea. I will meet you there in a few minutes."

• • •

The group congregates and we all enter together while George talks about the history of the lighthouse. Three boisterous children and parents who don't seem too interested in seeing that their kids behave create a much different dynamic than CynDee and I experienced on our visit. I don't really care, but I feel badly for Mark because I know he wants to hear every detail.

When we get up to the lookout area, we separate ourselves as much as possible and look out to the west. "Did you ever go upstairs in one of those old Victorian New England homes with a widow's peak?" I ask Mark.

"I have seen them but only from the outside. Why?"

"When CynDee and I were here, I kept looking out to sea like those women of old. I wondered where you were and when you would get back. And, now when I think of the fact you could have drowned. Well, I…"

The littlest of the three rascals starts screaming and will not stop. It's a total meltdown. Poor George decides to end our tour and get us back to the mainland as soon as possible. We don't argue. It seems like a long ride back. Mark tips George generously as we all part company. A very abrupt end to an otherwise beautifully delicious day.

"Ready for some wine on the hotel terrace?" Mark asks. With a nod, we make a beeline for the hotel.

"I can't believe we are the only ones out here, but I am glad for the peace and quiet."

"*Sláinte,*" Mark offers as we clink glasses.

"Back at the lighthouse, I was about to ask you if you wanted to talk about your near disaster at sea. It is such a major thing but you haven't really talked about it and its impact. I was so shocked it happened and so relieved you were OK, I didn't ask you much about it. It had to be life-changing. I would like very much to hear more."

"Yep. It was. Actually that is where I was going with this bit about story. In the hours after the incident, I thought a lot about the story of my life. I started mulling over Berry's words about being between stories and what that means on a personal level. You know, in general and for my own life right now. Part of any-one's grieving at the loss of a loved one or the ending of a career, or any other major event is putting their stories into perspective: what to hold on to, what to let go of, what changes, what is everlasting…all that." He takes a big sigh before continuing, "I truly believe that the stories we choose to tell ourselves create the world we choose to live in. And so I started thinking long and hard about my own."

"Wow, that is deep. CynDee may think we are eggheads, but I feel so appreciative that we can have deep, meaningful conversations like this. Thank you for sharing with me in this way," I say.

"CynDee is a kick and she is not the first person who has rolled her eyes at my spewing forth. I don't mean to be giving sermons all the time, but this is me and the way I process things."

"Yeah, and I love that about you. Keep going," I say as I touch his arm. "Please, tell me more."

"So, I am moved to commit myself to creating a new story, a new story for a new time. Dangling by the harness over the raging sea was like a real wake up call. Yes, it was fine to be gentle with myself through this grieving process, and yes it hasn't been that long since I retired, but it is time to boldly open myself to a new story.

"I want it to be a story informed by the insights we are gaining in this new millennium; I want it to be a story that incorporates love and service; I want it filled with joy and free of restraint. As they say, I want to fully live all the days of my life. When I reach Heaven, I want to know that I fulfilled my life here on earth."

"Wow, that stirs me to my core, Mark. It rings so true. On some level it seems it is how you live your life now, but I also hear that it is more—deeper, brighter in some way. Tell me more about why that is any different than what you have been doing and what it is that you want to change."

"Yeah!" he says as he takes a big gulp of wine. "Those are exactly the questions I have been living with these last few days. Thank you for getting what I am talking about."

"Hey! The dolphins have come. I think they want to applaud you for all this reflection. Look at them jump, like synchronized swimmers. They are so beautiful," I note.

"And playful. Reminding us to lighten up and live in joy, don't you think?" Mark adds.

"Yeah, and somehow, they communicate all that is important in the world: wisdom, hope, joy, being One with the Universe. It all is rolled up together."

We sit sipping wine and silently enjoying their antics until they choose to move on and we are left with ourselves. "I am feeling restless and I would love some more of those chocolate cake squares. Feel like walking down the beach to the steps, going up to the store and getting some snacks for tomorrow's road trip?"

"Sounds terrific. Let's do it."

As we walk toward the Old Road, Mark asks, "Do you want to revisit any of the places that you discovered over the last few days? Are there any lingering issues? Or would you like to do a prayer or ritual any place? We can stop on the way out to the highway tomorrow morning or we could do it now. What do you think?"

"You know, I was surprised that the ride back from the island didn't feel more emotional. Of course, that kid was screaming, but I felt as though I was fully present in this lifetime, not really thinking about Jane and the past life story at all. Maybe, it is like you are saying about it being time for a new story. And maybe now that I have seen and can put this past life story behind me, I, too, am free to create a new story."

"Yep. That makes sense."

"And here we are at the remnants of the Old Road. I actually am feeling light—and happy, happy that I found it. Not in a trivial, treasure hunt kind of way; more like upbeat, expansive. I suppose a shadow I did not even realize was darkening my spirit got lifted. I dunno, but I feel good about it all. And I appreciate your asking. It is important that I look back and see if things are cleared up. So, yes, please do come back with me to the places of the story.

"Besides, I have a feeling I will want to revisit it a lot as I write," I add. "It would be valuable to me if you could picture it with me. What if I show you the tower ruins in Shanagarry and then we drive further up the beach to Garryvoe? CynDee and I stopped at that beach on our way in. The hotel there overlooks the water and was quite inviting. How does that sound, or did you want to go back to the pub?"

"I love the idea. And when we stop just say if you want to process stuff or do a prayer or ritual. Then, we can go on to dinner, just the two of us. Shall we head back for the car? We can stop at the store on the way out of town."

"Just how many slices of chocolate cake are you planning to buy?" I tease him as we head back to the hotel to freshen up and take off again.

As we are about to pull out from the parking lot, Mark turns to me, "Mind if we ride up to the cliff walk first? It might be dark when we come back and I would like one more look."

"Fine with me," I say. "It is so beautiful, why not? And it is part of revisiting for a last time all the places of my Jane story."

"This is a spectacular walk. The view, the breeze, the sea spray. I love hearing the waves crash against the rock as the tide comes in. I often regret I didn't settle nearer the sea. I love lakes, but they aren't the same," he says.

"It is awesome. I am glad to hear your adventure at sea didn't ruin it for you."

"Never. I love it. I can almost see Cobh Harbour from here. Look. Did you and CynDee stop there?"

"No, we went straight to Drombeg," I respond. "I know it's where ships left for America and that it has a great museum. I was just too anxious to get back to the stone circle."

"We can go over if you want. We sailed into the harbor there and I felt the history of the place. I wouldn't mind spending more time there."

"I am more inclined to want to stop at the Rock of Cashel and maybe a stone circle, but we could get up early and stop if you want," I offer.

"Not necessarily. I just keep thinking about all those who left on famine ships. There's a story of change for you. Forced change is certainly a powerful motivator for new story. I think of those like Annie Moore and her children, immortalized in that magnificent harbor statue over in Cobh. We see them preparing to leave Ireland for America to start a new life, representing all those who emigrated; many out of need, often desperation, but also out of aspiration and hope. Talk about new stories. Such possibility, such promise in their hearts."

Mark is so eloquent and pure of heart, I am overwhelmed. I say nothing, but my presence and body language communicates that I want him to continue.

"It worries me sometimes that we all seem to wait for forced change like that. If we all would only right injustice, create beloved community."

"I remember one of the Sullivans talking about Cobh and how the English renamed it Queenstown. Then the Irish turned it back to Cobh with great pride and defiance. Lots of history there. I admit the dates and facts escape me. What I found memorable is the story of Queen Elizabeth coming to Cobh a few years ago. Amazing that she came, after all her uncle was blown up by the IRA. Even more amazingly, she was greeted warmly. I was so moved. Again, it is that power to change the narrative, begin a new chapter, perhaps an entirely new story," I say.

"Yep. The stories are not just in the ancient stones, they are all around us. But enough of that for now. Let's go get that chocolate before the store closes."

We revisit all the places of meaning in what I am going to call the Jane story, not the rape story, not the past life story, but the Jane story. It is Jane who tirelessly reached out to me, Jane who insisted I find the Old Road and insists that I tell the story. Mark is wonderful, walking with me, taking it all in and just allowing me to tell the story as it comes. It is not until we reach the cemetery that we start a discussion.

"You know, Abs, you have already begun telling the story. All that you just said as we walked was incredibly well told and powerfully moving. I am changed for having heard it. Others will be also, I have no doubt. You are bringing witness to the importance of keeping the Divine Feminine alive and for honoring sovereignty of each person, and each community as we strive to create Beloved Community. Who would have thought our fun romp to Ireland would include all this?"

"It has been amazing, in every way—and in ways I never imagined. Thank you for walking it with me and for giving me space to walk it on my own as well."

"Ditto. I feel the same. People throw around the term 'co-create' a lot. Some get the part about co-creating with the Universe, wherein we are open and allowing ourselves to walk with God. Some get how to walk side by side with another human being in that same openness and allowing. I find it challenging to do both. I know that doing so is a key part of the new story I want to create. Have I gone too egg-headed as CynDee would say?" Mark asks.

"Not sure what she would say, she has a healthy disrespect for newly coined buzz words, but I think she would agree with the aspiration. I do know that I love the way you so often express what I feel and want in my heart. Co-creation is a beautiful and apt word for it," I say as I slowly contemplate his words.

"Hmm. Good." He takes in my affirmation and continues, "I would like to get a selfie of us here in front of this Celtic cross before we head up to Garryvoe. I have always loved the Celtic cross, but it has added meaning for me now. Talk about co-creation: the circle symbolizing the Divine Feminine, the earth, community in balance with the cross symbolizing the Divine Masculine, the Ascension to Heaven and our Christ-presence. From now on, I will always see it as a symbol of this trip and what we have shared traveling to these sacred sites and our own balancing of male and female within ourselves."

The picture comes out well. A keeper, for sure.

• • •

The Garryvoe Hotel proves a perfect place for our last evening in East Cork. We are greeted warmly with a "you're very welcomed here" and then Irish *fáilte* as we are offered a table by the window looking out at the bay.

"Our lighthouse and island are front and center from here. What a view. You are right about it having a mystical vibe from a distance. Wow." Mark exudes enthusiasm and sets the tone for our private cocktail hour.

"I love sitting here with no worries, no goals to be met, nor any mandates to fulfill. I think I am more trusting that things will just unfold as they are meant to than I ever have been in my whole life. It's a great feeling," I find myself saying.

"You asked what is different about the new story I want to create (or co-create to use the new paradigm). And just now you said it: I want to be in the present, allowing life to unfold. I want to let go of structure and roles that no longer serve and I want to draw to me the people and resources and ideas that can assist me to live a life of meaning well into old age."

"You know, on one hand that doesn't sound very different from what I see you doing all the time. I know I said that earlier. But I do get that on a deeper level it is radically different. It is all about a new worldview, a new paradigm for understanding and living our lives, isn't it? The freedom of this trip has helped me realize that flow and being in the moment are keys to the changes I want to make in my life too."

"Yes, exactly, Abs. This is what I am trying to say."

"It also suggests to me that you want to be free of roles and expectations and a prescribed way of living. Where does that put our relationship? I mean there are all the issues of your family and your community. We have been so free here, but what about when we go back?"

"Well, that's part of where I was going when I started sharing my thoughts on co-creating a new story. It seems it is taking me all day to do it though." He gives a nervous laugh as he takes my hand and continues, "I want you to be part of my new story. Co-creation with the Universe for sure. Co-creation with you as well would bring it all together for me. You have become my *anam cara*, Abs. I want us to be together. I want to take life and our relationship wherever it is meant to go."

"That sounds like a beautiful challenge. Yes, I want that too. I have never felt more alive, freer and more trusting than I have these last few weeks. And, Mark Andrews, I am realizing I am in love with you."

In the background, I hear Jane's voice:

> *Blessings, my cara, Blessings for the stories you will tell, for the new story you will create, for the stories you and your man will create together. Serve the Mother, serve the Mother/Father God, serve in sovereignty and love, and help bring Divine Balance back to the world.*

BOOK CLUB QUESTIONS

Abby and Mark like the idea of being away from the watchful eye of friends and family as they explore their relationship.

What benefits do you see? Is it realistic?

What do you think of where they end up?

Lighthouses have intrigued Mark since he was a boy.

What do you think of his reasons?

In what ways are lighthouses a metaphor for life?

Stone circles have a similar draw for Abby.

What do you think of her initial interest? Of what develops?

How would you interpret her experiences? Is your interpretation more in keeping with Mark? With CynDee? Or with Abby? Or different?

The description of traveling by car along the southwest coast of Ireland provides the fabric that holds their experiences together.

What did you observe or learn about Ireland? About travel in general?

Have you had similar experiences? Have you seen any of the places they visited?

The idea of story is another central theme of the book.

Mark especially talks about the power of story and his desire to start a new story. Do you see the characters moving into new chapters or new stories in their lives as they return home?

What do you think of Abby's mandate to "tell the story" of the Divine Feminine and of women in ancient times?

Balancing male /female energies, honoring the Mother/Father God/Goddess as each individual views the Divine and the sacred places visited is another important theme. Mark and Abby come at it differently.

Describe how they differ and how they complement each other.

What are your views on the subject?

CynDee says she isn't as serious and academic as Abby and Mark; yet, she enjoys hanging out with them.

What did you think of her approach and reaction to events?

In what way does she add to the story of the stones?

"May ye find yourself amidst the stones" can be both a Celtic blessing and/ or a challenge for Abby, for all of us.

In what ways did the characters find themselves?

In what ways did you as a reader find yourself in their stories?

THE AUTHOR, JEANNE CRANE

I recently drove by the Western New York farmhouse where we lived until I was six. A large granite stone still sits under the maple tree from which my childhood swing hung. It reminded me of how magical that place had been to me. I smiled, wondering if "finding myself amidst the stones" had begun there.

Visioning at the Red Rocks of Sedona, meditating at the edge of a Zen garden in Kyoto, and absorbing the energy of the Ring of Brodgar on Orkney began a pattern for me, a way to deepen my spirituality and develop my higher consciousness. After I retired from coaching and consulting, I made pilgrimages and visits to many more sacred sites and stone circles. All were powerful, but surprisingly, the stones of southwest Ireland were especially stirring. This book sprang from my experiences there.

Like Abby, I sometimes have struggled to explain why I am drawn to those magnificent circles, but I knew I had to tell their story. I hope these pages will entertain you and transport you to your own experience "amidst the stones".

If you travel to Ireland, you can visit these marvelous places yourselves. All places, sites and travel information are real and accurate to the best of my ability. Only the characters and story line are fiction.

• • •

Please leave a review of the book on Amazon, visit my website to see pictures and/or to dialogue with me, and do consider this book for your book club. I enjoy giving presentations to libraries, Celtic festivals, etc., and I am available via Skype to speak with book clubs.

I would love to hear from you: Jeanne@JeanneCrane.com.

CELTIC BLESSINGS,
Jeanne Crane 2018
JeanneCrane.com

JEANNE'S OTHER BOOKS

Celtic Spirit: A Wee Journey to the Heart of It All

Snapshots of Ireland: Pictures and Notes on Travel
CORK
KERRY
CLARE and LIMERICK
GALWAY and the ARAN ISLANDS

Purchase books: Amazon